The Match Breaker Summer

The Match Breaker Summer

ANNIE RAINS

Underlined

Text copyright © 2022 by Annie Rains
Cover art copyright © 2022 by Jacqueline Li

GetUnderlined.com

Educators and librarians, for a variety of teaching tools, visit us at
RHTeachersLibrarians.com

Library of Congress Cataloging-in-Publication Data is available upon request.
ISBN 978-0-593-48155-4 (pbk.) — ISBN 978-0-593-48156-1 (ebook)

The text of this book is set in 11.5-point font.
Interior design by Cathy Bobak

Printed in the United States of America
10 9 8 7 6 5 4 3 2 1
First Edition

For Ralph, Doc, & Lydia.
With all my love, forever.
You inspire me more than anything.

CHAPTER ONE

Camp Time: Sunday. July 17.

> *I've been waiting for this moment my entire life. For the first time ever, I get to be a Camp Starling counselor. The first and last time.*

My cursive loops on the blank page of my camper's journal. This one has a purple leather cover with a tree embossed on the front. A lone bird soars in the right corner, which is what drew me to this specific journal. I don't take choosing the perfect camper's journal lightly. This one will stay with me over the next two weeks and document all the camp moments I never want to forget. That's especially important this year.

A lump tightens my throat as I lie on the bottom bunk in my empty cabin, staring up at the wood planks of the bed above me. The other counselors aren't here yet. It's just me and one big secret that presses in on me from all sides. I put my pen to paper and prepare to unload that secret—that's what journals are for—when I hear a rattling noise outside.

My spine straightens. What kind of bizarre sound was that? It reminds me of the obnoxious way my mom's boyfriend Dave shakes cubes of ice in his glass—only louder. The rattle is followed by a loud *SHHHHHHHHH*.

The only other people on the grounds right now are my mom—the owner of Camp Starling—and Dave, who gets to serve as assistant camp director just because he's dating my mom. Camp Starling is a camp for all ages to enjoy nature at its best. The next two weeks are designated specifically for teenaged girls and boys ages twelve through fifteen. Sixteen and up—me!—get to serve as camp counselors.

I hear the noise again and briefly wonder if it's my best friend, Nora. Nora is going to be the counselor in the cabin next door to mine. It's early, though, and Nora is a fashionably late kind of friend. I, on the other hand, view arrival times as a rule never to be broken. Actually, I view all rules as unbending lines in the sand.

The rattle and *SHHHHH* noises start again. I still myself and listen. It almost sounds as if it's right outside my cabin. Unable to contain my curiosity, I leave my journal to walk over and peek outside the door. There's no one there. Just Blue Lake, which is little more than a hop, skip, and a jump down a stone path ahead of me. To my left there's nothing but woods because Chickadee Cabin is the last before an expanse of tall pines and oaks. To my right . . .

I pull in a sharp breath. "What are you doing here?"

Hayden Bennett whirls to face me as he stops walking away

from my cabin. He has a surprised expression, as if he had no idea anyone else was here. Even though we've had plenty of classes together over the last couple years, I wouldn't say that Hayden and I are friends. He's that guy who's cute in theory, but who's always in trouble. I know this better than anyone because my mom is the principal of our high school. Usually when I stop in to see her, Hayden will be sitting outside her office, inside it, or he'll just be leaving. It's not that he does horrible things. He's just perpetually tardy, turns in his assignments late, and doodles on everything except paper.

I cross my arms over my chest. "This is private property," I tell him, waiting for an answer to why he's standing outside Chickadee Cabin. Camp Starling isn't even in the town where we live. It's a thirty-minute trip if my mom's the one driving. If I'm behind the wheel, it's more like forty because I only just got my license and I'm a cautious driver.

Maybe Hayden is a counselor here. I seriously doubt he filled out the application, though. Even if he did, my mom would never choose him. *Must be good with kids* is also a requirement. And from what I've seen, Hayden lacks people skills in general.

Case in point: instead of making conversation right now, he's just standing there. He kind of looks nervous, which is different from his usual apathetic demeanor. Even when he's outside my mom's office at school, he's slouched in the chair with his long dark bangs hanging over his eyes like he's just waiting to go inside to . . . what? I don't even know because I am never that unfazed about anything.

As I watch him, his eyes are wider than I've ever seen them, drawing me in to the color of his irises. They're brown. His gaze shifts from side to side. His feet are shifty too, making him look like he's ready to bolt. I notice the fabric messenger bag on his shoulder. It looks heavy and there's a bright green stain seeping through the canvas material. Before I can ask more questions, Hayden starts to back away.

His eyes dart around anywhere except to meet mine. What was he doing right before I peeked out of my cabin? I'm certain he was the source of the strange noises. "Hey, Pais. I, uh, didn't know anyone was here yet."

"Just me and my mom, *Principal* Manning," I tell him, emphasizing the word *principal* even though my mom takes that hat off during the summers. I'm just trying to ignite fear in Hayden's eyes. He doesn't look scared, though. Just suspect. "A few of the camp counselors are starting to arrive too." The counselors arrive one day before the campers. It gives us a chance to bond and review the rules before we take charge.

Hayden steps back and I can tell he's about to jet. I don't want him to go until I figure out why he's here to begin with, though. "We have counselor orientation this evening. Camp starts tomorrow," I tell him, trying to stall. "Today is Camper's Eve."

The skin between Hayden's dark eyes pinches softly. "Like Christmas Eve?"

I shrug. "Camper's Eve is what my dad used to call the afternoon before all the campers arrived for the first day. It might as well have been Christmas to him. He loved Camp Starling." I can feel my eyes suddenly burning and I know

4

they're glistening. Now I'm the one who wants to retreat. I don't talk about my dad much, and this is why.

Hayden looks mildly interested. "Used to? What does he call it now?"

Hayden didn't start attending my school until my seventh-grade year, right after I lost my dad. I guess he doesn't know my story. Why would he? I'm surprised he even knows my name. Or at least the first syllable of it. "My dad died when I was twelve."

Hayden looks at me for a long moment. Then his gaze drops to his feet. I notice that he's used a pen to draw all over his white Converse shoes. There's so much ink, they're practically black. I make out tiny streets and a cityscape. I think maybe there's a dragon on the toe of his other shoe. I look up at him again and his gaze swipes to the bag on his shoulder.

"My dad is gone too," Hayden says. "He doesn't have a good excuse. He just bolted one day." He shrugs like it's no big deal. Maybe it's not for him, but not having my father around is a huge deal to me.

"You never answered what you're doing here," I say more forcefully this time.

"I, uh, was just driving around and saw this place. I guess I wanted to see what it was."

He must think I'm gullible to buy such an obvious lie. No way would he waste gas to drive thirty minutes from his home for no good reason. "The Camp Starling sign at the front entrance should have clued you in that this place is a camp. At least for now," I mutter.

"What do you mean by that?" he asks.

Oops. I didn't mean to say that out loud. I shake my head. "N-nothing. Nothing I can control at least."

Hayden's gaze catches and holds mine. "You have more control than you think. Adults just like you to think you don't."

I watch him for a moment, wondering if he's right. If I could somehow reverse the huge tidal wave that's about to sweep my life off its axis. Once my mom makes up her mind, though, her decision is cemented. There's no wiggle room to compromise for what I want.

"A starling is a bird, right?" Hayden asks then.

I have to admit, I'm surprised and a little impressed that he knows this. "A starling is one of the most intelligent birds," I say. "They've actually outperformed tamarin monkeys in intelligence tests."

Hayden blinks.

I know a lot of random information about birds. It was my dad's thing and now it's kind of mine too.

"Wow. That's cool."

"Yeah." I quickly drop my gaze and deflect the attention back on him. "What's in your bag?" I take a step forward, but he takes several steps back, nearly tripping over his graffitied shoes.

"I'm sorry," he says again, looking at me for real this time. "I didn't know this was your mom's place. See you around, Pais."

"Paisley," I say, correcting him. Apparently he thinks he's

too cool to use my full name. He doesn't seem to hear me, though. He's already walking, half running, away. I watch as he veers off the path and into the woods that eventually lead to a fence that he'll need to clear before leaving the property. I have no doubt he'll be able to. He's an easy five foot ten, whereas I'm only five foot four standing tall. There's a parking lot beyond the fence. I'm guessing that's where his car is.

Again, I wonder what he was doing here and what that mysterious noise I heard before stepping out of my cabin was. I watch him disappear and another thought comes to mind. Since Mom and I are moving away from our hometown of Seabrook next month, I'm pretty sure that was the last time I'll ever lay eyes on Hayden Bennett.

❁

An hour later, I hear another noise outside Chickadee Cabin. It's not a rattle or a *SHHHH*. Instead, I hear footsteps, punctuated by Nora's muffled grunts as she lugs what's probably way too much stuff for two weeks of camp. I rush to the door, throw it open, and let out an excited shriek that surprises even myself. "You're here!"

She laughs as I pull her into the cabin. "Since we're sharing a car, I bugged Dad until he decided it would be easier to take me sooner than listen to me jabber for another second."

I understand exactly what she means. Nora is my best friend. I love her to pieces, but she does talk a lot. I, on the other hand, am the quiet one. I guess we even each other out. We've been best friends since third grade, when we were seated next to each other in class. I never got into trouble before Nora entered my life. Once she took the seat next to mine in third grade, though, it didn't matter that I was asking Nora to be quiet. Or reminding her that it wasn't the time for passing notes. Nope. I always got pinned right along with her. Needless to say, I disliked her at first. But then she shared her sugary snacks with me—the ones my mom would never buy. And when some bully tossed my lunch bag to the ground and stomped on it, Nora stomped on the bully's foot. In the third grade, that's the stuff best friends are made of. Now here we are, upcoming high school juniors and still inseparable.

Nora walks past me and eyes the bunks on the right side of the room. "Which bed is mine?"

Nora is only staying in Chickadee Cabin tonight. Tomorrow the campers arrive and she'll sleep in her assigned cabin with eight other girls. Chickadee has always been our cabin, ever since we were twelve.

"The last to arrive gets first pick. Camp Starling tradition," I remind her, even though that's a camper rule and we're finally counselors. "I thought you'd want the top bunk," I tell her.

Nora casts me a grin over her shoulder. "And you'd be right. You sure you don't mind?" she asks as a courtesy more than anything. She's already climbing the ladder on her way to stake her imaginary flag.

"Nope. I already put the sheets on it for you too."

"You are the best." Nora throws herself down on the top

mattress and sighs dramatically. "Last summer was wonderful, but this year we're in charge."

I clear my throat. "Actually, Mom and Dave are." And admitting that Dave has any authority at this place irritates me. He doesn't know anything about this camp. Unlike my mom and me, this is Dave's first year even stepping foot on the campgrounds. All because he and my mom met on some dating site nine months ago. He winked at her and she winked back. I'm no expert on the subject, but that's hardly romantic.

"You know what I mean," Nora says. "We get to tell the campers what to do. I've always wanted to be the boss," she says, gleefully.

She's not kidding either. Nora loves to tell others what to do. Some part of me thinks that's one reason we get along so well. Because I let her make most of the decisions about where we go and what we do. She's in the driver's seat, literally and figuratively. It's not that I can't think for myself. I'm usually just too busy thinking about other things, like schoolwork and swim team. And Camp Starling. I don't care about where or what I eat or what we watch on TV.

Nora sighs dramatically above me. "I have a feeling that this is going to be the most amazing summer ever, Paisley."

My eyes do that thing again. They well up with tears and I blink quickly and turn away so Nora doesn't catch me almost crying. I haven't told her the news yet. Usually I tell Nora everything as soon as there's anything remotely to tell. That's what best friends do.

Not this time, though. I promised my mom I wouldn't

tell anyone the news just yet. I only found out myself three days ago.

There I was, like Nora, thinking the best summer of my life was just around the corner. Then Mom and Dave sat me down on Thursday night to tell me that they had made a decision that would affect us all. I thought they were going to tell me they were engaged. Over the last couple months, I've seen the signs that they were getting serious. Dave has shifted from being a guest in our home to having free range of the fridge. He even attended the Manning family reunion with us in April. We took a family vacation at the start of my summer break last month and Dave was included even though he's not part of our family.

I wasn't exactly thrilled when I thought that was the big news they were going to spring on me. Dave is okay, but he's allergic to cats. So, now that he's spending so much time at our home, my cat, Spiral, is confined to my bedroom. The cat was there first. If anyone should be confined to one room in our house, it's Dave. He's also allergic to strawberries, which happen to be my favorite fruit. My mom never buys them anymore because what if Dave somehow eats one?

Turns out, an engagement wasn't the big news they wanted to tell me. Not even close.

"Paisley, honey," my mom said three days ago, taking hold of my hand. I noticed then that she didn't have on an engagement ring. That was my first clue that this news was bigger. "After these two weeks of camp, Dave is moving to be close to his mother. Her health is declining."

So they weren't getting married. They were breaking up.

"Oh." I looked at Dave. "I'm really sorry about your mom." And I sincerely was. I know how it feels to have a sick parent. My dad was sick for six months before he died. I wouldn't wish that on anyone. Not even Dave.

"His mother lives in Wyoming," my mom continued. She looked at Dave and back at me. "Paisley, honey, I know this might not be good news for you, but I've decided that we're moving to Wyoming with Dave."

As you can probably guess, I didn't take it well. I thought an engagement would be miserable news, but this was so much worse.

"If his mom is sick, why can't she move to Seabrook?" I asked, tears spilling onto my cheeks. "Why do we have to go there?"

"Because Wyoming is the only home she's ever known," my mom said gently.

"But this is the only home *I've* ever known!" I practically yelled at her. It wasn't fair. Even though this was a decision that affected us all, Mom and Dave had made it without me. There was no choice. "What about Camp Starling? North Carolina is like a thousand miles from Wyoming. How will we manage the campground from there?" This camp for teen girls and boys is only one of many things that are booked on the campground throughout the year. There is no way Mom could handle all the scheduling and upkeep from a million miles away.

My mom gave me a look. It was apologetic, but decided.

"This fall, I'm going to put the camp up for sale, Paisley. It hasn't been easy for me to manage on my own since your dad died. It'll be impossible after the move."

So there it was. This is the last hurrah for Camp Starling. My last Camper's Eve. It'll be my first and last time being a camp counselor here. My last summer in the town where I grew up. My last season of swimsuits and bare feet with Nora. Mom and Dave told me all of this on Thursday night and the For Sale sign went up in front of my house on Friday morning. Everything is about to change, and it's just too much to even think about.

"Paisley? Earth to Paisley Manning," Nora says from the top bunk. She rolls over and looks down at me. There's already a spattering of deep brown freckles on her nose from the sun.

I turn my back and pretend to look out the cabin window, catching my own reflection for a moment. No freckles for me. My skin isn't ghostly pale, but it isn't tan either. It's kind of the color of Hayden's canvas bag from earlier. My hair, in sharp contrast, is bright red, and the reason why my dad's nickname for me used to be Birdie—because I was "as bright and beautiful as a little bird." Even though technically the brightest and most beautiful birds are the males. Everyone knows that.

"Are you even listening?" Nora asks.

"Yeah. Of course, I—" My words stumble over each other when I notice something outside the window. I lean forward, plastering my hands to the glass. "Oh, no."

I hear Nora climb off the bunk bed and walk over to where

I'm standing, her flip-flops clapping softly against the soles of her feet. "What?" She stands to look over my shoulder.

I point at Cardinal Cabin, next to ours. "Look."

Nora sucks in an audible gasp. "Is that . . . spray paint?"

I nod quietly. Knowingly. It's still wet and one drop of paint is dripping down the side of the cabin. Painted in Oscar-the-Grouch green is a dragon with a long tail and outstretched wings. The detail is incredible. The dragon has a long snout and wide eyes that seem to be looking right at me. I would actually think it was pretty amazing artwork if the canvas weren't one of my dad's beloved cabins.

"Who would do that?" Nora asks in disbelief.

The color of the paint is the same as the stain on Hayden's bag. It's not a mystery to me who did this. I know *exactly* who's responsible.

CHAPTER TWO

The thing about having a cabin next to the woods is that cellphone reception is spotty. Every few steps, Nora holds up her phone and checks the bars as we walk toward where my mom and Dave are staying. My cellphone is dead because I failed to charge it last night, too caught up in the other details of camping.

"Still nothing?" I ask Nora, noting that several of the cabins have the same seaweed green paint snaking haphazardly across the sides. There was only one dragon. The rest of the graffiti consists of abstract designs that seem to have no real meaning. Not to my eye, at least.

What was Hayden thinking?

The first answer that pops into mind is that he was thinking he wouldn't get caught. And that would have been true if I hadn't heard him and stepped outside. I'm the only witness to his crime and the only thing standing between him not getting pinned for this and possibly getting into a whole heap of trouble. He might even be arrested. At the very least, he'll be grounded for the entire break. I know if it were me, I would be.

The thing is, it would never be me because I know the difference between right and wrong. I'm pretty sure Hayden does too, but he just doesn't care. I'm so angry at him right now I want to scream. I'm also embarrassed. Why would I ever confide in someone like him about my dad?

Nora lowers her phone and groans. "We might as well just walk there and tell your mom about this graffiti mess in person."

I nod, too overcome to speak as we continue the half-mile trek, walking barefoot side by side.

After a few minutes, Nora looks at me. "You're being quiet. Are you that upset about the spray paint?"

She knows how much the cabins mean to me, mostly because they meant so much to my dad. He helped build these cabins with his own hands. I have a whole scrapbook filled with pictures of him building each cabin and laying down the stone paths. He had a hand in everything here. In his day job, he was an accountant, which he used to joke was the most boring job in the galaxy. *"Way worse than Luke Skywalker's job of fighting off Stormtroopers."* But my dad hung on through tax season for camping season, when he got to play all summer here on Blue Lake.

I turn to Nora. "How dare Hayden Bennett trespass and mess this place up!" I explode. "Who does he think he is?"

Nora stops walking. Her jaw goes slack, showing me the

bright blue gum she's been chewing. "You saw Hayden here? With your own eyes?"

I nod quickly. "And he saw me. We spoke to each other. Although I didn't know what he'd done at the time. He was acting guilty, though."

"Hayden is guilty by nature," Nora mutters, giving me the impression that she's not a huge fan of his either. We've never really discussed Hayden before, which is odd because Nora has discussed the date-ability of all the other boys who go to our high school. "I thought we were just walking up to Principal Manning's cabin to tell her about the paint. I didn't realize we were also telling her who did it."

Nora always calls my mom Principal Manning. I mean, yes, my mom is the principal, but when we have sleepovers at my house, Nora still calls my mom Principal Manning. It makes me feel like I'm at school instead of home in my pj's. I can tell my mom wishes Nora would drop the title too.

"I can't believe him! I could just . . . *ugh!*" I nearly shout.

Nora looks surprised. "I don't think I've ever seen you this angry before. Your face is red."

I blow a breath up to cool my cheeks. "Dad wanted a natural wood finish for the outside of the cabins. No paint. Seeing the awful green color that Hayden doused the cabins with would have broken his camper's heart." Tears sting my eyes.

Nora puts a hand on my shoulder. She was there for me when my dad died. I had no idea what to do or how to act, but she just took charge in her Nora way. She's a huge reason why I got through that summer when I was twelve. I owe her a lot. "We'll make Hayden Bennett pay for this," she vows quietly.

I nod and set my sights on Eagle Cabin, where Mom is staying. All the cabins have a bird-themed title. Blue Jay. Raven. Cardinal. Bird-watching is one of the things we learn here at Camp Starling. Some of the kids think it's boring, but it's one of my favorite pastimes. I love wearing my binoculars around my neck and walking the long, weaving path through the woods while searching for a certain bird. My dad used to compare the day before camp to Christmas Eve. I would compare bird searching to the best Easter egg hunt there ever was.

We step up to Eagle Cabin and I lift my closed fist to make a staccato beat on the cabin door. My mouth is dry, as if we're actually standing outside the principal's office right now. Camp Starling isn't supposed to feel like school. Camper's Eve isn't supposed to come with any negative emotion. I blame Hayden for my sweaty palms and the rush of heat that fills my cheeks.

My mom opens the door and smiles at us. Principal Mom wears dress suits, a tight bun, and lipstick. Camp Mom wears a bright yellow T-shirt, a ponytail, and keeps a clean face—no makeup. Camp Mom rarely looks stressed, unlike Principal Mom. "Hi, girls," she says, looking between us expectantly.

"Hi, Principal Manning," Nora says.

Mom takes a visible breath. "Nora, please feel free to call me Ms. Ellen this summer, okay?" She's told Nora this at least a million times. If I accomplish anything this summer, it'll be to make Nora call my mom Ms. Ellen. My mom won't be her principal anymore, though. Because we're moving. Because of Dave.

Speaking of Dave, he steps up behind my mom and waves

17

with exaggerated enthusiasm. He's been trying too hard to make nice with me ever since they broke the news of the move. His cheesy jokes were only minor annoyances to me before. Now I can't stand to listen to them. I can barely stand to be in the same room with him. I blame Hayden for ruining Camper's Eve, and I credit Dave for ruining the rest of my teenage life.

"You two look very serious," my mom says.

Nora takes the lead, as always. "Principal Manning, someone has painted graffiti all over the side of Chickadee Cabin. Also, Blue Jay Cabin, Robin Egg, Sparrow, and Woodpecker." Nora slides her gaze over to me, passing the buck so I can do the honors of revealing the culprit.

"I ran into Hayden Bennett earlier," I say. "He was carrying a bag with paint stains that matched the color on the cabins."

My mom looks at me. "Are you sure it was Hayden that you saw, Paisley?"

I nod. "We spoke to each other."

Disappointment flickers in my mom's eyes. She turns to look at Dave over her shoulder. Dave doesn't know anything about being a Starling. It's bad enough that he's trying to fill my dad's shoes in my mom's life, but he's also vying for that role here.

I really don't think Dave will last the two weeks, though. He's super pale and from my experience, he'll have an unbearable sunburn by the end of this week. He's also bald, so if he doesn't keep a hat on his head, that's going to blister.

Mom sighs wearily. "Thanks for telling me, girls. I know Hayden's mom well. I'll assess the damage and give her a call." She puts a hand on my shoulder. I can feel her pep talk through the squeeze from her hand. It tells me that she understands everything. About today. And camp. The pending move. And Dave.

But how *could* she understand? When she was my age, she attended a camp, summer after summer. That's where she met and fell in love with my dad. That's why they decided to create a camp of their own, Camp Starling, because they had the perfect camp experience growing up. Mom couldn't know how I feel right now because she was never ripped away from everything she ever knew the way I will be next month.

Mom pulls her hand away and gives Dave a look that I catch.

He smiles at me, then rubs the back of his head, which I've realized is something he does when he's trying to think of something clever to say. "I guess your friend thought the cabins could use a little sprucing up before the big day."

I know I'm supposed to laugh at his weak joke. I get that Dave is trying, but I can't bring myself to reciprocate. Does that make me an awful human being? Instead of smiling, I frown as I retreat down the path with Nora, calling over my shoulder, "Hayden Bennett isn't my friend."

That's for sure.

❋

My first counselor orientation should be amazing. I've only been looking forward to it all year. Instead, I can barely listen

19

to the rules and expectations—which I already know by heart anyway—because my mind is on Hayden.

Good thing I'll never see him again, because if I did, I might totally go off on him. No more Miss Nice Girl.

"No one leaves the cabins after nine p.m.," my mom says. "It's lights-out because counselors and campers alike need to rest. Camp days are long and tiring."

Nora leans in and whispers as my mom reviews camp rules. "Who's going to be your camp crush this year?"

Camp crushes are as much a tradition as Campers' Breakfast and bird-watching. I take bird-watching a lot more seriously, though.

Humoring Nora, I look around at the guy counselors. There's only five because Isaiah broke his leg just before coming. My mom is working on finding a replacement for him. Otherwise, Dave will take that role. Those poor campers who'd get him as a counselor.

My gaze moves from left to right. First, there's Jacob, football player extraordinaire and all-around golden boy. Nora claimed him last year, even though I did kind of like him first.

Ricardo is tall and athletic. He's been coming here for years and is considered the camp clown. He can make me laugh, but I'm not sure we'd ever be able to hold a serious conversation.

In contrast to Ricardo, Dom is serious. He knows his bird facts as well as me. We could talk for hours for this reason. But he's always been more of a friend. I've never felt sparks with him, so I can rule him out.

Kyle and Joey are fairly new. They're brothers, both with light brown hair and deep summer tans, who just came to the boys and girls camp for the first time last year. Before that, they had only attended the all-boys camp that happens here in June. I don't know much about the two, other than they're ultra-competitive when it comes to camp challenges. Like me.

"I'm not sure," I say with a shrug, pinning my gaze back on my mom, who is now talking about what to do when campers wake in the mornings. They're to be escorted to the Bird Bath area to freshen up for the day. Then everyone reports to the Birdfeeder for chow, otherwise known as Campers' Breakfast.

I look at the guys again and find Jacob looking at me this time. He smiles and offers a small wave that I reciprocate. He is waving at me, right? My cheeks flare hot and I return to watching my mom, a nervous flutter in my chest like a moth batting around one of those outdoor lights.

"Did Jacob just wave at you?" Nora gasps. "Maybe he's into you, Paisley."

"Or maybe he's just being friendly," I whisper back. "Aren't you still into Jacob?"

"No way. That was last year, Paisley. This year I think Kyle is kind of cute," Nora says with a small giggle.

Camp crushes are serious business in some ways, but apparently, they also carry an expiration date. Nora has always been very take-charge when it comes to matchmaking. It's like she feels it's her duty to make sure everyone is paired up. Last year, she tried her hardest to make me and Isaiah talk. We became friends, yeah, but I wasn't doodling his name in my camper's journal or anything. Come to think of it, I've never doodled any guy's name in my camper's journal.

When my mom is done reviewing all the dos and don'ts

of being a counselor, she frees us to return to our cabins. We can sleep all together tonight because the campers don't arrive until mid-morning tomorrow. After that, it's one counselor and eight campers to each cabin.

Meghan and Maria step up beside me and Nora. Emma and Tisha join us too. In a nutshell, Meghan and Maria are twins on the outside, but Meghan is the extrovert and Maria is introverted. They remind me of Nora and myself in that way. Emma is the sweetheart of the group and Tisha is the queen of sarcasm. Nora, of course, thinks she's the boss of us all and maybe she's right.

"Everyone want to stay in Chickadee Cabin tonight?" Nora asks the other female counselors as we walk down the stone path toward the girls' cabins. "Paisley and I have already set up in there."

"Fine by me," Tisha says. "We better turn in early, though. Campers never sleep the first night. Tomorrow is going to be rough."

"And exciting," Emma says. There's a melodious tone to her voice. "Can you believe we're all counselors this year?"

"*We* were counselors last year," Meghan says of her and Maria. They're seventeen. "Trust me when I say you want to sleep tonight. Being a counselor is a lot more work than you expect."

Maria nods her agreement, but says nothing.

We reach Chickadee Cabin and everyone claims their bunk for the night.

"I think I'm going to talk to Kyle tomorrow during the

Trail of Fireflies," Nora announces. The Trail of Fireflies is a tradition on the first night of camp. Everyone walks the path searching for fireflies, but also connecting with their prospective crushes. "And Paisley wants to talk to Jacob," Nora informs the group.

"I never said that," I object.

"But he waved at you at the orientation," Nora says, as if this is proof that he will be my camp crush this year.

"Meghan?" Nora asks. "Who are you interested in?"

"I call Ricardo," she says.

"That leaves Joey and Dom," Nora says. "Tisha? Maria? Emma? Who are you going to fight over?"

"Leave us alone, Nora," Tisha complains. "Crushes aren't assigned. Maybe I'll talk to Kyle too," she says as an afterthought.

"But I just claimed him!" Nora rolls onto her side and frowns at Tisha on the bottom bunk across from her.

"Crushes can't be claimed. And I'm not interested in Kyle anyway. I was just pulling your leg," Tisha teases, rolling away from Nora toward the wall. "Good night, everyone!" she calls.

"Good night," Emma says.

I wait until everyone is quiet and I hear Nora's heavy breathing above me. Then I pull my camper's journal out from under my mattress and pop the cap off my purple gel pen, securing it in a fold of the thin quilt on my bunk. I turn to the second page and stare at it, waiting for my thoughts to meet me. The only thing I've been able to think about all afternoon is Hayden Bennett. Destruction of property is a crime, right?

Maybe he'll spend the summer in juvenile detention. That sounds awful to me, even though I have no idea what happens in a place like that.

I set my pen to the paper and start unloading all my worries.

> This is supposed to be the best summer ever. How can that be when I know it'll end in tears, and not the kind where you hug newfound friends and promise to see them again next year, same time, same place?

At some point, I realize that Nora's deep breathing has stopped. Is she awake? I know I promised my mom I would keep this secret under wraps, but I feel like if I don't tell someone right now, I'll combust. I need to talk to Nora. She's my best friend. Maybe she can help me figure out how to fix my life. "Nora?" I whisper into the dark.

I hear her roll around on the bunk above me.

"Nora, are you awake?" I'm suddenly desperate to unload my secrets to someone, something, anything other than this journal.

I hear her heavy breathing start back up, followed by a sleepy snort.

The thing about secrets is that they make you feel alone, which is how I feel in this moment. It's just been me and Mom since Dad died, but even she seems out of reach since Dave came into our lives.

I sigh, close my journal with my gel pen inside, and shove

it under my mattress where it'll be safe. Then I close my eyes and listen to the song of the cicadas outside, hoping that sleep finds me fast. Maybe when I wake up in the morning, this whole plan for the last summer at Camp Starling and the big move in August will all have been a bad dream.

CHAPTER THREE

Camp Time: Monday. July 18.

I've been nodding so long that I have a cramp in my neck. I stopped listening to what Nora was saying a while ago, back when she was telling me about her mom's sudden fixation with the Hallmark Channel. Apparently, combined with chocolate, it gives Ms. Dunlap all the endorphins she needs to work through her divorce from Nora's dad.

Note to self: watch Hallmark and eat chocolate if I ever have a broken heart.

The campers have been slowly arriving at the drop-off point all morning, and while nodding to Nora's stories, I've also been smiling in greeting to the kids. Some look so nervous that I worry they might throw up. I direct them to the community bathrooms, housed between the guys' and girls' cabins, an area known as The Bird Bath. Other kids show up and their eyes are suspiciously glassy. Then there are those kids who practically race out of their parents' vehicles without even turning back. Two weeks of parental freedom and summer fun? Yes, please.

Tisha walks over and stands beside us. Her dark hair is slicked back behind a fun bandana with a wild floral pattern today. Since last summer, she's grown at least two inches taller, making me officially the shortest among my friends. "Whatcha talking about?" She looks between Nora and me.

"Nora was just telling me about her mom's new obsession with Hallmark movies," I say. That effectively passes the conversation away from me so I can zone out and focus on the campers. I see a couple of the guy counselors huddled nearby and my gaze sticks on Jacob for a moment. He looks up and catches me watching him, which makes me look away. I check to see if Nora witnessed that interaction—because I'll never hear the end of it if she did—but she's too busy telling Tisha about all the things her mom is doing right now that add up to evidence of a midlife crisis. Even though I'm pretty sure Nora's mom is only in her thirties.

I glance at Jacob again. He's not looking in my direction any longer. Instead, he's talking to one of the boy campers who just arrived. I know Nora thinks so, but I'm not really sure Jacob is interested in me. He's tall with broad shoulders and plays football for another high school nearby. I'm more of a book nerd. He is a really nice guy, though. I'm sure we'd find common ground if we spent any amount of time together. I watch as he high-fives a camper. Good with kids—check. Then he waves at another guy heading in his direction.

The guy has his head tipped down but he looks vaguely familiar. He's wearing the camp counselor uniform—a yellow

T-shirt and olive green shorts. I wonder if he's Isaiah's replacement. The guy's black hair sweeps across his forehead and hangs low in his eyes. It takes me a moment to register who he is.

What is Hayden Bennett doing *here*? And why is he wearing *our* uniform? No way is he a counselor. Hayden has never attended Camp Starling a day in his life. As far as I know, the only time he's ever been at this campsite was yesterday when he illegally spray-painted several of the cabins. Is that why he's here? Has he come to beg for my mom's forgiveness? Or maybe he's here to gloat over the damage he's done. Well, I don't want to hear it. Because today is day one of Camp Starling and several of the campers will arrive to see that their cabin has ugly green swirls of paint all over the sides. And their experience will be less special because of it.

An angry fireball forms in the pit of my stomach. I imagine lifting it out with my hands and throwing it in Hayden's general direction. I don't want to hurt him, of course. Just blast that cool, unfazed, can't-touch-this look off his face. And singe our camp's colors off his body. Leaving his boxers intact, of course.

Before I know it, I'm stomping in his direction and then standing right in front of him. I pin my hands to my hips and lift my chin because he's several inches taller than me. I don't think I ever realized just how tall he is.

"Hey, Pais," he says in a relaxed tone. He's not exactly smiling, but there's a hint of a smile dancing in his brown eyes.

For a moment, I'm taken aback by the colors of his eyes at this range. We've never stood this close before. His eyes aren't just brown. They're a mixture of brown and green with golden flecks. It's as if some eye fairy with cans of spray paint of their own has made graffiti inside his irises in the most amazing way.

I blink, remembering the angry fireball in my belly. "What are you doing here?"

"The same thing you are, I suspect," he tells me.

But that's not possible. I earned this role, fair and square. I shake my head. Either he's disillusioned or mistaken, but he's wrong, nonetheless. I'm just about to tell him so when I hear my mom's voice coming up behind me.

"Hayden!"

I turn toward her. After what Hayden did yesterday, certainly she'll take over from here. I wait for my mom's lips to purse the way she does when she's upset. I'm expecting her blue eyes to narrow in over her nose and for her to fold her arms at her chest and demand to know what Hayden is doing back at Camp Starling. Instead, she smiles as if Hayden were an honored guest.

"I'm so glad you could make it. This is going to be a fantastic two weeks," she tells him.

"If you say so, Principal Manning." Hayden brushes his long black bangs out of his eyes as he looks at her.

"Please, call me Ms. Ellen when we're here at camp. That's what all the other kids will call me this summer."

"But he won't be here this summer," I tell her, trying my best to remain calm. Someone needs to escort Hayden off the premises before I lose it.

My mom's smile deepens as she looks at me. "Good news,

Paisley. Hayden is going to join you and the other counselors here over the next two weeks. He's going to run the arts and crafts program."

I feel my face scrunch. "We don't *have* an arts and crafts program."

"Maybe not in the past, but we do now," she says proudly.

I shake my head. "It's bad enough that you're closing the camp, but now you have to change everything about Camp Starling before you shut the doors?"

My mom narrows her gaze and lowers her voice. "We are not discussing that with anyone just yet, Paisley Grace. Remember?"

Uh-oh. First and middle name means she's mad. But so am I. "Hayden didn't attend orientation yesterday. I seriously doubt he even filled out the application or meets the camp counselor criteria."

My mom's hand finds my shoulder, and she gives it a gentle squeeze. "The criteria are more guidelines than requirements. And sometimes we bend those guidelines. In special circumstances."

"Special circumstances?" I repeat, not bothering to hide my frustration. "You mean like when someone completely disrespects private property and graffitis Dad's cabins?" I glare at Hayden. "You could have at least doodled birds instead of a stupid dragon. The theme here is birds, not like you'd know that."

My mom clears her throat. "That's enough, Paisley," she warns. "I was hoping you would show Hayden the ropes. Since he wasn't here for orientation yesterday, he'll learn faster if you share your expertise with him."

"But——" I start to say.

My mom's hand is still on my shoulder. She gives it another squeeze, but this time I know it's to silence me more than to offer comfort. "As you know, we're a counselor short because Isaiah broke his leg. Hayden has already apologized about yesterday. He, his mom, and I have worked out an agreement. He's going to undo his handiwork on the cabins while also helping out here at camp."

"So this is Hayden's punishment?" I gesture in Hayden's direction. "He spray-paints all over the cabins and instead of getting into trouble, he gets to come to summer camp? Which is pretty much an incentive to do more graffiti, if you ask me."

My mom's smile tilts and falls away. I see a flicker of disappointment in her eyes. I'm usually a nice person. Truly. I'm an afterschool tutor, and this past Christmas break, I volunteered at the nursing home where my grandmother lives. This guy has just gotten under my skin in the worst kind of way. He's broken the rules. Not only that, he somehow convinced my mother to break them too. The Manning family doesn't break rules. We're neat and orderly. We don't graffiti other people's property.

"We'll talk about this later, Paisley," my mom says. Her voice has taken on that stern principal tone. "Right now, if you don't mind, I'd like for you to show Hayden where Falcon Cabin is. Hayden will be the counselor there, along with Dave."

"But . . . ," I begin to protest.

My mom holds up a hand to stop me from saying anything more. It's not a request. It's a command. And I suspect if I refuse, I'll be in a lot more trouble than Hayden got into for spray-painting the cabins.

"Sure." I sweep my gaze in Hayden's general direction. I don't look at him directly. Instead, I start walking forward. He'll follow me if he wants to find his cabin. For all I care, he can get lost.

"Wait up, Pais," Hayden calls to me after we've passed several cabins on our trek down the central path that connects the girls' cabins to the boys'.

I slow down and wait for him to approach, keeping my back to him. "It's Paisley."

"You seem mad," he says.

"You think?" I ask, tone thick with sarcasm.

"Geesh, you're worse than your mom," he mutters behind me.

I whirl and face him now, making him skid to a stop in those awful graffitied shoes. Okay, they'd actually be kind of cool if they weren't on *his* feet. "Excuse me? You're comparing me to my mother? It seems to me she should be your favorite person right now. You're lucky she's letting you off easy after what you did."

Hayden holds up both hands. "Bad choice of words, okay? All I meant was you're tough. Like her."

The way he says it this time makes me think it might be a good thing. I feel this unwelcome warmth crawling through my chest—which makes me feel frustrated because I want to stay angry at him. For the entire summer if possible.

"What makes you think she's letting me off easy anyway?" Hayden asks. "Starting an art program from nothing is a lot of work. Not to mention scrubbing my artwork off the cabins and cleaning the toilets."

I laugh unexpectedly. "You're cleaning latrines? I guess that makes me feel slightly better."

Hayden doesn't look amused. He brushes those long, dark bangs out of his eyes. "I respect your mom, okay? If I had known this camp belonged to her, I never would have trespassed and painted those cabins."

I fold my arms over my chest. "Are you going to tell me the real reason you did that? Because I know you weren't just driving around aimlessly."

He looks down at his feet and doesn't answer.

"Whatever. I don't care." I shake my head and point to a cabin a few feet ahead of me. "There you go. Home sweet home. Luckily yours doesn't have any of the awful green paint on the side."

Hayden shoves his hands in the pockets of his long shorts. They're the right color, yes, but knee-length cargo shorts are not part of the uniform. "Your cabin will be the first one I fix," he promises.

"I doubt it'll come clean. It's paint. The wood will be stained forever because of you." Maybe my mom went easy on him, but I don't plan to. "All because you felt like being destructive. Just try not to ruin anything else with your art while you're here, okay?"

"Got it," he says.

I turn to walk away before I say anything else I might regret.

Because I do regret being so harsh toward him. I can't seem to help myself, though. Everything is out of sorts in my world right now. And the fact that Hayden Bennett is now a camp counselor is further proof of that.

I take a few steps, but guilt makes me turn back. Hayden looks lost, like some of the campers being dropped off earlier. I force myself to soften my tone of voice. "You're not alone in this. Dave will be rooming in the cabin with you and your campers. You'll be okay."

Hayden still looks uneasy. For a loner kid like him, I'm guessing so many roommates in a confined space might be his idea of a jail cell.

"Several of the guy counselors here are from our school," I tell him. "You know Ricardo, right?"

Hayden kicks a rock at his feet, drawing my attention to those shoes of his. They are not part of the camp dress code either. "Yeah. I don't think we've ever said a word to each other, though."

I'm not surprised. Ricardo isn't just a clown at camp. He's the class clown at school too. He likes to draw attention to himself, whereas Hayden seems to shrink away from the limelight—probably so he doesn't get sent to the principal's office more frequently than he already does. "Jacob plays football for Eastville High," I say. "If you know anything about quarterbacks or the NFL, that might get you an in with him."

Hayden shakes his head, his gaze dodging mine. "I'll just stay out of their way, and they'll stay out of mine. I don't need an in with anyone."

There are a lot of things I want to say in response to this comment. That's not how being at Camp Starling works. At camp, we're a team—one big, happy family. But maybe Hayden isn't used to having that kind of camaraderie in his life.

"We'll all meet in the common area in about an hour to go over camp expectations and rules with the campers," I say. "Since you're a counselor, you're already supposed to know those things, so do your best to pretend, okay?"

He gives a barely perceptible nod.

Good enough. I turn, eager to get back to Nora, Tisha, and the others. This is the extent of me "showing the ropes" to Hayden.

"Hey, Pais?"

I turn back, slightly annoyed. "It's *Paisley* to you," I remind him.

"Right. What did you mean earlier when you told your mom this place was shutting down?"

Now I look down at my feet. He wasn't supposed to hear that. "Just forget that. It doesn't matter."

"Is that the thing you were talking about yesterday? The thing you have no control over?"

He comes off so aloof at school. I'm surprised he remembers anything from our earlier conversation. "Look, I shouldn't have said anything in front of you. It's not common knowledge yet."

Hayden shoves his hands in his pockets. "I don't have any friends here. I won't tell anyone. Scout's honor." He holds up two fingers.

"I don't believe for a second that you were a Boy Scout," I say, putting my hands on my hips.

Hayden hesitates. "No, not a Scout. But my brother and I were both Little Rangers back in the day. We even had a camp-out here one summer."

There's a lot to process in that statement. Little Rangers is a camping and outdoor program for elementary-aged boys in our community. They use the Camp Starling grounds for a lot of their get-togethers. "I didn't know you had a brother." I've never seen Hayden hanging around with anyone at school, but maybe his brother is older. Or younger. "You camped here?"

Hayden nods. "It was a long time ago."

"I see." I want to ask more questions, but that would imply getting to know Hayden Bennett better and maybe even forming a truce. No way is that gonna happen.

"Why would your mom close this place?" he asks again.

I sigh and mutter, "Because she's following her heart and it's dragging us to Wyoming to be with Dave."

Hayden has this stare. It's intense and I can almost feel his thoughts circulating around in his head. I'm not sure why, but feeling his eyes on me makes me flustered. "Dave seems pretty okay."

"To you maybe. But he's single-handedly ruining my life."

"Then why don't you just break them up?" Hayden asks, as if that is the obvious solution. "Problem solved."

I laugh softly. Here I thought he was having deep thoughts and instead he's thinking of ways to conjure up mischief. "You would say something like that."

"What's that supposed to mean?"

"Well, you're forever in trouble at school. Of course your solution to my problem would be something that hurts someone else."

Hayden flinches slightly as if my words have tiny barbs. "Well, they're hurting you, aren't they?"

I swallow. He's right. The thought of moving away from everyone and everything I've ever known is painful. I don't want to discuss it with Hayden, though. I barely know him, and I definitely don't like him. "I don't know why I even told you all this." Especially since I haven't even told Nora yet. "Just please don't say anything, all right?"

"I told you I wouldn't," he says quietly. His intense stare is back, at least until that chunk of dark hair falls over his eyes.

"Well, I guess I have no choice but to trust you." I turn and walk away for real this time.

CHAPTER FOUR

I make it back to where Nora, Tisha, and Emma are still directing kids on where to go. For the most part, everyone has arrived. Camp Starling is a small camp. We don't accept more than ninety-six enrollments per camp and twelve counselors. Meghan and Maria turn to me as I approach. They're identical, so unless they're talking, I have no idea which one is which.

"Hi, Meghan." I take note of the one who smiles the quickest. She's wearing mini pearl stud earrings in her ears and her black hair is pulled back in a high ponytail, versus Maria, whose hair is pulled into a lower one. Noted.

Meghan's face lights up. "I've met all the kids who'll be in Seagull Cabin with me. They seem like a great group."

"Have you met your campers yet?" Maria asks me quietly.

I nod. I only got to meet them briefly because my mom ordered me to show Hayden the ropes. "Mine seem nice too."

"It's going to be a fantastic two weeks," Meghan says.

Have we always been so enthusiastic going into the first

day of summer camp? I guess so. The difference is I'm usually the leader of this pack of enthusiasm.

"For sure." I offer a smile in the twins' direction. There's a lump growing in my throat, though, making it hard to breathe.

"What's wrong?" Maria asks. "You seem off."

Now all my friends stop what they're doing and look at me with fresh eyes, agreeing that I don't quite look like myself.

I wrangle the loose strand of hair that slips in front of my eyes and tuck it behind my ear. "I just showed the new counselor, Hayden Bennett, to Falcon Cabin."

Nora's mouth falls open. "*The* Hayden Bennett? He can't be a counselor here. He isn't camp counselor material."

"Preaching to the choir," I say.

"And he's the one who spray-painted the cabins," Nora adds. "Is this his punishment? Because it doesn't fit the crime."

This causes a discussion over the graffiti incident from yesterday. Then Nora shares stories about Hayden with the others. Nothing too horrible. He graffitied the side of the drink machine in the students' court at school—that's why it's now catty-corner down the hall with the cafeteria. He refused to get up and read a report in front of the class when half the final grade was for the oral presentation.

"Maybe he's shy or something," Meghan says. She and Maria attend Eastview High just like Jacob.

"Or he just doesn't care about grades," Tisha adds.

"I heard he also used Sharpies to draw all over the guys' bathroom stalls," I say. "Some guy took pictures with his cellphone and showed the whole class. It was caricatures of several of the teachers. It was kind of funny, even though I'm pretty sure my mom didn't think so."

"Don't you guys think you're being a little harsh?" Emma finally asks. "I mean, if this guy is going to be a counselor here, like us, we need to put our differences aside and give him a clean slate."

Tisha frowns at our sweet friend. "Don't tell me you've already got a thing for this new guy."

Emma lays a hand on her chest. "Me? No." She shakes her head quickly. "I don't even know him. I just know how it feels to be the new kid on the block." Emma only moved to North Carolina two years ago. "It's not easy."

This makes me think of my upcoming junior year. I'll be at a new school too, all thanks to Dave. "Okay, fine," I say. "Hayden can have a clean slate about all the school stuff, but I can't forgive him for ruining the cabins. He doesn't get a clean slate on that."

"I guess we know who Paisley won't be crushing on this summer," Tisha says with a small laugh.

Nora scoffs. "As if. Paisley and Hayden are like oil and water. Paisley belongs with Jacob this summer anyway," she announces to the group, not for the first time.

I inwardly bristle even though I can admit Jacob is cute. Maybe I will try to connect with him this year, seeing that Nora isn't interested. Then again, I'm moving in less than a month. The home I've lived in all my life has a For Sale sign on the front lawn. Why start anything remotely romantic when my life is about to be turned inside out?

One hour later, all the campers are sitting attentively at the main camp gathering spot, otherwise known as the Birdfeeder. I realized a long time ago how cheesy that name was, but it's consistent with the whole bird theme here at Starling. And it's my dad's special brand of cheesy, not Dave's.

I slide my gaze to Dave, who is seated up front with my mom. She's done most of the talking, of course. She's already welcomed all the campers and given them an overview of what's going to take place during the next two weeks.

We're going to become one big camper family.

We're going to have a whole lot of fun.

We're going to swim, bird-watch, connect with nature, learn survival skills, kayak, sail, everything you can possibly want to do during the summer. All in two weeks.

These talks used to ramp up my enthusiasm, but my emotions feel flat, squashed by the news Mom and Dave delivered a few days ago. A mosquito bites me and I swat at it after he's already gotten a snack from my thigh. A small red bump rises in the place where he bit me. Note to self: use bug spray tomorrow. That's something I would normally remember, but I'm too distracted by all the chaos.

I swat at another mosquito and then slide my gaze over to Jacob. He's sitting with the kids in his cabin and listening attentively. I wait for heart flutters or some sign that he should be my camp crush this summer. Nothing. My gaze moves to Hayden next. I think he looks shell-shocked when he should be exhilarated right about now. My mom is making Camp Starling sound like the summer of his life. Everyone else around us looks pumped. I have my reasons for not catching the excitement, but what's Hayden's excuse?

I notice that Hayden has a notebook in his lap. He jots something down. Is he taking notes?

"We'll have team-building games and special challenges throughout these two weeks," my mom tells the group. "There are lots of opportunities to win ribbons. Then we'll have our traditional Starling All-Stars Competition at the end of next week. It will be the girls against the guys, and the victors will win the Starling All-Star trophy." Mom holds up a trophy with a tiny statue of a starling bird with its wings spread out. Every summer it moves between the guys and girls. Last summer the boys won by five points. I'm still not over the loss, even if it is some silly competition.

Nora elbows me and leans in to whisper, "Are you going to tell your mom's boyfriend to wear a hat? Otherwise, he's going to look like a lobster by the end of tomorrow."

I look at Dave and whisper back to Nora, "He's an adult. He knows how to take care of himself."

Nora harrumphs beside me. "My dad seems lost without my mom. I had to teach him how to scramble eggs last week."

I turn to look at her, my gaze catching on Hayden and find him watching me. He doesn't even look away or try to hide it. Instead, his eyes seem to say hi—if eyes can talk. All the guy counselors are sitting with their cabinmates, but Hayden is off to the side. Such a loner.

Nora elbows me again. "Are you even listening?"

She always says this because she's always talking. There's no way a friend can possibly absorb every word she's saying.

"Yeah, of course," I say with a nod, even though I'm not. Most of my attention is currently on Hayden. I redirect my attention to my mom and pretend to focus on what she's saying, but I really just want to know if Hayden is still watching me.

I chew my lower lip and bide my time until I can't hold my suspense any longer. I look over and find that he's not watching me anymore. Not at first, at least. But he seems to feel my eyes on him and he looks at me again.

My pulse jumps and I feel a little breathless. I'm about to look away, but Hayden holds something up to show me. A folded piece of paper. A note. I narrow my eyes to get a better look. Written on the front of the paper is a giant *P*—*P* for *Paisley.* Or *Pais* because he can't seem to understand that my name has two syllables in it.

Hayden tips his head in my direction as if to say the note is for me. Why would Hayden write me a note? What could it possibly say? And why do I care? I'd be happy if I didn't utter another word to him for the rest of camp.

I return to looking at my mom, but hard as I try, I can't focus. Instead, my annoyance with Hayden grows. He's still writing in that little notebook of his. Or maybe he's drawing. I've seen his work displayed in the art room at school. He has talent if he could just use the right medium versus the sides of vending machines and cabins.

He's supposed to be listening to my mom, but obviously he thinks he's too cool to take direction from an adult. What was it he said the other day? We have more control than we realize? Adults just want us to think that we don't. Or something along those lines. Then he'd made some crazy suggestion about breaking my mom and Dave up. It was the most ridiculous idea I've ever heard. Even if he was right. It would solve my problems.

When my mom is done talking, I tell Nora I need to do something. I don't give her an explanation. I just branch off and barge toward Hayden, half fueled by frustration and half by curiosity.

When I'm standing in front of him, he hands me the folded piece of paper.

"For me?" I ask, looking up at him.

He shrugs. "I couldn't find a pigeon to deliver it to you."

This makes me smile despite myself. I don't want to be charmed by the fact that he knows a few things about my favorite subject. But I am. "I just came over to tell you that I'll be watching you. If you make any more trouble, I'll tell my mom and she won't be lenient next time."

"I don't mind you watching me, Pais." His eyes are smiling again. I wonder momentarily if he's flirting with me, but that would be absurd. I'm definitely not what I imagine his type would be.

I huff as I take the paper and start to unfold it.

"Not here," he says, laying a hand over it, which basically means he's laying a hand over mine. I can't form a clear thought for a second because our skin is touching. "Put it in your pocket."

I stare at his hand until he removes it. "Fine," I finally say. Then I ask, "Why weren't you with the other guys?"

"Maybe the idea of team building doesn't appeal to everyone." Hayden kicks the dirt at his feet. Like I said, he thinks he's too cool for camp. And too cool for camp means too cool for me.

"Well, you should get to know your cabinmates. Those kids are going to be depending on you for guidance."

Poor kids. At least they have Dave. And the fact that I'm remotely grateful about Dave being here at Camp Starling annoys me as well.

"Anyway," Hayden says, ignoring my suggestion, "the note. In private."

⁂

Later that evening, as I stand with my group outside Chickadee Cabin, I pull out the note and carefully unfold it while holding my breath. I'm surprised to find that Hayden's handwriting is neat block letters.

I'M SORRY.

I blink, reread the message, and frown because the message is so unexpected. Is this a sincere apology? There's a hand-drawn rose beneath the words. I stare at the picture for a moment, wondering if the rose is for me or if he was just doodling because he was bored. Probably the latter. It's beautiful,

45

though. Every petal is so perfectly drawn that it almost looks real. He's really good at shading and adding depth.

Nora approaches me with a jar in her hand. "What's the piece of paper?" she asks.

I pull it against my chest before folding the paper back into its square form. I don't want to share it with anyone, least of all Nora, who will probably find something critical to say. Instead, I shove it into my pocket. "N-nothing."

She'd probably press me on the note if we weren't on a schedule. She's always late unless there are boys involved. "Okay. Well, it's time for us to head over to the Birdfeeder area with our jars. The fireflies are out. So are the guys."

I grab my jar and gesture to my group of campers to follow me. We walk alongside Nora's group, collecting Tisha's, Emma's, Meghan's, and Maria's groups as we pass their respective cabins.

When we reach the Birdfeeder, the guys are already there. All except Hayden, who is nowhere to be found. I wonder if he's already ditched his camp responsibilities. I wouldn't be surprised, although I would be a little disappointed. He needs to undo the damage he's done and make things right.

The counselors stand in front of the small group of campers, who all have plastic jars, coffee filters, and rubber bands. They're holding on to them, fidgeting, and chatting among themselves as they wait for us to lay out the rules.

Nora naturally takes the lead instructing the group. "Okay, campers extraordinaire! We're all going to head down Songbird Path with our jars. It's very important that you all stay on the path. No one ventures off. It's dark and there might be snakes that we can't see."

Jacob clears his throat beside her. "Although that's unlikely. Snakes will hear us coming and undoubtedly slither as far away as possible. Most are just as scared of you as you are of them."

Nora looks a little irritated that Jacob kind of disagreed with her in front of everyone. She not only likes to be in charge, she also likes to be right. "If you see a firefly, swing your jar over it and quickly place your coffee filter on the jar's opening so that it doesn't fly away."

"Make sure you don't hurt the firefly in the process," Dom adds. "We're going to release them back into the wild later and we want to make sure they're not injured."

"That's right," Nora agrees, looking less irritated by Dom's input.

I never knew what happened between Nora and Jacob last summer. I just assumed that the crush ended when camp did. But maybe there's more to the story. She certainly isn't eager to pick up where they left off. That's for sure.

"We'll finish our walk and convene back here in about an hour to release the fireflies," she says. "Sound fun?"

The campers nod and cheer.

"Okay, let's go!"

The campers start chatting excitedly. Nora, Jacob, and Kyle take the lead with the group. I hang back a little bit, walking in the middle of the group.

Tisha sidles up beside me as we walk. "If you're looking

for that guy from your school, he's not coming," she tells me. "I heard he's scrubbing paint off the cabins."

I turn to my friend, who is smiling back at me with a mouth full of braces. I hadn't even realized she'd gotten braces since last summer. "I wasn't looking for Hayden."

"Hmm. I saw you and him making googly eyes at each other earlier at the camper orientation. Bad boy or not, he's cute," she says. She's not like Nora though. She doesn't hold on to something and talk it to death. I guess that's one of the things that's been bugging me about Nora lately. She thinks she knows what's best for me, but I can think for myself.

Tisha and I continue to walk side by side. We're surrounded by campers who aren't really looking where they're going. They're too busy searching for fireflies. One boy marches right into me and steps on my foot.

"Ow!" I say.

Tisha has to reach out to steady me before I fall over.

The boy doesn't even glance back as he swings his jar at another twinkling light.

"I don't remember the Trail of Fireflies being so dangerous," Tisha says on a laugh.

"That's because we were the ones knocking our counselors down," I say.

"True." She turns to look behind her and then faces forward with a frown on her face.

"What's wrong?"

"Nothing. I just kind of thought I'd talk to Ricardo, but Meghan is already back there, making him laugh."

I glance back to see for myself. Then I look at her again.

"Ricardo laughs at everything. You can join them, you know? They're just talking."

Tisha shrugs. "Yeah, but Meghan told me she couldn't wait to say hello to him. She's way into him."

"Maybe you are too, though." I shrug. "Nothing's written in stone as far as who gets to talk to who." This sounds like something Hayden might say. We have choices. Control. What he really meant was that we don't have to follow the rules if we don't want to. I'm not agreeing to that by any means, but there are no rules about flirting, despite what Nora thinks. "Go," I say.

"What about you?" Tisha asks.

"I'm fine in the middle. I'll keep my eye out for the campers."

"And who will keep their eye out for you?" she asks.

I laugh. "Even though Nora is way up there in the front, I have my suspicions that she has eyes in the back of her head and she's watching my every move."

"She likes to have her hand in everything." Tisha smiles. "Okay, I'm turning back to hang with Meghan and Ricardo."

"Good luck." As soon as Tisha is gone, I dodge a jar that swings near my head.

"Good reflexes," someone says.

I look over and find Jacob walking beside me, which makes me instantly nervous in a good kind of way. "Oh, hey."

"Hey. Nora wanted to be alone with Kyle. It was kind of obvious. She kept insisting I come find you and keep you company," Jacob tells me.

I'm tempted to roll my eyes. "You don't have to walk with me."

"I know. But I wanted to anyway."

"Oh." I grow quiet for a moment. I can feel my cheeks burning. I must be distracted because another kid bumps into me while trying to catch a firefly.

"Got it!" the kid cheers excitedly.

"Got you," Jacob says quietly. He has one arm looped around my waist to keep me from tipping over and falling off the path. He lets go once I'm standing upright again.

"Um, thanks," I say, flustered beyond belief.

"No problem." Jacob smiles at me. It's a good smile. Perfectly symmetrical with matching dimples on both cheeks.

I swallow hard. Nora has a lot of opinions and she likes to be right. Maybe she's right about me and Jacob too, I think. Perhaps I should spend some time talking to him after all.

※

When we reach the end of Songbird Path and meet back up at the Birdfeeder, I'm tired and slightly giddy over the fact that Jacob walked with me the entire way. We talked and found out that we have a lot in common.

I glance around and see Nora chatting with Kyle. Tisha is talking to Ricardo and Meghan. And Maria is talking to Dom. Hayden still isn't here, which is a shame because the Trail of Fireflies is special. It's one of my favorite moments of camp.

"I'm going to go talk to the kids assigned to me," Jacob says. "It was good chatting with you, Paisley."

I nod as he starts to walk away. "See you around."

I decide to head over and talk to the girls from my cabin

too. They all seem to be getting along well. Most of them, at least. One girl named Simone is sitting by herself. She doesn't look sad or anything. Just lost in thought.

"You okay?" I ask, stepping up beside her.

She smiles at me. "Oh, yeah. That was fun. I've already released Sparkle. That's what I named my firefly."

I laugh at this. "Good. You don't want to hang out with the other girls from Chickadee Cabin?"

She looks over at the group and shakes her head. "I'm just getting a little alone time before we return to our cabin. My mom says I'm a daydreamer."

"Nothing wrong with that." I start to join the group of girls, but then I see Hayden in the distance. He's over by one of the cabins that he graffitied. "I'll be back in a minute," I tell Simone.

She follows my gaze to him and then looks at me again. "I'll just be here daydreaming."

"Sounds good." I pick up my pace the closer I get to Hayden. I'm not sure why I'm inclined to speak to him. Maybe because he apologized. Maybe because he didn't run off like I first thought. He's here undoing his damage. "Hey."

Hayden looks up from where he's squatting by one of the cabins. He has a brush and a bucket that I assume is filled with paint thinner. There's a look on his face, which makes me wonder if he's a little embarrassed. "Hey. Did you, uh, have fun catching lightning bugs?"

"I didn't catch any. The campers seemed to have fun though. And no fireflies were injured to my knowledge."

Hayden stands from his squatting position and I'm closer

to him than I realized. I tip my face back to look up at him and swallow thickly.

"Um, is the paint coming off?" I ask.

"Mostly. I'll have to go over it again," he says.

"Sounds like this isn't your first time scrubbing walls."

He chuckles, but doesn't cop to that fact.

"Anyway, we're about to be sent back to our cabins. Curfew is nine p.m.," I say.

"I know. I thought I'd just keep working until I finish this wall, though."

I shake my head. "Your campers will need you back at Falcon Cabin."

Hayden doesn't look worried. "Falcon Cabin has Dave. It's the only cabin with two counselors because your mom doesn't trust that I'll do a good job." He shrugs.

"Then prove her wrong," I say, irritated. "You have a responsibility to be with the kids in Falcon Cabin."

"And to scrub off this paint. And to run an arts and crafts program. Let's not forget cleaning the toilets." He picks up his brush and continues scrubbing. "I have lots of jobs. Just be glad I'm doing one of them, Pais."

"Paisley," I growl. "Whatever. Stay out here and get into more trouble. Maybe my mom will stick you with morning cooking too," I say sarcastically as I stomp away to rejoin the girls of Chickadee Cabin. I know my place. I'm a counselor and I belong with my group. Not on the outskirts with an infuriating rule breaker.

CHAPTER FIVE

Camp Time: Tuesday. July 19.

Camp starts with a bird call. I know the whole bird theme can be taken a little far, but my dad seemed to add something new every year. The Birdfeeder. The Bird Bath, where we all shower. The bird call through the speakers at six a.m. to wake everyone up. There'll be a second bird call fifteen minutes from now to signal everyone to the showers.

My eyes have been open for at least an hour already though. I've been listening to Tabitha's mouth-breathing above me while I write in my journal.

I jot down a few quick things and end my entry with one final thought.

I hope Dave doesn't brush up against poison ivy today (insert sarcasm).

I can say things like that in my journal because it's private. Just for me. And nice girl or not, sometimes I have unkind thoughts.

"Make the birds stop!" Simone whines from the other side of the room.

I look over to see her arm draped over her eyes. She's in a bottom bunk too. Simone has brown skin and dark hair. From here I see the fluorescent pink polish on her nails. Tabitha snorts from above me, like she's startled awake by the sound of Simone's voice. I hear her flop around beneath her sheet.

"Morning already?" she groans.

I close my journal, roll to my side, and shove it under my mattress while everyone's eyes are still shut. I don't want anyone to know where I keep my most private thoughts. Then I lie back for a moment and listen to the sound of birds. "I believe that's a robin's call," I tell my campers. Mom changes the sounds up each day because that's what my dad used to do. We keep all his traditions and, in a way, that keeps his spirit alive here.

I swallow, remembering that Mom is going to sell Camp Starling. Because of Dave. "Robins are territorial," I say, not that anyone is awake enough to listen to me. "They settle their disputes by singing and puffing out their red chests." If only that would work for me to get rid of Dave.

I sit up, drape my legs off the bed, and lift my arms overhead, yawning as if I'm tired too. Mornings are my prime time, though. I feel like springing onto my feet and running around to complete my routine. I walk over to my trunk and pull out some clothes and other essentials for the day.

"All right, everyone, time to start stirring. We want to head over to The Bird Bath early," I tell the half-awake girls. "If we're first in line for the showers, we'll be first in line for breakfast. And trust me, you don't want to miss out on Campers' Breakfast." Campers' Breakfast is another of Dad's traditions. It's the breakfast of all breakfasts intended to fuel a long day of fun and learning.

The girls barely stir at the sound of my voice.

I clap my hands softly the way my past cabin counselors used to do to get their campers' attention. "Time to wake up."

"Yes, *Principal Manning*," Maddie says sarcastically from the bunk above Simone's. Maddie is an upcoming sophomore at my school. That makes her just a year younger than me. Her eyes crack open and I think maybe I catch an eye roll. She obviously doesn't like being told what to do.

I try not to take Maddie's attitude personally as I grab my toiletry bag. Slowly the other girls start to sit up, stretch, and chatter among themselves. Maddie is the last to climb off her bunk. She's also the last to grab her things, making us slightly late getting to the Bird Bath. We aren't first in line, but at least we aren't last. That would be Nora's group, because Nora is always fashionably late. I predict that she'll later complain about the food being picked over and cold once she's inside the Birdfeeder.

The girls of Chickadee Cabin step into the shower area, dip in for a quick rinse, then dress and brush their teeth. I do the same before standing in front of the mirror and taking a moment to pull my damp hair into a ponytail. Excitement for the day ahead claws through me, along with a hungry growl in my belly that's grown louder since I left my bunk.

Campers' Breakfast happens at the Birdfeeder, which is a large log cabin that houses the kitchen. Outside the cabin, there's a series of covered shelters with picnic tables set up for the campers to eat at. It's one of my favorite parts of the day. Mom hires a small staff to work the kitchen for lunch and dinner, but breakfast has always been prepared by Mom and Dad. Mom usually enlists my Aunt Jenny and Uncle Leon too. Aunt Jenny manages the elementary school's cafeteria in Seabrook, so she's great at meal prep. They typically make buckets of grits, pans of eggs, and stacks of pancakes. It's insane, really, but Dad used to insist on waking extra early to cook.

As the Chickadee Cabin girls and I walk to the Birdfeeder, I hear a *psst*. I whirl and come face to face with Hayden. I wave the girls on toward the food and stop to talk to him, ignoring the little jump of my pulse when our eyes meet.

"Hey. How was your first night?" I ask.

He shrugs a shoulder. "It's rough sleeping in a cabin with people I don't know. I slept in the hammock behind my cabin instead."

"You slept outside?" I shake my head. "You're not supposed to leave your cabin after dark." He was there for the campers' orientation. He should know that.

"Since Dave was inside, I figured I'd stand watch on the outside. That'll be my justification, at least. If your mom asks."

"A night guard. Like a duck."

Hayden grins at me. "A duck?"

I can't believe I just compared Hayden to a duck. No wonder I've never had a boyfriend in my life. "Some ducks sleep with one eye open," I explain. "To watch for predators."

He looks amused as we continue toward the Birdfeeder. I assume his campers are already inside, probably led by Dave since Hayden didn't even sleep in a bunk.

"So what can I expect from today?" he finally asks.

I'm still mad at him, but to his credit, he was cleaning up the cabins last night. And from what I could see he was doing a good job even if he ignored the curfew. "Well, Mom is probably cooking breakfast right now. There's going to be so much delicious food. She wakes early on camp days," I tell Hayden. "Camp days require lots of fuel. That's what my dad used to say." I look down at my feet for a moment. There's something about Hayden that makes me keep bringing up my dad. Maybe it's because he doesn't have a father at home either.

We step inside the Birdfeeder log cabin and I expect to smell salty bacon in the air, hear the sizzle of a grill in the back, and see my mom rushing around with trays of food. That's not what I see, though. Hayden and I stop walking and stand there for a moment, both of us taking in the scene.

Mom walks up behind me and her hands brace my shoulders, giving them a soft squeeze. "Good morning, Paisley. Good morning, Hayden," she says with a cheery voice.

I turn to look at her. She must be sick for the food not to be ready yet. Something must be wrong. She looks fine, though.

Her cheeks are rosy and her smile is bright. "What's going on? Where's the food?"

"Oh." She nods as if she hadn't realized I'd be wondering. "Dave had an excellent idea."

"Dave," I repeat, already having a feeling I'm going to dislike what she's about to say.

"He thought it was a little excessive for me to make so much trouble for myself cooking all the breakfast items that I normally make. I was making the list of foods yesterday and preparing to run to the grocery store. Dave suggested that I just get crates of fresh fruit, granola bars, and juice to set out for the campers. That will be so much easier for everyone involved."

"But you love cooking Campers' Breakfast," I say, feeling a little heartbroken at the idea. Fruit and granola bars is not Campers' Breakfast. Dad would never have suggested this.

"Yes, I do love cooking, but it's nice to switch things up once in a while, Paisley." She gives me a meaningful look and I know she's talking about everything else too.

"I think I just lost my appetite," I say, turning to leave. "I'll be back before my campers are finished eating." Which shouldn't take long considering it's all just finger foods.

Hayden catches up with me. "Hey. You okay?" Concern knits the skin between his dark eyes.

I blow out a breath and turn to face him. "No, I'm not okay. Campers' Breakfast is not fruit and granola. Not on the first full morning at least." My arms splay out to my sides as I talk and I know I'm possibly overreacting, but I can't help it. Campers' Breakfast is supposed to be a hot-cooked meal that makes the campers feel less like they're miles from home and more like they're with family.

Dave chuckles as he walks by us. "Someone must be hangry this morning." He doesn't seem to know what Hayden and I are talking about, just that I'm upset. He waves cheerily on the way to where we just left my mother.

I growl under my breath.

"You really don't like him, huh?" Hayden asks.

I'm not sure what makes me open up to Hayden, but I need to get this off my chest. "No, I really, *really* don't."

"You told me that he's the reason you're selling this camp and moving?"

Tears sting my eyes. "Because of Dave, I'm moving away from the only home I've ever known." I nibble at my lower lip. Sometimes that helps keep me from crying when I want to.

Hayden doesn't say anything for a long moment. "I still think my matchbreaker plan is a good one."

"You mean your idea about breaking my mom and Dave up?" I ask.

"It has a nice ring to it, don't you think? Instead of matchmakers, we'd be match*breakers*."

"We?" I lift a brow. As if I'd ever team up with Hayden Bennett.

"Well, you'd need someone who's willing to break the rules a little bit," he says.

"You?" I fold my arms across my chest.

"If your mom and Dave aren't together, you don't have to move to Wyoming. And you don't sell Camp Starling."

I blink, wishing his idea didn't appeal to me so much. I

don't have any other options, though. Mom and Dave didn't give me a choice in any of this.

Hayden shrugs. "Believe it or not, I don't want this place to shut down either."

This should surprise me, but it doesn't. "Because you came here once? With your brother?" I ask, remembering.

"Yeah." He shoves his hands in his pockets. "The dragon I drew on the side of that cabin was for him. He had a thing for dragons back in the day."

"Had?" I ask, finding myself interested in Hayden's motivation.

He looks away for a moment, his attention moving to the bushes. "People grow out of things," he says in explanation.

I get that, maybe better than most. After my dad died, I grew up and out of things quickly. I didn't want to play with dolls as much. I mostly just wanted to read and disappear into some other world that wasn't my own. Or follow Nora around like a baby bird.

A group of campers walk by us, heading toward the Bird-feeder. They won't be getting the huge Campers' Breakfast that has always been integral to Camp Starling mornings. Instead, they'll be getting a granola bar.

"I wouldn't even know how to go about breaking up a couple," I tell Hayden finally. I've never even had a boyfriend. I know nothing of romance or relationships.

"But you're considering the matchbreaker idea?" he asks, looking pleased. His dark eyes are actually twinkling, or maybe that's just the rising sun above the tree line.

"I *might* be considering it," I admit.

"Great. Let me think about our tactics. I'll find you," he says. Then he starts to walk toward the Birdfeeder.

"Wait," I call. "Where are you going?"

He looks over his shoulder. "I happen to like granola bars. Also, I'm a counselor. I should probably find my campers and hang with them."

That's what I should be doing too—even if I'm less than thrilled about the change in breakfast plans. How is it that I'm taking cues from the camp's bad boy? That makes as little sense as the rest of the things in my upside-down life right now. "Right. See you there," I say, staying put. I don't want Hayden to think I'm walking with him. We're not friends. Not even a little bit—even if I'm considering teaming with him to fix my life.

CHAPTER SIX

The first task of the day involves swimming relay races to the end of the pier and back. It's just friendly competition between the cabins, but the cabin who finishes the relay first gets the first blue ribbon of camp.

I've always gotten a little competitive about the ribbons. I know they're just pieces of material, but as a camper, I always brought home a half dozen to put inside my Camp Starling Memory Box along with the camper's journal from that summer. Even though I'm a counselor this year, I still want that first-place ribbon to go to the girls of Chickadee Cabin.

My heart kicks up a notch as I give the instructions to my cabinmates. Maddie seems disinterested, of course. Is it just me or does she not like camp? Once I'm done reviewing the task, I stand back as the campers argue over how to order themselves in line. I kind of miss being part of the groups. Just last year, I was young enough to take part in the challenges. I would have jumped at the swimming challenge because that's my strong suit. I started lessons before I could talk—one of those Baby and Me classes with my dad. He used to say he was the only father in the group, but I don't think he minded. I'm on the swim team at school too and I usually place in my competitions.

Nora must have noticed the frown on my face because she bumps her shoulder against mine. "I'll race you tonight if that makes you feel better." Nora tends to be slightly self-centered and a lot bossy, but she also looks out for me in ways like this. She knows me, through and through. We are yin and yang, that's for sure.

"Do you miss being a camper already too?" I ask.

She nods, but she doesn't understand the half of it. Knowing this is Camp Starling's last year hangs like a dark cloud over this summer, making it hard to enjoy. I don't want that for Nora or the others. I never thought so before, but sometimes ignorance really is bliss.

The girls pair up for the races. One girl from each of the six girls' cabins. The girls stand at the edge of the lake and then Emma gets them started by blowing her whistle. All six girls jump into the water with excited shrieks, quickly swimming toward the end of the pier.

I glance across Blue Lake and see the boys' team doing the same thing from a pier farther down the lake. I try to pick out Hayden, but from this distance I can't. I'm not sure why I'm looking for him. It's not because I like him or anything. To prove that to myself, I look for Jacob as well. All the guys look like blots of color, though. All except Dave. He's bigger than everyone else and is wearing his yellow and olive-green camp leadership colors. It still gets away from me that he is the assistant director when he has no idea what's even going on.

The shrieks from the water in front of me draw my attention back to the girls. One of them, Simone, is flailing twenty feet out from shore. She's in trouble, and no one else seems to be moving toward her. Instead, all eyes are wide, watching her from blood-drained faces with slackened jaws. Everyone is frozen, including the lifeguard, who seems to be waiting to determine if this is a life-or-death situation. In my mind, it doesn't matter. If someone needs help, you go to them.

Before I even know what's happening, my feet start running. I'm pretty sure Simone is having a swimmer's cramp, even though breakfast was much more than thirty minutes ago. I've had this happen before, and it'll quickly turn an easy lap into something dangerous.

I sprint into the water, my body momentarily shocked by the cold. I keep moving forward anyway. My arms cut through the water's surface taking me to Simone as fast as I can possibly swim. I've won a blue ribbon every summer for the last four years for speed and skill.

"It's okay, Simone!" I call out between breaths. "I'm coming! Stay calm!"

Half of Simone's face dips below the water. Her eyes are wide. She kicks her way back up to the surface, but it's a weak kick. Her leg is cramping and she's fatiguing quickly.

"I'm going to grab you. Don't cling to me," I call out when

I'm just a couple feet away. My breaths are labored by now too. "I'll hold you, but you've got to promise not to pull me under."

Simone's gaze connects with mine. Her pupils are so large that her brown eyes look almost black. "Okay," she calls weakly.

I know I can't take her promise at face value. That's because she's scared. I swim around her and wrap one arm across her chest. "I got you." I look between the lakeshore and the pier. It'll be quicker to make it to the end of the pier because both me and Simone are exhausted at this point.

Kicking as hard as I can and using the one arm I have to propel myself, I launch us in that direction. The lifeguard meets us halfway and takes over assisting Simone, which is a huge relief. By the time they reach the pier, Nora, Meghan, Maria, and Tisha have run to the end to help. Nora reaches a hand to pull Simone up first. Then Meghan and Maria help the lifeguard up.

Tisha offers a hand to help me. She yanks on my arm with an exaggerated groan until I collapse onto the pier, lying flat on my back. She kneels beside me, staring down at my face. "You all right?" she asks.

I blow out a breath and close my eyes against the beating sun.

"Paisley?" Tisha asks again. "Do you need me to find your mom?"

"No," I finally say. I open my eyes to look at her. "Is Simone okay?"

Tisha glances over her shoulder where Nora, Emma, Meghan,

and Maria have taken Simone back to the shore. "She's sitting up and seems to be fine. Your mom is over there too."

I expel another breath. "That's good."

I sit up because if my mom sees me lying back, she'll get worried. Tisha wraps her arm around my shoulder. "You know, now that we're counselors, there are no ribbons for us at the end. That heroic thing you just did would have definitely gotten you one, though."

I give her a small smile. "You think?"

"I know."

I sigh. "All that matters is that Simone is okay. But I, on the other hand, am sopping wet."

"You better go change," she says. "I'll watch your campers for you."

"Thanks." I stand on shaky legs as the adrenaline pumping through me starts to die down. I've never saved someone's life before. It was kind of cool. Exhilarating. And exhausting. This experience will definitely be going into my camper's journal tonight.

※

At lunchtime, I sit with the girls of Chickadee Cabin while the other counselors sit with their campers. I miss sitting with Nora, Tisha, Emma, Meghan, and Maria. That's one of the many things that's different about this summer. When we were just campers, we sat together. We did everything together without a care in the world. This summer, I seem to have a million cares on my shoulders.

I pick up my PB&J sandwich and take a bite. I also have a sliced apple, a scoop of baked beans, and a bag of chips.

Simone slides into the chair across from me with her melamine tray loaded with the same items as mine. I somehow have a feeling that, just because I kind of saved her life, she's now going to cling to me for the rest of camp. "Thank you," she says for the dozenth time.

"It was nothing." I chew my bite of sandwich and look around for Hayden. He's sitting with a table of boys and surprisingly, I see him talking with them. He's even smiling. I find myself grinning as I watch, hoping that means he's having a good time. It's his first camp experience, so he should. That's the only reason I care. Everyone should enjoy their first summer of camp, even if they're nearly aged out and only got here as a punishment.

Simone glances over her shoulder to see who I'm looking at.

I quickly look down at my food and busy myself by grabbing an apple slice.

"He's cute," Simone whispers, flushing. Simone is twelve or thirteen, I think. I remember getting crushes on the camp counselors at her age. I wasn't like Nora, though. I never tried to talk to my crushes. I usually did the opposite and ignored them, even when they spoke to me. "Oh, I didn't mean I thought he was cute for me," Simone amends, seeming to read my mind. "You were the one looking at him just now. I meant he's cute for you."

I want to tell her that I don't think Hayden is all that cute. But, of course, that would be a lie. If Nora caught me looking at him, she wouldn't call him cute. Nora would tell me that

Hayden Bennett is not my type. That we're too different. That he's trouble with a capital T whereas I'm that girl who never gets detention. I lose sleep if a teacher so much as gives me a warning look. Nora would say that Hayden and I couldn't possibly have anything in common. And she'd be right on all accounts. Probably.

I lift my eyes and watch Hayden again. He's telling something to the camper across the table from him. The kid is probably twelve. He's small for his age too. The kid is watching Hayden the way Simone has been looking at me ever since I pulled her out of the water. The kid is probably just so relieved to have an older kid talking to him and making him feel important.

I look at the other guy counselors. Jacob is focused on his food while seated with the younger kids. He's there and technically doing his job, but he's not interacting with the campers the way Hayden is. Neither is Ricardo, although Ricardo does appear to be trying, at least.

Something warm moves through my chest and I look at Simone again. "Yeah, he's kind of cute." I wouldn't admit that to Nora in a million summers, though.

Simone grins back at me as if we have a little secret. Then she grabs an apple slice and dips it into the little cup of caramel they gave us just like I'm doing, swirling it clockwise around the container. "I won't tell anyone you think so," she promises.

※

After lunch, I snag Hayden to the side. "So, I've been think-ing about what you said, and I'm in."

Hayden looks at me like he has no idea what I'm talking about. "What I said?"

"About breaking up my mom and Dave. Let's do it."

Hayden glances in each direction, like he's making sure we're alone. We aren't, not really, but no one is paying atten-tion to us. Everyone is chattering excitedly about camp things. "Are you sure?"

"She doesn't really want to stay with Dave forever. She only thinks she does. But she'll eventually be miserable. And so will I."

Hayden gives me a long, hard look as if he's trying to de-cide if I'm serious. "All right. Well, I've been mulling on the idea too. I think the key is making Dave as miserable as possi-ble while he's here. To show your mom and everyone a differ-ent side of the lovable, happy-go-lucky guy we're seeing now."

I nod slowly. "Yeah, I like that idea." I think for a moment, but the Birdfeeder area is so loud with chatter that it's hard to get a clear thought in my head. Finally, something comes to me. "We're about to go on a healthy walk," I say. Campers always take a healthy walk down Songbird Path after lunch. "We could put honey in Dave's sunblock. So when he lathers it on, he becomes a bug magnet. Bugs are way worse in the woods. And trying to keep up with energetic campers while bugs are biting at you is hard." I look at Hayden with a grow-ing grin.

Hayden looks impressed. "You thought I was good at being

bad, and here I thought that Paisley Manning was just good."
It's the first time he's said my full name without shortening
it. Just when I was kind of starting to like the shortened version. Hayden watches the campers around us for a moment.
"I'll walk with Dave so I can witness his unraveling firsthand.
I need to stick with my campers anyway and prove myself to
be a team player."

Without thinking, I shove a playful hand against Hayden's
chest, knocking him a few inches back. "A team player sleeps
in the cabin with his roommates," I say. "You should start
there."

There's a twinkle in Hayden's dark eyes. "A true camper
sleeps under the stars."

I feel my heart stumble around in my chest. I find those
words poetic in a way that surprises me.

"Have you ever slept under the stars, Pais?" he asks.

I shake my head. "No. And I'm still a true camper."

I take a few retreating steps, needing to create distance and
go snag some honey to squeeze into Dave's sunblock before
the walk. Maybe the prank is low-hanging fruit, but it's the
best idea I have right now. "Good luck with the camp festivi-
ties," I call behind me.

"I somehow sense you don't think me or Dave can handle
these next two weeks?"

My grin feels silly as it stretches through my sun-kissed
cheeks. "Him, definitely not. You?" I shrug. "I hope so." I turn
quickly before Hayden can see me blush. Was I just flirting
with him? Certainly not. I head toward the Birdfeeder kitchen.
I happen to know where there are honey packets inside. Adding

one or two to Dave's sunblock won't hurt anything. Honey is all natural. It's sweet. And while the bugs flock to Dave this afternoon, maybe it'll help convince him to bug off from this camp.

※

The healthy walk is exactly what it sounds like. It's a leisurely walk down Songbird Path after lunch before any afternoon activities. I'm walking with the girls in my cabin. Well, they're all walking behind me except for Simone. My attention isn't on my campers, though. It's on Dave, farther up ahead. Hayden is walking beside him.

I watch gleefully as Dave pauses mid-step to smack the back of his leg. Then he swats at something on his arm. He's a bug magnet, and while I feel somewhat guilty, I'm also giddy over the possibility that he might just decide that camp isn't his thing and go home.

Okay, I know that's a long shot. Someone doesn't go home just because of a few mosquitoes, but there's also the fact that he's already getting a mild sunburn. And he's sweating to the point that he looks like he's melting. And we're only on day two.

"You seem awfully happy," Simone notes. "Did you get to talk to the guy or something?"

She's asking about Hayden.

"Yeah, but it wasn't anything like you're thinking. We're just friends." Co-conspirators really.

Simone nods. "Cool."

Maddie groans behind us. "What are we doing after this lame walk?" she complains.

I take a breath before answering. Maddie has been subtly bucking my lead and the things of this camp since the moment she arrived. I get that I'm only a year older than her, but I'm still in charge of our cabin. "This walk is good for us," I say. "And afterward we're all going to take the kayaks out on the lake for some paddling practice."

"That sounds amazing," Tabitha says, walking beside Maddie.

"I can paddle at home. I have a creek behind my house," Maddie informs us, unenthused.

"Great. Then you already know how it's done. You can partner with one of the girls who doesn't."

"Like me," Tabitha offers, raising a hand. "I've never been in a kayak before."

Maddie frowns, but at least she doesn't say anything else.

I redirect my attention to Dave several yards ahead. He's waving his arms around, just a little bit at first, but then he seems to flail in a panic. The campers around him all back away. He must really dislike bugs.

Perfect!

"What's wrong with Dave?" Simone asks, her tone full of awe.

I shrug, tempering the smile that wants to curl on my lips. "Some campers just can't handle the outdoors, I guess."

"And they eventually get used to it?" Simone asks, looking at me.

I shrug. "Or they go home." *Hopefully.*

CHAPTER SEVEN

Turns out, Dave wasn't panicking over a mosquito. He was being chased by bees. And he's allergic.

The bad news is that he got stung by one.

The good news is he had an EpiPen handy and he'll be just fine.

After the walk, I search for my mom because I am consumed by guilt and I need to come clean about what I did to Dave. I know she'll be horribly disappointed in me and I'll probably be cleaning latrines just like Hayden, but a guilty conscience is unbearable. I finally find my mom behind one of the cabins. She's leaning against the side and looking down at her cellphone. She looks up, startled for just a second and then smiles warmly at me. Her smile used to set me at ease on a rough day. Moms can fix anything after all. At least I used to think so. But then my dad died. She couldn't fix that. She was sad and lonely for a couple years, just going through the motions. I was too, and she couldn't fix that either. But we got through it, the two of us, together.

"This is the only place I can get reception," she says in explanation as to why she's hiding behind a cabin.

"I thought you didn't like cellphones at camp anyway."

She shakes her head. "I don't. I just need to keep in touch with Dave and check on how he's doing. He was stung by a bee," she says.

"Yeah, I heard." Guilt twists and ties my insides into tiny knots.

"Poor Dave. He's having a hard time so far. He's just . . . not exactly a woodsy guy," Mom says. "It's nice to have him here to help, but he's—"

"Indoorsy," I supply.

My mom nods. "Yes, perfect word choice."

"Pale and not very athletic," I add, unable to help myself.

My mom frowns. "I'll have you know that Dave played tennis in college."

"Well, that's a ball sport, I guess. Not like the ones Dad played." I know, I know. I'm laying it on a little too thick. My dad played basketball in college, though. He could also kick a football around at Thanksgiving and spike a volleyball like it was his job.

Mom narrows her eyes. "Dave is nothing like your dad, Paisley. He's not supposed to be. I could never find someone to replace your father, so why would I even try?"

I hold my tongue. If no one can replace Dad, why did my mom go on an online dating site to find Dave? Why did she let him romance her and convince her to mess up our entire lives? "You know, people have long-distance relationships. If Dave wants to move to Wyoming to be close to his mother, we can still stay here, Mom. You two can see each other over the holidays. You can FaceTime," I suggest.

My mom's lips part. "Long-distance relationships rarely work. And I don't want to be without Dave. We're talking about marriage, Paisley."

"But you're not actually engaged," I point out, holding up a finger. "And there'll be no motivation for him to pop the question if you move us to Wyoming."

That V between Mom's eyes deepens. "Where is this even coming from?"

"It's just, well . . ." I trail off, choosing my words carefully. Should I confess what I did first or tell her all the things I'm feeling that led up to what I did? I'm torn because I always try to do the right thing. Mom has been through so much, and I don't want to add to her stress. I should get a say about our lives too, though, right? "I just think . . ."

I hear her phone buzz in her hand.

She looks down and shakes her head as she stands up. "I'm sorry, sweetie. Your Aunt Jenny needs me."

I need my mom too, I want to say. That's why I came all the way out here looking for her. "I just . . . there was something I needed to talk to you about, Mom. It's important."

"Can we talk later, Birdie?" she asks.

My mom typically uses my dad's nickname for me when she's feeling guilty about not spending enough time with me. Or when she wants to remind me of my dad. I don't need reminding of him, though. I'm not the one who's forgotten Dad and all the things that were important to him. *She* is.

"Sure," I say, but she doesn't even hear me because she's

already walking away to put out a proverbial fire somewhere. Meanwhile, the little sparks in my belly are igniting. Forget guilty consciences, confessions, and doing the right thing. Mission Matchbreaker is back on.

⚛

Later that afternoon, the campers and counselors gather at the lake's edge for a little beginner's kayaking. After some brief instructions, the campers break into teams of two, put on their floatation devices, and climb aboard their vessels.

The counselors are kayaking along with them in designated bright yellow kayaks. The bright yellow delineates where the camp leadership is in case there's a problem. I really hope I don't need to jump in and pull someone out of the water again. Simone is already following me around like a baby duck.

I look out across the water, surprised to see that the guy campers are on the lake at the same time as us. For the most part, we're sticking to opposite sides of the lake today. While the girls are coming in from the left, the guy campers are coming in from the right. We're making even diagonals, like an arrowhead pointing to the landing across the lake.

I paddle hard and quick with Nora in front of me. Of course she's in the front. There was never any discussion about that. I wouldn't have argued anyway. Nora keeps glancing back at the guys. She can hardly focus for looking at . . . Kyle? Last I heard, that's who her camp crush was. I follow

76

her gaze to see and then I catch an eyeful of jet-black hair. Hayden is in one of the bright yellow kayaks, his arms moving fast and quick just like mine. He's in a kayak with Jacob, which I find surprising.

Nora frowns back at me. "Why did you stop paddling? I can't do this on my own, Paisley!"

Oh. Right. Nora is good at checking out the guys and staying on task. Me, not so much. I start moving again, but I can't help looking over every few rows to see where Hayden is. I spot a yellow kayak way far behind and realize it's Dave. He must be okay after that bee sting. But he's practically still on shore with his kayak. I almost feel bad for the guy. Almost.

"Row!" Nora demands over her shoulder.

Right. Eyes and brain on the mission ahead, which is watching out for our campers and making it to the landing spot. I paddle harder, faster, my heart racing so hard that it might jump out of my chest. I glance over and see that Hayden's kayak is starting to move ahead of ours, not that this is a race, but still. My competitive streak comes out when I'm at camp.

"Row!" Nora demands again.

I startle at the loudness of her voice and drop my paddle. Then I lurch to reach for it and fall overboard into the water. In the process, Nora attempts to catch me and she splashes into the water too. She screeches so loudly that I'm sure she's being attacked by a shark, but this is fresh water and it's a lake. There are no sharks here. Just an old rumor about piranhas that isn't true. Once Nora catches her breath, she turns to glare at me, sparks firing in her green eyes. "What was that, Paisley?"

"I'm sorry," I say. "I'm not sure what happened." I am sure, though. I was distracted.

"Are you two okay?" someone calls out to us.

Both Nora and I direct our attention to the new voice. Hayden. He and Jacob have turned their kayak around to come help us.

"Yeah," I say, shocked that they would do such a thing.

"No," Nora says. "I'm soaking wet, thanks to Paisley."

I grimace. Then I watch Hayden climb into our kayak while Jacob stays in theirs.

"Let's split you two up," Jacob offers, his gaze landing on me. "Come on, Paisley. You can ride in this one."

I hesitate because some part of me wants to ride with Hayden. I know I'm supposed to be into Jacob, at least according to Nora, but . . .

"Perfect. I'll be with Hayden." Nora is already reaching for our kayak, where Hayden is waiting for her. Nora is going to be so mad at me later for embarrassing her in front of her campers. And for putting her in a situation where she lands herself in a kayak with Hayden Bennett.

I swim toward Jacob in the other kayak, hesitating when he reaches out his hand to help me climb aboard.

I slip my palm against his and wait for sparks. Climbing aboard a kayak from the water is awkward, though. There's no graceful way to fling your leg over the side of the kayak and roll inside. Once I'm in, I glance over at Nora and Hayden in the other kayak, surprised to find Nora smiling. Well, that's a good sign at least. Maybe she'll let me live after all.

"Ready?" Jacob asks me.

"R-ready," I say, shivering now that I'm out of the water. "Thank you, Jacob."

"My pleasure." He smiles back at me.

No butterflies. No sparks. No nothing.

I glance over at Hayden. He's watching me too. He offers me a tiny smile and then I feel it—warmth from a tiny spark. It seems to grow as our kayaks start moving toward the landing on the opposite side of the lake. And I can't help wishing that I was the one in the kayak with Hayden.

CHAPTER EIGHT

Later that night, I'm trying not to feel bummed about all that went wrong today as the campfire roars ahead of me. Dozens of glowing embers float toward the sky like tiny wishes. That's what I used to think, at least. When I was young, my dad and I would see one break off from the fire and we'd take turns making a wish, one for every ember, until we ran out of wishes.

Right now, my wishes are fizzling on my tongue. I have too much on my mind as I sit quietly, watching the flames lick the air. I feel someone plop down beside me and I sigh because I don't really feel like talking. Then I look over and realize it's Hayden. He's been mostly MIA since the kayaks. I'm pretty sure he was cleaning the bathrooms. I have to give him credit. He's done everything Mom asked him to do and he's still here.

"Whatcha doing?" he asks now.

My heart thumps an extra beat at the realization of how close he's sitting. "Wishing on fire embers."

He turns to watch the fire for a moment, seeming to analyze what I've said. "Aren't you supposed to wish on things that fall from the sky? And not things that float up to the sky?"

"I don't think that's a rule." I roll my lips together. Maybe I don't feel like talking about relevant stuff right now, but irrelevant stuff seems okay. "There *are* rules to wishes, you know?"

"Oh?" He folds his knees in front of him, clasping his hands together. "I think I should be aware of all the wish-making rules. So I can break them all." He cast me a mischievous grin. If I had one rule for choosing a crush prior to this summer, it would have been to pick a guy who colored inside the lines. Note to self: Create rules for who to crush on after this summer. It would be pretty pointless to do so right now, because once you have a crush, it's hard to uncrush. And I'm pretty sure I'm crushing hard on Hayden based on the embers floating around in my belly and chest right now.

"So what happened with Dave in the woods today?" I ask. "I heard he got stung."

Hayden looks at me. "Just like you planned, he was a bug magnet out there. Mosquitos, flies, bees. It was hard to watch."

I nibble my lower lip and face the fire. "I didn't plan on the bees. Or that he'd be allergic to them."

Hayden grimaces. "Yeah. Me either. That's tough. Before the whole bee sting incident, I might have also pointed out paw prints and suggested to Dave they could've belonged to a bear," Hayden confesses. "Dave looked completely freaked."

"There's no way it was bear prints," I say. "We've only ever seen a bear once on this property. The fences keep them away."

"Just helping your cause." Hayden glances over. "The poor guy kept jumping at every noise until the bees started swarming around him."

"I feel awful. That sounds like a horrible experience. But maybe it will be enough to scare him off from Camp Starling."

Hayden eyes me. "Is that what you're wishing for on the fire's embers?"

I look at the fire again. "Something like that."

Hayden shifts beside me. From my peripheral vision, I see him watch the fire too. After a moment, he says, "Okay, tell me these wish-making rules."

I pull in a breath, thinking about my response. "Well, one rule about wishes is that you can't wish to undo something that's already happened. Wishes can't time-travel."

"Hmm. Good point," Hayden says. There's an easiness about him as he sits beside me. Usually when I'm sitting next to a guy, my palms get sweaty and my breaths grow shallow. Guys make me nervous. I don't feel that way with Hayden, though. Mainly because he's not a Jacob. What I mean to say is, Jacob is the golden boy at camp. He always has been. Hayden, on the other hand, is not one of the guys that girls whisper about excitedly.

"What are the other rules about making wishes?" he asks.

"Well," I say, "you also can't wish bad stuff on people."

Hayden bumps his arm against mine. I feel the sensation run through me like a shockwave. "So, no wishing for Dave to come face to face with a bear while he's here?"

I frown. "I don't want Dave to get hurt or be sick. The bee

sting was a total accident and I feel kind of rotten about it. All I want is for Dave to leave my mom and me alone. We were happy before he came along."

"You're not happy now?" Hayden asks, his tone serious.

I look at him, noticing the reflection of an ember in his brown eyes. Without thinking, I make a wish: *I wish that I could stay right here.* I don't need to reverse time, but can't we just stop it for a little while? Because this moment feels perfect somehow.

"You okay?" he asks, eyes narrowing.

I look away, and just like the fire's ember, the moment sizzles out. Hayden isn't the one for me. I should be paying attention to Jacob. "Yeah. Another rule about wishes is that wishing them doesn't make them come true."

"That kind of defeats the whole purpose of wishing then," Hayden says. "You should just call it *hoping.*"

I heave a sigh. "Exactly. And hoping leads to disappointment these days."

Hayden bumps against me again. This warmness oozes through me, not from the fire's glow, but from Hayden. "Cheer up. It's not the end of the world."

"Just the end of mine," I mutter. "Unless I figure out this whole matchbreaker idea of yours."

Hayden starts to say something. His shoulder is still against mine, distracting me from my thoughts. Then Nora plops down in front of us, her gaze darting from me to him. I feel a little hiccup of worry because Nora is likely to harass me later for hanging out with Hayden versus her and the other counselors. She'll probably recap all the mischief Hayden has ever gotten into including the graffiti on the cabins.

Looking at her right now, though, you wouldn't know she'd ever thought anything judgmental of Hayden. She's grinning at him and blinking a little faster than usual. Her cheeks are a deep shade of pink. Not the kind from too much sun either.

"So how are you liking your first camp experience?" she asks Hayden, giving him her undivided attention.

"More than I thought I would."

"You didn't think you'd like it here?" she asks. She seems sincerely interested in his response.

"This isn't really my scene." He shrugs. "Or I didn't think it was. It's kind of a cool place, though, I guess."

"Well, I love it here. This is my fourth year coming," Nora tells him. She pulls her ponytail in front of her shoulder and twirls the hair with her fingers. "Do you think you'll come back again next summer?"

I worry momentarily that Hayden will give away my secret about Camp Starling closing its doors, but instead he offers another quick shrug. "I don't know. Maybe."

"What do you normally do during the summers?" she asks. As soon as Hayden answers one question, Nora seems to have one more at the ready.

I sit there and listen, feeling almost invisible as they talk. I'm also a little baffled. Nora is talking to Hayden almost as intently as she used to with Jacob last summer, which is crazy, because there's no way she has a thing for Hayden Bennett. Is there?

A ribbon of jealousy runs through me. By normal standards, Nora is prettier than me. She's had way more boyfriends than I have—I've had exactly none—and she's great at flirting. I'm kind of the sidekick who's fun to be friends with, but not the one guys are interested in taking to the movies and holding hands with in the dark. That's Nora.

I watch as Nora and Hayden talk, feeling invisible just like I did when Dave started hanging around my mom. Mom and Dave would get lost in their own conversations and then suddenly remember poor Paisley and try to rope me into whatever they were doing or talking about. Finally, I just spared them the effort and started making myself scarce when Dave was around, claiming that I needed to study at the library or meet up with my friends for some kind of social thing. Sometimes it was true. Other times, I was just on my own somewhere. There's nothing worse than being a third wheel.

"Pais?"

I blink and look at Hayden when he calls my name. "Hmm?"

There's a bit of humor in his eyes. "I asked you a question, but you were a million miles away. Making more wishes on fire embers?"

"Wishes on fire embers?" Nora repeats, as if that would be an absurd thing to do.

I'm starting to realize that maybe I don't actually tell Nora everything like I thought I did. I just tell her the things I know she won't think are crazy.

"You mean wishing on falling stars?" she asks.

Hayden's expression subtly changes, as if he's realizing

that I only shared that thought with him. I'm not sure why my cheeks burn, but they do. Maybe because I'm sharing a lot of things with only him these days.

"What was the question?" I ask Hayden. "Sorry, I was lost in thought."

"That's okay. I just asked how it feels to be someone's hero."

"Oh. You heard about Simone, huh?" I ask.

Hayden smiles. "Who hasn't? Everyone's been talking about it."

I'm blushing even harder now.

"Well, you're a hero too," Nora tells Hayden. I notice that she doesn't include Jacob. "You paddled out to my rescue earlier on the lake." I also notice that she doesn't include me.

"You and Pais weren't in any real danger," Hayden tells her. "You had on life jackets. Simone was going under from what I hear."

A nervous smile flutters on Nora's lips. "True. I guess Paisley was the one who dove into the water and pulled Simone out. Any one of us was ready to do the same thing, of course. It's kind of our job as counselors." Her words are just running over each other, one after another, just like her questions a minute ago. There's something sheepish as she glances in my direction. Does she realize she's minimizing what I did this morning? Because I'm realizing it. I'm realizing that Nora minimizes a lot of things about me.

"No one else dove into the water to help Simone, though, right?" Hayden asks.

"The lifeguard did. Paisley just beat her to it. I was about to dive in too," Nora says. "I could have." She gives him a nervous smile. Nora is rarely ever nervous.

I hold my tongue to keep from calling her bluff. She wouldn't have dived in because she wouldn't have wanted to get her hair and clothes wet. Maybe our kayak capsizing is karma for her hesitation.

Hayden looks at me. His smile is back and so are the butterflies in my stomach. "Well, I think you're the hero of the day. You should be proud of yourself."

I get caught for a moment in his stare. I can't blink, can hardly breathe. Then Nora agrees, her voice coming out a little too loudly.

"Yes, that's true. You got to Simone first, Paisley. Good job." She smiles again, looking to Hayden with an expression almost as if she's seeking his approval.

That's when I know. Nora always has that approval-seeking tendency with her crushes. She is totally crushing on Hayden. Which is awkward. And unlike her. And disappointing because as competitive as I can be, I can't compete with Nora when it comes to winning over a guy.

☀

Later, as I walk with the girl campers back to the west side, Nora is in stride beside me. There's this worry building inside me, billowing like smoke from the campfire earlier. As long as she doesn't tell me she likes Hayden, I can pretend that I don't know. I can convince myself the way she's acting is just in my imagination. And I'm not saying I have any feelings for Hayden, but as long as I don't *know* know that Nora does, I could if I wanted to. He would be fair game.

"I like Hayden," Nora blurts out before erupting into hyper giggles. She claps a hand over her mouth and looks at me with wide green eyes. "I can't believe I just said that. He's not my type at all. But he's so cute, don't you think?" She looks at me expectantly.

"Um, yeah. I guess so." I lock my hair behind my ear, suddenly feeling sick to my stomach. "If you like that kind of guy."

"You mean the total bad-boy type?" She laughs again. It's high-pitched and nervous. "I'm shocked that I do, but I was watching him today, after he helped me in the lake, and he's kind of cool, you know?"

Once again, she fails to point out that Hayden and Jacob came to help both of us.

"He's also interesting. And funny. He's gotten a bad rap as a troublemaker, but he's not really. He's more of an artist. I mean, I wouldn't expect you to think he's great because, well, you're more of a Jacob girl."

"A what?" I draw back.

"Come on. You know it's true. You and Jacob are perfect for each other. And I think he likes you. Meanwhile, I'm perfect for Hayden." She giggles again.

I feel miserable as I listen, and I'm not even sure why. All I know is camp is very different this year. Nothing is the same.

Everything feels off, including my friendship with Nora. It occurs to me that if we hadn't been friends since third grade, I might not even really get along with her right now. I never thought someone could outgrow a friend, especially the friends-forever type. But maybe, just maybe, I have.

❊

As I lay in my bunk that night, listening to the whispers of the girls in my cabin, I reach for my camper's journal under my mattress, careful to make sure no one sees my hiding place. Then I uncap the purple gel pen tucked inside and press it to the paper.

> Day two was a big fat flop. I might have added honey to Dave's sunblock which in turn led to Dave needing his EpiPen, but it wasn't enough to run him off.
>
> The good news is that I did kind of save someone's life. But I capsized my and Nora's kayak and somehow lost the ~~guy I like~~

I stop writing and draw a line through those last three words. Not the guy *I* like. The guy Nora likes. There's this small ache in my heart. Once, in sixth grade, Nora and I both had a crush on Cody Johnson. Sixth grade was the year that Nora suddenly began to hang out with the guys she was into. That was when I first made the decision that best friends could not like the same guy—ever. Because friends were more important than crushes. And even if we're not exactly feeling like besties lately, that's still true.

I put my pen back to paper and write:

I'm sure tomorrow will be better. It has to be.

CHAPTER NINE

Camp Time: Wednesday. July 20.

My body is sore as I stretch beneath my blanket. It's the good kind of muscle ache that you get from using your body all day at camp. I open my eyes and breathe in the fresh air of our cabin. I'm the first one awake. The sun is barely up as I climb out from beneath my blanket and slip my feet into a pair of flip-flops. Then I quietly gather my clothes for the day and head out to the Bird Bath to dress and freshen up before my cabinmates.

I may have gone to bed with downcast spirits, but everything is fresh and new in the morning. As I head out of the bathroom area, Simone is standing there, waiting for me.

"Oh. Hi, Simone."

She smiles. Her dark hair is pulled back in a clip today. "I saw you wake up, so I followed you."

"I like to get a head start. Especially since I'm a counselor this year. As a camper, you really shouldn't be walking on the paths this early without a buddy," I say. Not that it isn't safe, but it's one of the rules. Counselors have more liberty.

"Well, I was with you. Kind of," Simone says.

"Except I didn't know you were with me. So if something happened to you, I wouldn't know that I was supposed to be looking for you."

"Right." Simone nods, her smile faltering. "Sorry."

I shake my head. "No, it's okay. Now you know. It's best to stick with a partner. Another camper," I add, because I'm getting the feeling that Simone has grown attached to me since yesterday. That's not necessarily a bad thing but hanging around a counselor usually means a camper hasn't found anyone else they feel comfortable with yet. I make a mental note to connect her with another camper today to be sure she has a friend here. "I'll walk you back to the cabin."

We turn to head back.

"I saw you get those honey packets from the kitchen yesterday," Simone says, a bit sheepishly.

My insides freeze. "Oh? Well, I really love honey." It's not a lie. I do.

"I saw you messing with Mr. Dave's stuff too."

I hedge. "I was just returning his sunblock. I borrowed it." Okay, *that* is a lie. What am I supposed to say, though?

"Oh." Simone seems to accept my explanation. I wonder what she thought I was doing. What if she knows the truth? Will she rat me out?

"So, um, where do you live?" I ask, changing the subject as quickly as possible.

"In Clifton. It's about an hour from here. I found this place online and begged my mom and dad to let me come," she says with a small laugh. "My parents are such control freaks. They don't let me do anything. Like, even getting them to agree to allow me to sleep over at a friend's house is a huge deal. I'm actually surprised they said yes to me coming here."

"Well, I'm glad you convinced them," I tell her. "Camp Starling is my favorite place in the whole world."

"Really?" Simone looks surprised. "Your favorite place lacks internet, fast food, and pretty much all the basic requirements for a teenager."

"True. But it's where I feel closest to my dad. He died when I was twelve," I tell her.

Usually, when I tell people about my dad dying, they get weird, like they don't know what to say. It's a good way to ruin a conversation.

Simone looks over at me. "That must have been hard. I can't imagine losing my dad so young. You must be tough."

This makes me laugh quietly. "I don't think so. I cried for the first year or so." And sometimes I still cry when I'm alone. But mostly I just write my feelings in a journal.

"Crying doesn't mean you're not tough." Simone sounds way older than her age. I'm actually kind of surprised that I'm enjoying our conversation, more than I've enjoyed chatting with my own best friend so far this week. "My grandma Panda says a tough cookie is one that keeps being put in the oven, but refuses to crumble under the heat."

There's so much to process in that statement. "Your grandma's name is Panda?"

Simone grins. "Well, that's what I called her when I was young. I guess it stuck. It's kind of a nickname now."

I laugh again as we approach Chickadee Cabin. The green spray paint is mostly gone. There's still a faint tint to the wood if you know where to look for it. It almost looks like it was meant to be that way, though. Maybe it was. Maybe Hayden was fated to randomly spray the cabins for no good reason so that he'd get sentenced to two weeks of camp.

The other girls are all stirring as we walk into Chickadee Cabin. Tabitha's cheeks are sun-kissed from yesterday. So are Mandy's. Maddie is sitting up in her bunk. I smile at her, but she doesn't smile back.

"Okay, everyone, grab your clothes and things. We'll hit the Bird Bath first and then walk to breakfast together." I hope my mom has come to her senses and gone back to the true Campers' Breakfast instead of fruit and granola. When we reach the Birdfeeder twenty minutes later, however, it's evident that she hasn't.

Hayden steps up beside me as my campers beeline toward the food. They don't seem to care what's being served, but I do.

"Hey, Pais," he says.

My heart leaps for a moment, but then I look around and catch Nora eying us. Right. Her crush. "Hi," I say, telling myself that I'm not crushing on Hayden anyway. We're just friends, which is surprising in and of itself. I mean, yeah, I find him cute. And funny. He's also easy to talk to. That doesn't mean I want to date him. "Did you sleep in the cabin last night?"

He shakes his head. "I'm a duck, remember?"

I give him an amused look. "So, how do you feel about cooking?"

He cocks a brow. "I'm an amazing cook. My mom used to give my brother and me lessons."

There's that mention of his brother again. I'm about to ask him about it, when Hayden shoves his hands into his shorts' pockets and says, "What kind of food are you planning to cook?"

"Breakfast foods."

Hayden nods. "That just so happens to be my specialty."

"Great. Meet me here tomorrow, an hour early? Campers' Breakfast is meant to be something more than this," I tell him. "I think you and I should remind my mom what she seems to have forgotten. And put Dave in his place for trying to change things. Camp Starling has always had Campers' Breakfast. It was my dad's tradition. Are you in?"

"Sure." Hayden bumps his arm against mine. This is something he's started doing with me, and I kind of like it. Just like I kind of like the way he shortens my name. But it's also starting to feel like flirting. My gaze immediately moves to Nora, who thankfully isn't watching anymore. But I still feel guilty. I look at Hayden and clarify what's going on between us. I need to label this thing between us for my own sanity. "You know, I think you and I are becoming friends."

"That's cool. I've never had a girl friend before." He steps away before I can say anything.

He said *girl friend*, two separate words, as in I'm a girl

and his friend. A friend who's a girl. Not someone he's dating. Because we're not dating. I'm not even interested in him that way, I tell myself, still standing there rooted in place, my thoughts swirling around in a dust cloud in my head. It's a lie, of course. Just like the one I told Simone earlier. Once you tell one lie, it's easier to tell the next. There won't be a third lie though. I'm not a liar. I'm just a teenaged girl who's desperate.

※

Three hours later, I see Dave heading my way before he reaches me. Everyone else is taking a healthy walk after lunch in order to give Hayden time to set up the picnic tables for his arts and crafts program. My campers are hanging out with Meghan's and Maria's groups. I stayed back to offer Hayden my help. Mom did ask me to show Hayden the ropes, after all.

"What are you doing with the campers this afternoon?" I shift back and forth on my feet as I watch Hayden set paper plates on the tables.

He looks up as if he didn't realize I was standing there. "Well, your mom kind of gave me a short notice on doing this. And limited supplies. I found boxes of white T-shirts with the Camp Starling logos on them in the shed. Your mom said they were from several years ago. Kind of like promotional stuff that went unused."

"I remember those. What are you planning to do with them?" I ask.

"Tie-dyeing." Hayden winks at me. "You want to be my assistant?"

I laugh softly. Not because he's funny in a Ricardo kind of way. I guess the laughter is this giddy feeling bubbling up out of me every time I see Hayden now. It's absurd and I wish it didn't happen, especially since I know that Nora likes him. "I've never tie-dyed anything before in my life."

"It's easy. I'll show you how. Your mom said all the campers can wear their shirts tomorrow."

"Wow. That's a really cool idea." And it's something we've never done here at Camp Starling, just like granola for breakfast and the arts and crafts program.

Hayden shrugs, his gaze catching mine and sticking, holding. "It should be fun."

"For sure," I say, another laugh tumbling off my lips. I remind myself of Nora and how she behaves around the guys she likes.

Hayden gestures to several boxes that he's already laid out on the pavement. "Help me sort these shirts into piles based on size? The campers will pick up one shirt each and take it to the tables. I'll rope the other counselors in to help out."

I think of Nora and wonder if she'll try to take my place as Hayden's assistant. Just the thought makes me feel this tension inside me, tightening my chest. "I definitely don't mind assisting you," I offer, partly because I want to, and the other part because I want to own this role before Nora snatches it away from me.

"Great. I've already prepared the dye inside the squirt bottles. Each table will have two bowls of cold water and rubber bands. It's pretty straightforward," he tells me.

I head over to the boxes of shirts and start pulling them

out, making piles of smalls, mediums, and larges. "You say it's straightforward, but these are campers who have left their parents for two weeks. Anything goes."

Hayden chuckles and catches my eye again. The moment is all butterflies and campfire embers dancing around in my chest. "Thanks for the warning, partner."

"Partner, huh? I thought you were more of a solo kind of guy," I say, remembering that Hayden doesn't even sleep inside his cabin.

"Well, I usually am. You and I kind of make a nice team, though, don't we?"

I redirect my attention to the shirts, wondering at my uptick in heart rate. Did my heart actually just skip a beat? "Yeah, I guess so." When I'm done sorting the shirts, I turn back to him. He's laid out vinyl tablecloths on the picnic tables. The bowls of water are sitting at the centers of the tables just waiting for the campers to come find a seat.

We work together, making easy conversation. Hayden makes me laugh repeatedly and I momentarily forget all the things that are currently stressing me out, like my mom and Dave getting married, the move, and selling Camp Starling.

Fifteen minutes later, we both turn toward the sound of a few early campers heading our way. Nora and Jacob are with them. Nora's eyes narrow when she sees me with Hayden. *Uh-oh*. I distance myself from Hayden and straighten the piles of rubber bands, as if they need any type of organization. Soon all the campers have grabbed a T-shirt and are seated at a table. The girls and guys are free to mingle for arts and crafts time, but they mostly stay with their cabinmates. Hayden explains the rules to both the campers and the counselors and everyone starts tying their shirts.

I kind of step back and watch once everyone is working on autopilot.

"Paisley?" Dave steps up beside me. His voice is loaded with enthusiasm, which I would normally find endearing, but this is Dave we're talking about. "Beautiful day out here, huh?"

"Mm-hmm." I keep my focus on the campers. Watching over them is my job here this summer after all, even if they don't need me at this very moment.

Dave seems to look around in appreciation. "It's great that you've gotten to grow up at a place like this, coming here every summer."

I turn and look at him. Good thing I'm wearing sunglasses to cover my *are-you-serious* eyes. "Every year of my childhood until next year. Then my childhood is being cut short because we're leaving and Camp Starling is closing forever," I remind him. I hold my tongue and don't add that it's all his fault.

Dave grows quiet for a long moment. "Well, you'll be headed to college before you know it. That's like one long week of camp." He chuckles, but I don't laugh with him.

"College kids need summer jobs. And being a camp counselor looks good on applications. Only, I don't think being a counselor once is enough to count," I say.

Dave shifts beside me. He rubs the back of his head the way he does when he's thinking extra hard. "Well, there are camps in Wyoming, you know?" he says, voice full of enthusiasm as if I'm twelve.

"That's where you grew up, right?" I ask.

"Cheyenne, Wyoming. It's the biggest city in the state." He smiles as if he's made headway in the conversation.

"So what camp did you go to when you were growing up?" I ask, putting on a smile and looking at him. My smile is forced, of course.

Dave's enthusiasm takes a notable dive. Now he almost looks crestfallen. "Well, I didn't go to camp, Paisley."

Ah ha! I feel a little surge of victory. Of course he didn't attend camp because he's not like me and my mom. He's not a Manning. He doesn't have the great outdoors in his blood. "I guess it's true, what they say about opposites attracting. Because Mom loves camping, just like my dad did." I'm secretly proud of myself for finding this unexpected rub in the conversation. "Camping was all my parents ever talked about, they loved it so much. It's hard to even imagine that you and Mom have anything in common without a love of camping."

"I didn't say I didn't love camping," Dave says. "I'm giving it my all out here this week. It's just, my family couldn't afford to send me to camp when I was growing up. We were what one might call poor. My parents didn't have extra money for things that weren't essential." He shrugs as if it's no big deal, but his shoulders suddenly look like they're carrying a heavy weight.

I've had friends whose parents struggled financially. It's not easy for them. "I didn't know," I say, feeling bad for the way I've treated Dave. Don't get me wrong. I don't regret wanting him and my mom to break up, but everyone deserves their day in camp.

"Times were hard. As a result, I acted out and got myself into quite a bit of trouble back in my day." He watches Hayden interacting with the campers as they squirt dye onto their rubber-band-bound shirts, a small smile playing at the corners of his mouth. "I guess that's why I convinced your mom to let your friend Hayden be at camp this summer instead of bringing in the authorities."

I swallow thickly. "That's why?"

Dave nods and looks at me. "Yeah. I know it would have meant a lot to me as a city kid to have something like this to look forward to. But hey, better late than never, right? I get to have the full camp experience this summer with you and your mom. What could be better?" His smile bounces back in full force, like one of those rubber bands, showing me a piece of his lunch wedged between his front teeth.

Better would be if this wasn't Dave's first and last camp. He doesn't understand or appreciate how amazing this place is. Not really. Not like my dad, who built this place with his own hands.

"Well, since you've never been to camp, you don't understand what Campers' Breakfast is," I say, holding my ground and ignoring the empathy I feel at knowing that Dave wasn't afforded the things I deem a huge part of who I am. "Campers' Breakfast is not granola bars and fruit."

Dave rubs the back of his neck again. "Oh. I was just trying to make your mom's job easier. She has a big responsibility here at the camp all by herself."

"She's not all by herself. She has me. She's always had me."

I push my sunglasses up on the crown of my head and look Dave directly in the eyes. "So Hayden and I are making Campers' Breakfast in the morning for everyone."

"On your own?" Dave asks.

"I'm calling in reinforcements." Which means my Aunt Jenny and Uncle Leon, who help with camp every year. "Tomorrow, breakfast is going to be the way it's supposed to at Camp Starling. The way my dad would have insisted it was. It's a surprise for my mom so don't tell her," I say as I walk off to observe the campers continue to make their tie-dyed shirts, leaving Dave standing there and rubbing the back of his head.

CHAPTER TEN

After Hayden's arts and crafts program, the campers are given some free time on the grounds. Instead of following them, I ask Meghan to watch my group for me while I dip into Mom's cabin and use her cellphone to call Aunt Jenny and Uncle Leon. Technically, it's against the rules for a camper to be in my mom's cabin, but I'm her daughter and a counselor, and this is an emergency. Kind of. Because what is Camp Starling without Campers' Breakfast?

I walk inside her quarters and find her phone on the bedside table. I pull up Aunt Jenny's contact, and press CALL.

"Hi, Aunt Jenny," I say after she answers.

"Paisley?" Aunt Jenny asks when she hears my voice. "Is everything all right, sweetheart?"

"Everything's fine, aside from the fact that it's Day Three and we've only had granola bars and fruit for breakfast so far." Aunt Jenny is my dad's sister so she understands exactly how much Camp Starling meant to him. When Dad was going to camp every summer as a teen and falling in love with my mom, Aunt Jenny was going to camp as well. She has always been part of Camp Starling from the very beginning, willing to help with anything my parents needed.

"I know that change is hard, Birdie. But that's how your mom is doing things this year. She's simplifying."

"Dad wouldn't have wanted it this way," I argue.

"Honey . . ." My aunt trails off.

"I have money," I tell her. I babysit a kid down the street and I've been saving the earnings over the last year. Granted, I was saving the money to go to the Audubon Day Camp for Bird Lovers during winter break this year. "I want to surprise my mom tomorrow," I tell Aunt Jenny, "and give the campers a true Campers' Breakfast. I know my mom is only going along with granola and fruit because it's easier and that's what Dave suggested. It's not really what she prefers, though. I just want to do things the right way, the Camp Starling way, for one morning. Will you and Uncle Leon help me? Please."

Aunt Jenny hedges. I know she's probably wondering if this is going behind my mom's back. My Aunt Jenny is the nicest person. She always helps out a ton at camp. She's already been helping this week, supervising the campers during the daily activities.

"Dave is ruining everything, Aunt Jenny. He doesn't even know how to kayak. He could hardly keep up with the activities yesterday." I don't mention that while he couldn't keep up, I capsized myself and Nora.

"Dave seems like a really nice guy, sweetheart. And more importantly, he makes your mom happy."

"She only *thinks* she's happy," I counter. "And besides," I add, deciding I might try the angle of Dave never having experienced camp, "Dave told me this is his first camp experience. He needs to experience a Campers' Breakfast."

Aunt Jenny releases a breath into the receiver. "Okay. But save your money. Your uncle and I will buy the food and be at the Birdfeeder at five a.m. tomorrow to help cook."

I bounce on my heels. "I'll be there with reinforcements too. It's going to be amazing. Thank you, thank you, thank you!"

"You're welcome, sweetheart," she says. "See you tomorrow."

I hang up the phone and slip out of Mom's cabin, looking around to make sure no one sees me. All clear. Then I return to camp before anyone even notices I'm gone.

"Where were you?" a voice asks as I approach the group.

I whirl to face Simone.

Okay, anyone except Simone.

"Just working on a little surprise," I say. "You'll see tomorrow. Did I miss anything?" It's just been downtime for the last hour, where campers get to relax outside and make friends with other campers.

Simone nibbles at her lower lip, looking a little sheepish. "Your friend Nora, the other counselor? She's spent the entire time you were away talking to your, um . . ."

"My what?" I ask, brows bunching.

"The guy counselor you've been talking to a lot. The one you seem to like."

I look around, my gaze zeroing in on Nora. Sure enough, she's over there with Hayden, her arms gesturing wildly as she tells him something. My heart sinks as I watch the two of them. He laughs at whatever she says, which shouldn't crush me, but it totally does.

"You should go over there," Simone suggests. "He was looking for you while you were gone."

"He was?" I ask, hope lifting my spirits.

"I'm guessing he'd rather be talking to you," Simone says.

Watching him talk to Nora, I'm not so sure about that. What guy wouldn't rather be with her? She's funny, smart, pretty.

Simone nudges me, pushing a hand against my arm. "Go. I'm thirteen and even I know that you have to fight for your crush."

"He's not my crush," I protest, but the words come out weak. "But I do need to tell Hayden something. For camp." I nod to myself, gathering my resolve and offering Simone a smile. For a thirteen-year-old, she's pretty cool. A lot cooler than I was at her age. Then again, at her age, I was still reeling from losing my dad. I was lost, following Nora around like Simone has followed me this week. Nora was my one constant back then in an otherwise broken world. She doesn't feel like that this summer, though.

Nora looks up as I head toward her and Hayden. He looks up too, and maybe his smile grows bigger. That could be my imagination.

"Hey, Paisley," Nora says. "Where have you been?"

I guess people did notice that I had been MIA for a little bit. "I, uh, well . . ." I look at Hayden. "I've been working on the arrangements for tomorrow morning. For breakfast. You're still helping me, right?"

One corner of his mouth quirks as he bats his dark hair out of his eyes. "Wouldn't miss it."

"Great." Warm gooeyness spreads through my rib cage, spreading up around my heart space. Simone is right. Resist it all I want, but I totally have a thing for Hayden.

"What's going on at breakfast?" Nora has this tone to her voice. Nora hates to be left out of the loop on things.

"Oh, Hayden and I are going to revive Campers' Breakfast for everyone. My Aunt Jenny and Uncle Leon are coming out to help. It'll be a surprise for my mom, so don't say anything. I don't want her to know about it." Because I'm afraid if she did, she'd put a stop to it.

Nora looks between me and Hayden. "You and Hayden are setting this up?"

I know when Nora is jealous. There's this spark in her eyes. You can actually see it. Green with jealousy is a real thing with her. "Why didn't you invite me to help?" Her eyebrows lower. For a moment, I see hurt in her expression. I didn't mean to leave her out.

"Making breakfast requires getting up an hour earlier, Nora. And it's not necessary for you to do that. Hayden and I can totally handle this."

Nora looks stiff. "I can wake up early, Paisley. Since when do we keep things from each other?"

That question feels loaded. If she only knew how many things I was keeping from her this summer.

"And since when are you and Hayden in cahoots?" Nora blurts. "You don't even like him, but suddenly you're cooking breakfast with him?"

I cast Hayden an apologetic smile. It's true, I didn't like him before camp. He did graffiti the cabins, after all. I like him now, though.

"You can wake up early and help us if you want to, Nora. It's just, Hayden offered. He says he's good at cooking breakfast, so . . ." I trail off.

"So you're using me," Hayden supplies, teasing and lifting the mood. "Again."

I shrug, but I don't dare look at him. Nora is already jealous and maybe she has hurt feelings too. I'm worried my cheeks are hot and flushed. If I look at Hayden, what would she see on my face? "Something like that," I tell him, looking at the ground instead. In my peripheral vision, I see his graffitied shoes, which don't annoy me anymore. Now I think they're pretty cool.

Hayden chuckles, which seems to fuel Nora's frustration. I see it on her face when I look back up. The skin of her neck and chest has red blotches and her smile is tight.

"Great. It's settled, then. I'm helping with breakfast tomorrow," she says, softening her tone. "Waking up an hour early is not a huge deal. I'm your best friend"—she stresses *best friend*—"so you can count on me for anything. Just like I can count on you."

She doesn't have to finish that statement for me to know what she's implying. She can count on me not to steal the guy she's into. Message received loud and clear. And I'm not trying to. I'm actively trying *not* to like Hayden. It's just . . . not working.

❋

Camp Time: Thursday. July 21.

Campers' Breakfast is the most important meal of the day. That's what Dad used to say.

The smell of grease floats on the cool summer morning air. Yes, grease has a scent. The air feels thicker. It's harder to breathe. I hear the soft sizzle and pop as my Uncle Leon and Hayden manage cooking the meat while me, Nora, and my Aunt Jenny prepare mile-high stacks of pancakes. Each camper gets three silver dollar cakes, but there are ninety-six campers in total, so you do the math. That's a lot of pancakes.

My mind wanders to memories of me, my mom, and my dad cooking these meals. I was a lot younger back then, but I could still help in small ways. Aunt Jenny and Uncle Leon cooked as well. We were up before the birds and having the time of our lives. I miss those days. The food was definitely made with love, and it tasted better because of it. At least in my memory.

I glance over at Nora, who has been giving me the silent treatment so far this morning. I thought maybe she was just tired. She's not a morning person, after all. But then my Aunt Jenny started asking her questions and now she's chattering away about all things high school while effectively ignoring me. Aunt Jenny keeps trying to rope me in on the conversation, but Nora keeps blocking me out. She's upset with me, and I'm left to guess at the reason. Probably because I made plans with Hayden and excluded her, and she thinks I'm moving in on her turf. But he was kind of my turf first. She just doesn't know that.

"You excited about going into junior year, Birdie?" my aunt asks me as she adds to the growing stacks of cakes.

I look up. My lack of excitement must be evident on my face because my aunt pauses and frowns.

"It won't be so bad. You'll see," she says.

"Why would it be bad?" Nora is looking between us now. "At least we won't be lowerclassmen anymore. Being a lowerclassman is the worst," she says dramatically. Even though Nora is not a morning person, she's full of her usual flair and drama at this early hour.

"Well, a new school is hard." Aunt Jenny shakes her head and continues working with the pancakes on the griddle. "But you're only the new kid for the first couple of months. If you just hang on, it'll be like you've always been there."

"We're not going anywhere different," Nora says. "We'll be returning to the same school this year."

I don't respond. Neither does Aunt Jenny.

Nora puts her spatula down and turns to me with an audible huff. "What is your aunt talking about, Paisley?"

I catch my aunt's eye and I can tell she realizes she's totally misspoken. She probably assumed I would have told Nora that

I was moving next month. "N-nothing." I shake my head, feeling my ponytail scrape along the back of my neck.

Nora growls, the sound echoing through the Birdfeeder. "I thought we were best friends. But you're not acting like a best friend this week. Since when do we keep secrets from each other?"

"I'm not," I say.

"You are!" She shakes her head. "Are you moving or something?"

I hedge, but don't answer. I'm not supposed to tell anyone yet. Even though I told Hayden.

Nora growls again, and instead of picking the spatula back up, she storms off, heading in the direction of the girls' cabins.

"I'm so sorry," Aunt Jenny says, her voice soft and low. "I didn't realize you hadn't told her yet. Why haven't you, Birdie?"

I turn the pancake on the griddle in front of me, working on autopilot. I'm trying hard not to let my eyes well up. "Mom asked me not to. And I only just found out myself right before camp started. I'm still in denial, I guess. Maybe if I don't tell anyone about the move, it won't happen."

Aunt Jenny puts her hand on my back. "Leaving your home, your school, and your friends. That's not easy. But change can be a good thing. It doesn't have to be bad."

I look at her. "What about Camp Starling? Dad built this place. We're just going to sell it?"

Aunt Jenny looks taken aback for a moment. "Your mom didn't mention that to me yet."

"Oh." Maybe I wasn't supposed to say that much. Mom hasn't even spoken to the Realtor yet. "Please don't tell her I told you."

Aunt Jenny lifts her hand from my back and returns to cooking pancakes. "For this morning, let's just focus on Campers' Breakfast, shall we? The rest of our worries can wait."

I force a smile, my gaze catching on Hayden, who is watching me. Then my gaze moves to Dave walking toward the Birdfeeder area.

"What is he doing here?" I mutter.

Aunt Jenny follows my gaze. "Oh, it looks like Dave is joining us."

"I didn't invite him," I say.

And it's early yet for preparing granola and fruit.

Dave steps up and I immediately notice his yellow shirt, which is now also red and green. He seems to inspect what's happening. "This must be the famous Campers' Breakfast," he says. He pretends to push up his sleeves, even though he's not wearing long sleeves. I swear, this is the cheesiest man on earth.

"What happened to your shirt?" Aunt Jenny asks.

Dave looks down. "I tie-dyed it with Hayden yesterday. Pretty cool, huh? I think I might dye all my shirts this way. What do you think, Hayden? Will you help me?"

Hayden casts me a guilty look, as if agreeing to help Dave is going against me somehow. "Sure. No problem."

"Great." Dave rubs his hands together. "So how can I help with breakfast?" He turns to my Uncle Leon and Hayden. "It looks like the men are in charge of cooking the meat. Argh," he says in a caveman kind of way. "Give me a tool and meat I'll make."

Hayden steps away from the grill he's manning. "You can take over for me. I'll get the fruit ready."

"Fruit isn't part of Campers' Breakfast," I call out.

Hayden turns back to me. "Yeah, but some of the campers might like it, right? Can't we put out both?"

Everyone's looking at me to make the call. Because this whole thing was my idea to begin with.

Aunt Jenny's hand finds my back again, and I can hear her voice inside my head. *Change can be a good thing.*

I look at Hayden, not Dave, and nod. "Okay. Fine."

CHAPTER ELEVEN

So, this is how my Campers' Breakfast surprise went down.

Mom woke up and went to the Birdfeeder to get the fruit and granola out for the campers before the second Bird Call at six-thirty. She was surprised, of course. There was a big smile on her face along with a sheen of tears in her eyes. She hugged me, as I imagined she would, but there was no talk about how Dad would have been so proud. Or how wrong she was to go along with Dave's suggestion that we serve fruit and granola this year at breakfast.

Nope. Instead, after leaving me, my mom stepped over to Dave, momentarily raved over his tie-dyed counselor shirt— *"How adorable!"*—and then embraced him too. I heard her say, "I can't believe you were in on this."

I nearly lost the breakfast that I hadn't even eaten yet.

"I wasn't. This was all Paisley's doing," Dave told her, gesturing at me.

Mom wouldn't take her eyes off Dave, though. "But you're out here helping. Just another reason that I love you."

Aunt Jenny must have seen something in my expression because she placed her hand on my shoulder. Her words silently replayed in my mind. *Change can be a good thing.* If that was true, why did it have to feel so awful?

So, once breakfast was over, I cleaned up with the help of the girls from Chickadee Cabin. Simone was a huge help. Maddie, not so much. Afterward, I told Simone about my fight with Nora, which I know is kind of weird. Simone is a camper and I'm the counselor. I'm supposed to be supporting her, not vice versa. But she's a great listener and I just had to tell someone. That leads me to now.

"Nora has always been my best friend, but for some reason, we're just not getting along this summer," I say.

"Some reason?" Simone looks over at me as we walk. "You don't know why?"

We're heading toward the trails because today is the day we focus on bird-watching. Mom's best friend from childhood always comes to Camp Starling on Day Four because she's an ornithologist. Her job is to study and teach people about birds of all varieties, which is a huge passion of mine. Maybe I'll even go to school to study ornithology one day. There's a zoology and wildlife degree I was interested in at one of the universities in North Carolina. Who knows if there's anything like that in Wyoming.

"I guess I do know why Nora and I aren't getting along," I tell Simone. "Nora and I have never kept secrets from each other."

"So you should come clean," Simone suggests, as if the answer is obvious.

"The thing is, I think coming clean will drive us farther apart. In fact, I know it will." Because I'm moving fifteen hundred miles away. I actually Google-mapped the distance right before camp started. How much farther can we get?

"You don't know that for sure. The truth might bring you back together."

"Are you sure you're just thirteen?" I ask.

"Fairly certain. I'll be an adult in five years. Then I can move out and live my life my way," she says.

I'm sixteen and I've never had this thought in my entire life until Dave came along. I only have to put up with his cheesiness for another two years before I can leave for college.

"I don't know why you think your life is so upside down right now," Simone says, "but I think it's like that for everyone."

I stop walking and look at her. I've already asked this question, but I ask again. "You're only thirteen?"

Simone grins and hides her face in a small swooping movement. Her dark hair spills along one cheek. "Yeah. And since you think I'm so mature and all, take my advice and go make up with your friend. If it drives you farther away, then at least you tried."

"I'm the camp counselor here. I'm the one who's supposed to be giving *you* advice and helping *you* navigate your time here."

"Oh?" Simone looks at me expectantly. "Whatcha got?"

I think for a moment and then point at Tabitha and Mandy. "You need to make friends your own age. Go hang out with some of your cabinmates."

Simone's expression twists into a frown. "They aren't as impressed with my maturity as you are."

"Then act your age and be immature," I say, giving her a teasing shove toward the girls. "And I'll act mine and be mature."

Simone sticks her hand out to shake. "Deal."

I slip my hand against hers and smile. "Deal."

❋

"The American Oystercatcher can be found in the outdoors of coastal North Carolina," the ornithologist tells us mid-morning.

I'm barely listening because I know all the birds and their information by heart. I could practically give this bird-watching lesson at this point. And maybe one day I would have if Camp Starling didn't have one foot in the grave.

"Hey. We need to talk," I whisper to Nora, coming up beside her on the trail.

Nora doesn't even look at me. She's actively ignoring me and paying more attention to this bird-watcher tour than I've ever known her to.

"Nora, please. I don't like being upset with each other."

Nora stops walking and turns to me with her hands on her hips. "Are you upset with me? Because you have no reason to be."

"No." I shake my head quickly, making me feel momentarily dizzy. Maybe I haven't drunk enough water today. Hydration is key at camp. "You're the one who's acting like you're mad at me."

"I'm not acting," she says. "I *am* mad at you. You're keeping things from me. What did your Aunt Jenny mean at breakfast? What's going on, Paisley? How can we be best friends if you're not telling me things?"

I exhale softly. "I told my mom I wouldn't say anything, okay? And I didn't know how I would tell you anyway."

Nora looks at me expectantly. Campers are passing by us on the trail, so we step off to the side. Simone gives me a reassuring smile as she passes me with the group of girls from Chickadee Cabin. I smile back, but it feels awkward and shaky.

"Is this about Dave?" Nora asks.

I nod. "As you know, he and my mom are pretty serious. They've even been discussing marriage. Well, there's more than just a looming engagement." I pull in a long-suffering breath. "Dave is from Wyoming. His mom still lives there and she isn't doing too well. So Mom and Dave have decided that we're all moving there this fall."

"What?" Nora explodes.

Campers turn back to stare at us. The bird lecturer stops lecturing and looks at us too, her eyes widening beneath her wide-rim hat.

"Sorry," I say. "Everything is okay."

"No, nothing is okay," Nora whisper-yells at me. "This is not okay. You can't move. We've been best friends forever. We're supposed to finish high school together and then be roommates in college," she says.

That has always been our plan. Ever since third grade.

"I know." Nora and I step off to the side as more campers pass by us on Songbird Path. "I can't believe this is happening. I don't want to move to Wyoming. I don't want Mom to sell Camp Starling."

Nora's mouth drops open at that last tidbit of knowledge.

"Yeah. There's also that," I say.

"No wonder you've been acting so strangely. You haven't been yourself at all, and now I know why." Nora's shoulders visibly round like she's carrying a heavy weight too. Secrets are like that, and I feel a little guilty about unloading mine on her.

We're the last in the group, so I start walking and Nora follows along. We're quiet for a long time as she digests the information that I've already known for a week.

"I can't believe this," she finally says. "What are we going to do?"

I debate whether I should tell her about the matchbreaker plan. But I guess if I'm going to stop keeping secrets, I should stop keeping all of them. "Hayden and I have a plan. It might not work."

"So that's why you two have been hanging around each other so much," she says, almost in relief. As if she was worried it might be for another reason, like oh, say, we liked one another.

"That's why," I confirm.

"What's the plan?" she asks. "How can I help? Because if it gets you to stay, I'll do anything."

"Well, so far the plan has been to make Dave so miserable that he leaves Camp Starling early. Mom and I love camping. We love camp. I thought that if she saw how completely clueless Dave was in all things camp-related, she'd see that he's not the one for her."

"Really? That's your plan?" Nora is obviously unimpressed.

"I might need to tweak my angle. The main thing is that I need to break Mom and Dave up. That's the only way to keep everything from changing. It was Hayden's idea."

"Evil genius," Nora says more to herself than to me. Now that his name is involved, she seems exponentially more impressed with the whole scheme.

I clear my throat. "I haven't really needed to do much to show Dave as incompetent here. He kind of screws things up on his own anyway," I say. "He's a horrible camper. He has no clue what he's even doing out here."

"It's true." She cackles loudly and gains a look from the bird lecturer again. Nora lowers her voice. "When he was roasting marshmallows for his s'mores the other night, he kept catching his marshmallow on fire. Did you see him?" she asks.

At that time, I was too busy wishing on embers and staring into Hayden's eyes. "No."

Nora shakes her head on a laugh. "The marshmallows caught fire and then he stomped the flames out with his boot. He wasted like half a bag before he gave up. What kind of camper can't even roast a marshmallow?"

"The worst kind of camper," I say. "So that's where I'm at. I'm out of ideas. Mission Matchbreaker is floundering."

"Mission Matchbreaker?" Nora asks.

"Hayden's idea. Our main goal is to make Dave miserable."

Nora hums thoughtfully beside me. "When I was going out with Felix this year, I was head over heels for him until the so-called honeymoon period was over. Then all his disgusting habits came out, like the way he sneezed into his hand but never washed or sanitized afterward. Or the way he chewed his nails to the nub. I realized that I couldn't hold his hand without getting grossed out. And I couldn't stand spending a second longer with him."

"I'm pretty sure Mom has already discovered Dave's disgusting habits. And she loves him anyway."

Nora and I continue to walk. "How bad do you want to break them up?" she finally asks.

"Bad," I say. "I don't belong in Wyoming. I belong here and so does Mom."

"Okay, then I have an idea that will definitely work," Nora says.

Hope gathers at the center of my chest. "Let's hear it."

"Since my mom and dad's divorce, I have realized this secret with both of them when they're dating new people."

"To be honest, I'm pretty sick of secrets. But I'm desperate."

Nora presses the fingertips of her hands together in a classic evil-genius gesture. "No matter how much my mom and dad like someone, there's always one person they love more. One person they'll choose over their new flame. Every. Single. Time."

I lift a brow in question. "Who?"

"Me. And I'm sure your mom is the same." Mischief flashes

in Nora's green eyes. "If it comes down to you or Dave, Principal Manning will totally choose you."

What is it with Nora calling my mom Principal Manning? "My mom doesn't have to choose, though," I say. "She has us both."

Nora shakes her head. "You're too easy, Paisley. You said you wanted to stay, right?"

I nod.

"Then you need to fight. You and Dave are in the honeymoon period right now too. He's disgustingly nice to you but only because he's still dating your mom. Do you really think he'll still be that same nice guy once they're married?"

I've never thought about that before, but I assumed he would be. Dave is a lovable goof. I can't see him being any other way.

"What do I do?" I ask, increasingly panicked.

"Test the waters. Make him mad. Ruin his favorite things. Bring the honeymoon period to a crashing halt and show your mom who Dave really is. Then give your mom a choice. You or him." Nora lifts her chin proudly, as if she's cracked some ancient code. "Trust me. You're not going anywhere, Paisley. You and Camp Starling are here to stay. If anyone is leaving, it's Dave, and he's not taking you with him. Not on my watch."

❋

As I lie in bed that night, I pull out my camper's journal and purple gel pen and roll over onto my elbows to write. I like to think of these journals as a wastebasket for all my mental vomit. I just put my pen to paper and let all my thoughts pour out of me.

Who am I anymore? I don't even recognize myself. It's been a week since Mom told me we're moving and I think I'm having some sort of mid-teenaged-years crisis—if that's even a thing.

I told Nora what's going on and now she's in on Mission Matchbreaker too. She wants me to push all of Dave's buttons so we can see his ugly side come out before it's too late. Before my mom uproots us both to Wyoming. I've never really been a button-pusher despite Mom's insistence that I push hers sometimes. And it goes against my nature to want to upset someone. I like to make people happy.

BUT, all I need to do is remind myself that my mom will be so unhappy in the near future if her plan plays out. Not just me. She loves being a principal at Seabrook High. She loves our town and we're close to family here—our family. Our whole life is here.

So, anytime I have second thoughts, I'll just remember that and press all the buttons I can find until I hit the one that turns cheesy, annoying, cackling Dave into someone my mom would never want to be with.

CHAPTER TWELVE

Camp Time: Friday. July 22.

I get up super early once again the next morning and make breakfast with the help of Hayden, my aunt, and my uncle. My aunt and uncle volunteered to foot the cost of breakfast for the rest of camp. My mom tried to turn them down, but Aunt Jenny can be pretty insistent. She is my dad's sister, after all.

Even though no one invited him, Dave has joined us too, wearing another tie-dyed counselor shirt. Nora also walks up just before the bird call goes off inviting campers to the Bird-feeder for chow.

Dave has a knack for making large pancakes that he flips in the air. It's almost like a circus performance, and I wonder if Dave missed his calling as one of those actors for those toddler shows on cable TV. You know, the ones with impossibly wide clown smiles and exaggerated movements.

How does Dave have this much energy so early in the

morning anyway? I don't even think he's had a cup of coffee yet. My mom always says she's not breathing until she's had her first cup. I'd venture to say it's actually two cups before she's making any kind of sense. Just another tally mark for why she and Dave don't belong together.

While Dave flips pancakes, my Uncle Leon eggs him on with a juvenile chant like they're the young campers. *"Dave, Dave, Dave. Flip, flip, flip! Don't drop it,"* he chants in a sing-song voice.

Eating up the attention, Dave flips the pancake higher into the air and then he does a spin before catching one with his spatula and landing it back on the griddle. "How do ya like that?" he asks with an energetic laugh that cuts through the chilly morning.

I just watch. We're all having so much fun that I momentarily forget that I'm supposed to be pushing Dave's buttons as part of Mission Make Dave Miserable. I blink and look at Nora, catching a flash of mischief in her eyes. Nora has never really had a problem being direct and to the point, at the risk of being rude. Don't get me wrong. She's very nice, but sometimes she speaks her mind without regard to whether it hurts someone else's feelings. Like that time at the beginning of our freshman year when our friend Jess showed up to the Welcome Back Dance in a dress.

"People don't wear dresses to the dances in high school," Nora informed Jess. "That's so middle school. Ripped jeans and cropped tops next time."

I suspect Jess spent the next two hours mortified and

wishing she could just go home and hide under the covers. Neither Jess nor I danced with anyone that night. Her excuse was the dress. Mine was that no one wanted to be caught with their arms around the principal's daughter. There's a definite downside to having my mom as a school administrator. The upside is that the teachers are all extremely nice to me. And to be honest, none of the guys would have probably danced with me anyway.

"Look at that, Paisley," Dave calls to me. "A heart-shaped pancake."

I lift my gaze and glance into his pan. Seriously, I think Dave must have been one of those entertainment chefs in a former life. Or a backup for Barney the purple dinosaur back in the nineties.

"Don't break that heart," Uncle Leon calls, which Dave finds hilarious. They both laugh hysterically at this and then Uncle Leon briefly breaks into a rendition of "Achy Breaky Heart," a song I only know because it was made into a hit by Miley Cyrus's dad.

I return to stirring grits and then look up and catch Hayden's eyes. Instead of mischief, I see humor. He's also having fun. I think he kind of likes Dave. I think Dave likes him too. He apparently sees himself in Hayden, which blows my mind because Dave and Hayden are nothing alike.

Dave flips another cake high into the air and spins. Then he calls out, "Ouch!" as he lets a pancake fall to the ground. "I think I pulled a muscle with that last pancake toss. Maybe I'm getting too old to play with my food." He looks up and gives me a wink. "Can't go getting hurt on the first week of camp now, can I, Paisley?"

I hold my tongue. If you can't say anything nice, don't say anything at all. That's what Dad would say. But that's not the point of being a matchbreaker. The point is to take that heart-shaped pancake and break it, just like Uncle Leon said. Sorry, Miley Cyrus's dad, Mission Achy Breaky Heart's a go. "It would be a shame to go home at the halfway point," I say. "I mean, it happens. Some people just aren't cut out for camp." I shrug and avert my gaze because of my guilt. "If flipping pancakes causes you to pull a muscle, maybe that's a clue that your muscles are . . . I don't know, weak."

My gaze flutters up just in time to see Dave's smile slink off his face. I feel horrible.

"Your mom loves me just the way I am," Dave says, his voice lifting jovially, but not to the same level as it was. I instinctively know my words stung him like that bee the other day.

"Yeah, well Mom loves me just the way I am too, even though she wishes I'd condition my hair more and stop biting my nails."

Everything around me is silent for a moment. Even the birds' chattering seems to halt for a beat. If I look up right now, I know the humor in Hayden's eyes will be gone. Maybe I'd even see disappointment there, which is ironic because he's the one who stirs up trouble, not me. This whole match-breaker thing was his idea to begin with. I can't help it if he suddenly decided he likes Dave.

"Hmm," Dave finally says. "I guess you're right, Paisley.

Maybe I could stand to condition my hair too." When I look up, Dave winks playfully at me again and then pats his bald head, which already has a slight sunburn, probably because his sunscreen is more honey than protection. He still hasn't figured that out.

I don't smile or laugh. Instead, I sigh under my breath because, despite my best efforts, Dave's buttons are unsuccessfully pushed.

❋

"Watch out!" someone calls behind me sometime after breakfast.

I whirl just in time to see a Frisbee spinning toward me and I reflexively reach out to catch it.

"Good catch!" Tabitha calls. She, Simone, and Mandy are positioned in a triangle as they toss around the disk.

Friday is Camp Starling's Fun Day. That means the water toys are out and the campers are unleashed for all the fun they can have. There are large island floats on the lake and paddleboards out for use as well. The badminton nets are up, and there are piles of Frisbees and every other land toy you can possibly think of.

Fun Fridays are the best. As a counselor, maybe they're not quite as fun because I'm dodging and making sure no one gets hurt. Even so, I'm having a good time living vicariously through the campers from Chickadee Cabin.

I curl the Frisbee into my side and toss it back in Tabitha's direction. She jumps high to snatch it from the air and the game continues.

"Don't think I didn't know what you were doing at breakfast," Hayden says, stepping up beside me.

I turn and look at him. "Was I that obvious?"

"Just to me probably." He shrugs casually. I used to think this guy was apathetic and that he just didn't care. Now I know differently.

"It was Nora's idea," I say.

"Your new partner in crime?"

I give him a teasing smile. "You're not as good at mischief as I thought you'd be."

There's something sheepish in his expression. "Sorry. Breaking up happy couples is new to me." He shoves his hands in his pockets. "And Dave is pretty cool in a not-cool kind of way. Maybe he'd make a great stepdad one day."

"In Wyoming?" my voice dips low. "No." I shake my head.

A beat of silence passes between us, broken by the chirp of a tiny brown-and-white bird hopping around near the brush.

I point at it. "That's a song sparrow," I tell him.

Hayden observes it for a moment. "It kind of blends into its environment."

"Camouflage." I nod. "To protect it from predators. You might not see it, but you will definitely hear it if you pay attention. The song sparrow loves to sing."

When I look up, Hayden is watching me.

It makes me nervous, but in a good kind of way. "The song sparrow's heart beats four hundred fifty times a minute," I tell him. It feels like my heart is beating that fast right about now too. So fast I can barely pull in a full breath.

"Do you know the names of all the birds here?" he asks.

I hug my arms around myself, feeling a little self-conscious. "It's weird, huh?"

"I don't know. I think it's actually kind of cool."

I look at Hayden, chewing on my next words, wondering if I should speak them. "My friend Nora is pretty nice."

Hayden meets my gaze. "Yeah. She's great."

Just the fact that he agrees sends my spirits plummeting. I swallow hard, hoping nothing shows on my face. "She likes you."

"I know," he says.

"You do?"

He shrugs a shoulder. This seems to be his default gesture. "Your friend isn't exactly subtle."

"Subtlety isn't her strong point," I hedge. "Well, there's an ice cream social tomorrow night." Camp Starling always hires an ice cream vendor at the midpoint of camp. "You could hang out together." When Hayden doesn't immediately respond, I look up at him.

He's looking at me with something unreadable on his expression. "You're going too, aren't you?"

I nod.

"Who are you planning to sit with? Jacob?" he asks.

"Why would you suggest him?"

"I've seen you two talking a couple times. I think he's into you."

I shrug. "I don't know about that. I don't usually garner a lot of attention from guys," I say.

His eyes narrow. "Why is that?"

My cheeks are heating and it's not because of the sun's rays. "I guess I'm kind of like that song sparrow. I don't stand out."

"You stand out to me," Hayden says.

My heart rides up in my throat. Is he flirting with me? I'm not sure. I don't know what to think or say. "Anyway, you'll be eating ice cream with Nora."

"I don't like ice cream, Pais. And I'm not really one for social get-togethers. The only reason I'd even consider going is because you'll be there."

My mouth gapes open. I have to mentally remind myself to close it. "You're a camp counselor. You have to go tomorrow night," I say. Which is not the smoothest thing to say to a guy who basically just said he was going out of his way to do something he never does because he wants to be with you. That's romantic, right? Definitely the most romantic thing a guy has ever said to me.

Hayden looks out at the campers on Blue Lake. "I'm not sure I'm cut out for this gig. I mean, I haven't saved anyone's life yet."

"You helped me and Nora when our kayak capsized."

He looks at me again, his gaze holding mine for a long moment. It's hard to breathe when he's looking directly into my eyes. It's like he's holding my journal and reading the pages. Like he knows what I'm thinking. If that were true, though, he'd know that Nora isn't the only one with a huge crush on him. He shrugs and looks away. "I've got a week left here. Maybe I'll redeem myself and prove to be a great counselor after all. See you around," he calls over his shoulder, starting to step away.

Without thinking, I grab his hand. "My best friend likes you. What am I supposed to do?"

I worry that the question makes absolutely no sense, but he seems to understand exactly what I mean as he turns back to face me. "One of the things I like about you, Pais—what I've always liked about you—is that you seem to understand right from wrong. Not everyone does. So I guess, to answer your question, you should do whatever feels right."

He lets go of my hand, turns again, and walks away.

I watch him, my breaths coming out labored as if I've been running up a hill. I haven't been doing what feels right lately. I've been doing what feels the opposite of right. But everything in my life is wrong at the moment. Except for him. When I look at Hayden and he looks at me, everything feels perfect.

CHAPTER THIRTEEN

Nora is talking faster than I can possibly process her words. All except one word: Hayden. She keeps saying his name and getting my attention.

"So you're going to have to ramp up your efforts to split up your mom and Dave if we're going to make this work," Nora finally says, turning to look at me.

We're sitting on a picnic table while the campers are off in clusters, huddled together and talking excitedly. These were always some of my favorite times of camp in years past. This is when secrets are spilled. Not that we ever really had any secrets before this year. This seems to be my summer of secrets.

Maria and Meghan climb onto the picnic bench beside us. Emma too.

"What are you two talking about?" Meghan asks.

"Nothing," I say quickly.

But Nora leans in. "We're going to break up Paisley's mom and Dave," she tells them, oozing enthusiasm.

Maria pulls back and claps a hand over her mouth. "What? Why?" she asks when she finally peels her hand away.

I give Nora a look to shut her up, but either Nora can't interpret the daggers coming out of my eyeballs or she's ignoring me. "Because Principal Manning is following Dave to Wyoming, where his family is from."

Now Meghan pulls back and claps a hand over her mouth just like her sister did. Her eyes are wide. "No. You can't move away."

"Who's moving? I hope it's you, Nora," Tisha says sarcastically as she sits down across from me.

Nora rolls her eyes as she looks at our friend. "Paisley. Unless we help her. We have T minus one week left of camp. We need to get serious, ladies."

"Shh. Quiet your voice," I say. "I don't want people to hear us talking about this. No one is even supposed to know about the move yet. It's a secret."

"One you apparently told Hayden before me," Nora says with a hint of resentment.

"Hayden Bennett?" Maria asks. "Why did you tell him?"

"Because he was there and I needed to talk to someone." And his eyes were warm and his presence was surprisingly inviting. He felt like a friend I'd known forever even though we barely knew each other before this summer.

"Well, I'm planning on talking to him tomorrow night at the ice cream social," Nora says. "So if you need someone to talk to, talk to us right now. We're listening."

I ignore the little ache of jealousy in my chest over the

fact that Nora wants to talk to Hayden as I look between all my friends. "Okay. Well, I don't want to leave Seabrook. I don't want to move to Wyoming. You guys are my best friends."

"We're not guys," Tisha points out. "I take offense." She's joking, though. This is just how Tisha is.

"But I like Dave," Meghan says. "He's really nice."

Nora reaches across the table and jabs a finger into Meghan's shoulder. "Maybe so, but he's taking Paisley away from us. Is that what you want?"

"Of course not." Meghan frowns.

"Can't you just tell your mom and Dave that you don't want to move?" Emma asks innocently.

"I did." Although, to be fair, I didn't tell them as much as I cried and ran to my room. "We haven't discussed it since. I think my mom has just assumed that I've accepted my fate and that I'll adjust. She loves to say how resilient kids are. I tried to talk to her when I walked up on her outside the cabin the other day, but she's just not hearing me."

"Hmm." Nora has a deep look of concentration on her face. "You've tried painting Dave in a negative light."

I nod. "And really, he does that on his own. It's almost endearing."

Tisha raises a hand. "I can vouch for that. I saw him slip off the lake trampolines into the water the other day. He came up laughing and instead of letting everyone make fun of him behind his back, he led the show by making fun of himself for a hot minute. Then it was over."

Emma shrugs. "He's like that adorable geek all grown up. He's hard not to like."

Nora nods resolutely. "And you've tried pushing his buttons," she says to me.

"Dave doesn't have buttons. He doesn't get upset over anything," I say. "He's never going to fly off the handle and yell at me. He's just not."

We all sit there with thoughtful looks on our faces.

Then Nora reaches for my hand and squeezes. "I'm going to think about this situation all night. I'm not going to let you down."

I know she's just trying to help, and I appreciate it. But sometimes Nora's help makes things worse. Nora is not like Dave in the sense that her flaws aren't very endearing. They're frustrating.

Maria's hand covers Nora's and then Meghan's covers Maria's and Emma's. Tisha lays her hand on top.

"We're all in this together," Tisha says. "I mean, if you go to Wyoming, we aren't going with you. We're staying. But we'll do anything to keep this move from happening."

I smile. "Thanks, guys." I look at Tisha and correct myself. "Girls. But all I need is your friendship. I'll figure this out on my own. I don't want any of you to do anything. Really. I've got this."

They all pull their hands away.

Nora looks skeptical. "Really?"

"Yeah." I nod resolutely.

"Okay, but no more secrets. We need to know what's going

on with you," Nora says, giving me a meaningful look. "All of it."

I trace an X over the left side of my chest. "Cross my heart."

"Good." Her hand falls back over mine, followed by Maria's, Meghan's, Emma's, and Tisha's. "Best friends forever."

✺

Camp Time: Saturday. July 23.

Today in camp, we're learning archery, which is very Princess Merida. I even have the red hair like Merida except mine is stick straight even with the crazy humidity on this lake.

The arrows have rubber tips, but those rubber tips can still hurt if you get in their path. Especially in the upper thigh, where I took a hit last summer. I had a bruise for a month.

Simone is still sticking close to me, although I've noticed that she's made friends with Tabitha and Mandy from our cabin. Watching them kind of reminds me of when Nora and I first met Meghan, Maria, Tisha, and Emma. We were all cabin-mates too. We were so different, but also the same in the fact that we were experiencing camp life together. There's a bond that happens between cabinmates. A sisterhood.

"I need to check on the other girls," I tell Simone.

She whirls to look at me, pointing her bow and arrow right at my chest.

I hold up my hands in surrender, then use my hand to move

the arrow's tip away from me. "Hey! Point that thing somewhere else!"

"Oh. Sorry." She immediately aims the bow at the ground.

"Try to keep it aimed at the target," I say, noticing that Dave is standing between two of the said targets. I'm not sure what he thinks he's doing, but standing there with that brightly colored tie-dyed shirt is just asking to be hit. "It helps to point it a little left of the target," I say before my conscience can kick in. "In case there's wind."

"To the left," Simone repeats. "Got it."

"Great." When I walk over and check on Tabitha, I tell her it's helpful to aim a little right of the target, even though the wind isn't even blowing in that direction. I mean, those rubber tips hurt, but they won't injure you. And any true camper would know not to stand anywhere in the vicinity of a target with arrows pointed in your direction. It's just common sense.

I keep walking and check on all the other Chickadee Cabin campers, adjusting their technique as I go. My Aunt Jenny is here with the girl campers today too. Uncle Leon is on the boys' side. We also have two archery instructors, a husband-and-wife duo.

I guess you might say that Camp Starling is a mixed bag of outdoor fun and skills. I will probably never use a bow and arrow in real life, but I'll also likely never build my own shelter in the woods for survival or navigate the water by sailboat outside of camp.

"How are you doing?" My mom walks up behind me and rests one hand on my shoulder, drawing my attention to the slight sunburn I have there.

I turn just slightly, finding shade under her oversize wide-rim hat. "I'm okay."

"One week of camp down. One more to go. How does it feel to be a camp counselor this year? Is it everything you dreamed it would be?"

"It feels . . . different," I say. "Everything feels different this summer, though."

Her eyes are sympathetic as she looks at me. "Different isn't always bad."

Why does everyone keep saying that? "It isn't always good either." I release a pent-up breath. "I'm sorry. I'm not trying to be negative."

"I know. You're just being honest, and I appreciate that. I want to know how you're feeling. You don't need to hide it from me."

My heart rate picks up speed. Maybe Emma was right. Maybe it all comes down to just having an honest and calm conversation with my mom and telling her that I don't want to move away. No one consulted with me about this after all. They just informed me.

"Well, honestly, Mom, no one asked me how I feel about selling this camp. You and Dave just told me it was happening. How is that fair?"

My mom looks surprised. "I didn't ask because the camp belongs to me. I own it. I'm the adult and you're the child."

"I'm sixteen. In two years, I'll be an adult and this camp belongs to our family. That's what you and Dad always said, at least. Dave is not family and you made the decision with him. Why?"

"Paisley," my mom says softly. "There's a lot more to running a camp than being a counselor for two weeks in a summer. When you turn eighteen, you'll want to go to college. Not worry with all the upkeep that comes along with running this place."

"But, Mom." I open my mouth to say more, but then Dave cries out.

"Oww!" he crows in the distance.

I turn my head just in time to see him clutch his leg and hit the ground. *Bull's-eye!* I think it was Simone who made the winning shot.

Mom rushes in his direction. I'm not worried about Dave, though. He'll be okay. I, on the other hand, will not, because I'm not sure my mom even heard what I was trying to say. I'm not sure she ever truly hears me. She's in principal mode, calling all the shots for our family. And she still thinks I'm some kid, even though I'm not anymore. I should have a say in Camp Starling. And on whether we move. Following Dave to Wyoming will be a huge mistake. We don't belong there. We belong here.

CHAPTER FOURTEEN

Camp Time: Saturday evening. July 23.

I'm sitting outside at the Birdfeeder. The ice cream truck that my mom hired is here and everyone is being served up two scoops—no more, no less. This isn't Baskin-Robbins. We don't have thirty-one flavors, but there is a lot for everyone to choose from.

"You always choose plain-Jane vanilla, Paisley," Nora laments across the picnic table from me. "You don't even pick a topping."

All my friends look at my cup.

"Leave her alone, Nora," Tisha says with a slight eye roll.

"What? I'm not being mean. I'm just trying to push Paisley to be more adventurous. What's wrong with that?" Nora asks.

I'm not really paying attention to the conversation. I'm too busy looking for Hayden. He's not here, even though he said he would be. He's finished cleaning the cabins and I think my mom only had him clean the latrines once and only to make a point. You do the crime, you do the time. Where is he?

"Who are you looking for?" Nora asks.

I look down into my cup and shake my head. "My mom." I pick up my spoon and carve it into the vanilla cream. "I don't see her or Dave."

"I bet they're love-birding." Emma slips a spoonful of strawberry ice cream into her mouth with a huge smile.

"Love-birding?" Tisha asks, not bothering to contain her eye roll. Then again, she never bothers to contain it. "I'm pretty sure that's not a real verb."

"Camp Starling has a bird theme. I'm going with it." Emma spoons more ice cream into her mouth.

"You're probably right." I wasn't looking for my mom or Dave, but now, thanks to Emma, I'm wondering where they are and guessing that she's correct and Mom and Dave are in fact love-birding.

"Hey." Hayden is suddenly standing at the head of our table with his cup of ice cream in hand. My heart lifts into my throat. Before I can say anything, Nora scoots over and makes room for him to sit beside her on the wooden picnic bench.

"Saved you a seat," she says with a wide smile. Her freckles have gotten dark in the sun this week. I have friends who cover their freckles with makeup. Not Nora. She only gets prettier with hers.

Hayden glances over at me before sitting down. "Thanks."

Nora leans into him, her shoulder pressed to his as she looks into his cup. "Ah, good choice. See, Paisley? You have to be adventurous with your ice cream selection. Vanilla is so boring."

I look at Hayden's cup too. He has peanut butter–chocolate with syrup on top.

"I don't know. I think vanilla is cool." Hayden meets my gaze.

A million butterflies compete for wing space in my chest. Fighting a crush that's already rooted is next to impossible.

"What's cool about vanilla?" Nora asks in disbelief. She almost sounds upset that Hayden would stick up for me and my ice cream choice.

"If Pais likes it, that's what's cool about it." He spoons some ice cream into his mouth, meeting my gaze across the picnic table.

My cheeks are burning even though we're eating an ice-cold treat. It's partly because of him and partly because my friends are all staring at me.

"Well, I didn't choose my ice cream to be cool either," Nora says. "I just chose it because I like it."

"Then why are you criticizing Pais for choosing vanilla?" Hayden asks. It's confrontational in a way, but he still looks relaxed.

Nora goes quiet for a moment, which is so uncharacteristic of her that it worries me. "I was just teasing. That's what friends do, Hayden." She bumps her shoulder against his again. "That's what guys and girls do too."

"Oh?" He glances over at her, catching her eye for just a moment.

All the ice cream's sweetness in my belly turns sour. I can't help it. I want to be the one sitting shoulder to shoulder with him. I don't want to stand back and just let Nora have him. She's had a million crushes who've all reciprocated her feelings. Hayden is mine.

"There's nothing friendly about picking on me or my vanilla," I say digging my spoon into my cup. "I mean, it's ice cream, Nora. What did vanilla ice cream ever do to you?"

Hayden ducks his head as he suppresses a laugh.

"And when guys and girls tease each other, it's called flirting, not criticizing," I add. "And criticizing is all you seem to do these days. At least where I'm concerned."

Nora's mouth drops open. "Well, you've never had a boyfriend so how would you know anything about flirting, Paisley?"

I look at Hayden and hold his gaze even longer than Nora held it a moment earlier. "I think I'd know."

⁕

Later that night, I reach under my bunk and my hand searches for my journal. For a moment, my fingers don't feel it and a rush of panic zips through me. Then my hand hits the hard spine and I expel a breath. Phew. I don't know what I'd do if my journal turned up missing.

I pull it to me, open it, and uncap my purple gel pen, pressing it to the lined paper.

So I think for the first time ever, I let a guy come between me and my best friend. That's because I

*really like Hayden. Every time I see him, I'm sure
of it. And when Nora flirts with him, I want to
explode because she can attract any guy's eye. Why
does she need to go after the one guy that gives me
embers and butterflies? And why, when I finally
have a guy interested in me, do I have to move?*

*I know the answer. It's because of Dave. Even
though I'm starting to give up, my brain is still
entertaining this whole Mission Matchbreaker thing.
Just this afternoon, I was fantasizing about putting
Mr. Cheez-It himself on a rigged kayak in the
middle of Blue Lake. In my fantasy, he struggles
to keep it balanced and eventually just tips over.
Splash.*

*I am a nice person. Really. So why are
thoughts like these running through my head? I'm
blaming that on Dave as well. Everything that's
wrong in my whole world right now is Dave's
fault.*

Something knocks against my cabin window as I'm writing. I sit up in my bunk and look around. All the other campers in Chickadee Cabin are fast asleep including Simone, who
takes the longest to drift off. I'm usually waiting on her to
doze off so I can reach for my journal.

Something hits the window again, making a sharp sound
against the glass. I get up and walk over to look out the window. It takes a moment for my eyes to focus to the dark. Then
I see Hayden standing outside in the moonlight. My heart

bubbles up into my throat. Guys are not supposed to be on this side of camp after dark.

I walk to the cabin door and open it as quietly as I can. Then I step outside, closing the door behind me. "What are you doing out here?" I whisper.

His hands are in his shorts pockets. In the moonlight, he has this mysterious look to him. "I couldn't sleep and wanted to see you. You know, without the others."

"It's against the rules," I remind him.

"I know. And you'll be breaking the rules if you come down to the lake for a walk with me." A mischievous smile forms on his mouth.

I look down at Blue Lake and back at Hayden. "You're a bad influence, you know that?"

"So I'm told. My intentions are good, though, if that makes a difference."

I tilt my head to one side. "So you're not trying to go skinny dipping out there in the lake?"

Hayden's jaw drops and his eyes widen. Then he lifts both hands in a defensive motion. "I just want to walk, I promise."

I burst into loud laughter and immediately clap a hand over my mouth to quiet myself. I don't want to wake the rest of the campers.

"I can't believe you just suggested that," Hayden says, moving closer so that no one hears us.

"I didn't suggest it. I was only joking." I shake my head. I can't control what comes out of my mouth when I'm with Hayden. Or my heart rate. Or anything, it seems.

"So the lake? To sit and talk," Hayden clarifies. "That's it. I'm not getting in that water after dark. I've heard there's piranhas or something in there."

"That's a long-running rumor at Camp Starling." I laugh again, again clapping a hand over my mouth.

Hayden smiles. "You're pretty good at being bad, but you've got to work on not getting caught, Pais."

I grin as we begin to walk side by side toward the lake. "And evidently I also need to rethink my boring taste in ice cream flavors."

"Vanilla is classic, not boring. And Nora is jealous."

"Of me?" Our arms bump together as we walk.

"Why not you? You're smart, nice, pretty."

I can't believe he just called me pretty. "You've seen Nora, right? She's the most beautiful girl in the rising junior class."

"Yeah. I guess she's pretty too, in an obvious sort of way."

"So my beauty isn't obvious? It's hidden?" I ask.

Hayden shakes his head. "Putting words in my mouth, Pais. I think you're pretty in a classy, vanilla ice cream kind of way. A lot of people don't realize how great vanilla ice cream is because they're blinded by all the other flashy flavors and toppings. But those people are missing out, in my opinion."

We reach the bank of the lake and stop walking to stare out at the water. Then I feel Hayden's hand reach out for mine. I let him hold it as we say nothing for a long time. "You are peanut butter–chocolate ice cream," I finally say. "Which, if you think about it, is the rebel of all ice creams. Peanut butter was never meant to go inside ice cream." I turn to him. "It's a rule breaker, just like you."

"I'll have you know that I've been on my best behavior since I've been here. I don't think I've broken any rules."

"Being out past nine is against the rules. And you're always out past nine because you refuse to sleep in the cabin," I remind him. "Which I still don't understand."

He shrugs a shoulder. "I guess I'm just a loner."

"No one wants to be alone."

"Sometimes being alone is better than getting close to people who will just end up rejecting you anyway," he says quietly.

I swallow, wondering if he's talking about his dad. Hayden doesn't have a lot of friends at school. I always kind of assumed it was by choice, but I know firsthand how mean kids can be. "If you give people a chance to get to know you, they won't reject you. Especially the kids here. Camp Starling is a family. Maybe it's corny, but this is my safe place. You don't have to worry about anyone rejecting you here."

"I wish I could trust that," he says.

I squeeze his hand. "Kids must have treated you pretty rotten for you to be so cynical."

He casts me a look. "Cynical, huh?"

I shrug a shoulder.

He blows out a breath. "I guess that's true. Art isn't as cool as athletics. At least not in some circles."

"Well, neither are birds, but I don't care."

Hayden shakes his head. "One of the things I like about you."

"What's that?" I ask.

"You don't care that you're different. You're unique. I've never met anyone quite like you."

I find myself smiling. "Thanks."

He looks down for a moment. When he looks back up, he's smiling too. "Anyway, I like how you stood up for yourself with your friends tonight. I don't want us to come between you and Nora though."

Us. That word catches me by surprise. "Hayden, there can't really be an us. I'm moving next month. Unless our little plan somehow works."

His expression is solemn. "Dave is tougher than I've given him credit for. Bug bites, bee stings, an arrow to the behind."

I giggle again. "It was his upper thigh."

Hayden is still holding my hand, his palm warm against mine. There are a million butterflies competing for wing space in my chest and a trillion stars in my eyes. There are also a trillion tiny cracks splintering in my heart because the first guy I've ever really liked, and the first to hold my hand, is only a temporary fixture in my life.

"See? Breaking the rules can be fun, right?"

I angle my body toward his. The wind off the lake blows my hair around my face, tickling my cheek and my nose. "Is that why you're always hanging around my mom's office at school? Because breaking the rules is fun?"

"Getting caught is the opposite of fun." Hayden just stares at me and for a moment, I see the reflection of stars in his eyes too. My heart thumps inside my chest. "I don't know why I get in trouble so much. I oversleep because I'm up drawing comics. Then I wake up late and get to school late. I draw instead of doing my homework and never turn it in on time."

"So you suffer for your art?" I ask, teasing him.

"Something like that. Speaking of art, I have something for you."

I lower my gaze as he reaches into his pocket and pulls out a piece of folded-up paper. It reminds me of the note he gave me on the first night of camp. "What is that?"

He presses the paper into the palm of my hand. "For you. Open it."

I take my time unfolding the paper until I see a sketch of a bird. Not just any bird. "It's a song sparrow." I look up at him.

"Like the one you pointed out the other day. I thought it was beautiful. It stood out to me, like you."

I'm not sure what to say, or what this even means. He drew me a picture of a bird. His favorite thing meets mine. "Thank you, Hayden."

"You're welcome."

I pull in a deep breath. "Well, we shouldn't stay out too late because I don't want to get in trouble."

Hayden nods. "I'll walk you back to your cabin. But first . . ."

I lift my brows in question.

Hayden points up at the sky and we both look up. "I also arranged for a shooting star for you to wish on."

I lower my gaze to give him a skeptical look. "You can't arrange for shooting stars. They just fall when you least expect it."

"Kind of like us?" Hayden asks.

My lips separate but no words come out. I can't pull my gaze from his. "I guess so," I finally say, thinking I know what's about to happen, but also knowing that can't possibly be true. No way is Hayden about to kiss me. No way am I about to have my first kiss—which is supposed to be awkward and regrettable by all my friends' accounts—under a sky full of the most romantic twinkling stars. The stars are reflected so perfectly in the lake beside us that it feels like we're standing in the center of our own little galaxy. Just the two of us.

No way is this about to happen. In fact, I must have fallen asleep in my bunk and this is actually a dream. Yeah, that's what this is.

"Is this a dream?" I ask, just to make sure.

Teasing me, Hayden reaches out and softly pinches the skin on my forearm.

"Ouch." I smile up at him.

"Not a dream," he determines. "I was beginning to wonder myself."

"Then why didn't you pinch your own arm?"

He tips his head back in a small laugh, his eyes skimming the sky. Then he points. "Up there!"

I look up just in time to watch a shooting star zip through the sky, a tiny fireball that burns out at the end of a long tail.

I'm breathless and amazed. "I can't believe we just saw that."

"And you said falling stars couldn't be planned." Hayden looks at me.

I shake my head. "I don't know how you did that, but I'm impressed."

Hayden lifts his arm to touch my forearm again, but he doesn't pinch me this time. Instead, he trails his index finger down my skin leaving goose bumps in its wake. I shiver in the best kind of way. I still can't believe this is happening, even as Hayden leans forward, his gaze meeting mine, silently requesting permission as he moves painstakingly slow.

I don't back away. I don't turn my head. I don't even blink or breathe. Instead, I wait for him to kiss me, and when he does, my body turns ablaze just like that shooting star, melting me into a puddle of goo.

The world disappears while our lips are pressed together. That's why I don't hear anyone approaching. I don't see the light from a flashlight either. I don't know we're about to be busted breaking camp rules—more than one—until someone clears her throat.

I leap back, nearly stumbling into the lake, but Hayden catches me. I'm out of breath for so many reasons, good and bad. "Nora!"

Nora's gaze bounces between me and Hayden. Her expression shifts under the moonlight, from surprise to hurt and finally anger. She crosses her arms over her chest, narrowing her green eyes on me. "What are you doing out here, Paisley?"

"I . . . well, I . . . I could ask you the same," I finally say.

"I came out here looking for you. You weren't in your cabin."

"I asked her to take a walk with me," Hayden tells Nora.

Nora doesn't look at him. "You're breaking curfew, Paisley. Who's watching your campers?"

"They're asleep," I say. "Everything is fine and this is just a short walk."

"That ends with a long kiss?" Nora's tone is hard and defensive.

I have no idea what to say. I knew that Nora liked Hayden, but I like him too. Why can't I have what I want sometimes? Why do I always have to bend to everyone else's desires? "I didn't want to hurt your feelings."

"My feelings?" Nora asks. "Why would breaking curfew with Hayden hurt my feelings?"

"Because you like him," I say, quietly.

Nora shakes her head as if that's not true. I think she's embarrassed. "No, I don't. I don't care who you kiss, Paisley."

Now I breathe a laugh. "Oh, really? That's why you're pushing Jacob on me this summer? Why you always try to decide everyone's camp crushes every year?" I ask, voice rising.

"What's wrong with being helpful?" Nora asks.

"By helpful, you mean controlling?"

Nora's mouth falls open. She pulls a hand to her chest. "Is it my fault that you follow me around like you have no idea what to do or say at school? No one's controlling you, Paisley. The reason you feel that way is because you don't know how to think for yourself."

"What?" I practically yell.

Hayden's hand finds my shoulder. "Okay, calm down, you two," he says, but neither of us are listening to him.

"I mean, that's probably why you're out here kissing Hayden," Nora says. "I told you I was interested in him, and since you can't seem to think for yourself, you decided that you are too. It's like the time you cut your hair just because I did."

Every cell in my body is erupting red-hot lava. "You encouraged me to cut my hair because you regretted cutting yours so short, and you didn't want to be the only one in class who couldn't even pull your hair into a ponytail. My haircut was a pity cut," I tell her.

Nora gasps. Her cheeks are turning a dark shade of pink.

"And I'm out here kissing Hayden because he asked me, not you, to come on a walk with him. You just can't stand the fact that I have something you don't."

Nora takes a step backward. She doesn't look angry anymore. "Of course you have something I don't. You have everything, Paisley. You had two parents who loved each other and a mom who thinks you're amazing. You have all As and you always win the swim meets. All I have are two parents who fight over me, not because they want to spend time with their daughter, but because they want to hurt each other." She takes another step backward. "I always thought I at least had you in my corner. But it looks like I was wrong. You're sneaking around behind my back and lying to my face."

"I'm not lying," I say quietly.

"Of course you are. You're lying to me, your mom, everyone. But most of all, if you think you're doing your mom or me or any of the people you're keeping secrets from this summer a favor, you're lying to yourself." Nora's eyes are suspiciously shiny. She looks between me and Hayden one more time and then turns to leave.

I think about calling her name and stopping her, but my heart is beating too hard. I feel a rush of a million emotions. That warning about first kisses usually being awkward or one big disaster? Yeah, mine went from amazing to awful in a millisecond. But only because seeing me and Hayden together broke Nora's heart. She can pretend that it didn't, but I know her better than that. When Nora is hurt, she lashes out. But the thing is, she usually lashes out with complete honesty. She doesn't lie—unlike me apparently. She's right. I've been lying to everyone.

"Are you okay?" Hayden asks, reaching for my hand.

I look up and shake my head. "No. I'm not okay at all."

CHAPTER FIFTEEN

Camp Time: Sunday. July 24.

Sunday at Camp Starling is always Family Day. It's the midpoint of our camp, and families are invited to come visit with their camper and see what they've been learning.

Since my parents own Camp Starling, this day has always been a little weird for me. I usually hang back and spy on others, fascinated by the inner workings of different families. I remember the first time that Nora's parents came to Family Day. We were twelve. That was before my dad died. Her parents were still together back then, but even I could see that they shouldn't be.

I'd leaned up against a cabin with my favorite ball cap shading my face. The sun was blistering and the farmer's tan on my back was proof. I was totally eavesdropping, but I was twelve and I felt kind of bad for Nora. She was my best friend and cabinmate. I had slept over at her house a few times and had some idea of what her home life was like. I knew her mom and dad were demanding.

"Nora, have you been applying your sunblock? Your skin is so red," her mother had grumbled that day when I was eavesdropping. "You're going to have wrinkled and pruned skin just like your Nana's if you're not careful."

"You don't tell a kid that!" Nora's father had snapped. "Your skin is beautiful, bumblebee. And my mother's skin is beautiful too." He shot a pointed look at Nora's mother.

I was watching it all. Nora turned to offer me a shy smile, which struck me as odd because I had never known there to be anything timid about Nora until that moment.

Today is really no different. Nora's parents are both here to visit, sitting on opposite sides of the picnic table from each other. They seem to be competing for her attention, which she withholds equally from both.

"Are you making sure to wear your sunglasses? You don't want lines around your eyes a decade from now," Ms. Dunlap says.

Nora gives her mother a faint nod. "Yep." Nora is such a take-charge person except when she's with her parents. With them, she seems resigned. Her shoulders are slumped forward and she has a disinterested look on her face. Adults who don't know Nora would probably assume she has what they call a teenager attitude. I know Nora better than that, though. It's not that she doesn't care. It's that she cares too much about what her mother thinks. And try as she may, she can't please her mom. Nora has no control over her family dynamics.

"Nora, sit up straight, for goodness' sake. I knew I should have enrolled you in ballet classes when you were five. It would have made a world of difference in your posture."

Mr. Dunlap doesn't even chastise his ex-wife anymore. He's probably realized he has no control either.

Nora glances around and her gaze lands on me, spying on her just like I did when I was twelve. Her forced smile wilts into a deep frown and she looks away quickly as she straightens a bit. She's still mad at me about last night. That's okay because I haven't gotten over the things she said to me either.

I turn and continue walking between the tables. My mom is here all day, every day. My aunt and uncle come a lot too. I don't need a Family Day, so my role today is to point people in the direction of the bathrooms, where to get water, or to introduce myself as one of the counselors.

I continue walking past the campers and their families until I spot Hayden who, to be honest, is exactly who I was looking for. I'm expecting for him to be alone, but he's not. He's sitting with a thin woman with short black hair, the same color as his. Is that his mom? Hayden said his father wasn't in the picture and I guess I just figured his mom wasn't very involved, because, if she was, why would he always be in detention?

The woman looks nice, though. She's wearing a pair of white denim shorts and a pink-and-black-striped T-shirt. She has bangle bracelets on her wrists and a locket necklace around her neck. I wonder if Hayden's and his brother's pictures are inside. The brother I've never seen. The one I didn't even know existed until Hayden mentioned him the other day.

Watching Hayden with his mom, the two of them laughing and seemingly close, I realize I don't know as much about Hayden as I thought. Most of what I think I know, I've just assumed. But I want to know more.

He looks up and catches me watching. I was totally spying on him. I freeze. His smile puts me at ease, though, and he gestures me over to meet his mom. Last night was my first kiss and today I'm meeting his family, which kind of feels like a big deal. This seems like so much more than a summer crush. It's more like the kind of summer romance that crushes hearts.

I walk over, my chest rising with shallow breaths. What if his mom doesn't like me? Will that change how Hayden feels? "Um, hi," I say.

"Mom, this is the girl I told you about. Paisley Manning."

It feels weird to hear him say my full name. I shake Ms. Bennett's hand. "Nice to meet you."

"You too, Paisley. So you're the one who busted my son painting the cabins and got him sentenced to summer camp," she says with a serious expression.

My mouth drops and my gaze darts to Hayden's. "Oh. I, well, um . . ."

Ms. Bennett laughs softly and gives my hand a reassuring squeeze. "I want to thank you for that because Hayden has apparently been having the time of his life out here. He's been talking my ear off about all the fun goings-on. And your name keeps popping up."

I exhale a breath. "This is a wonderful place. I've always loved being at Camp Starling."

"Maybe Hayden should stir up more trouble next summer

159

so that he can land himself back here for camp." She points a finger at him. "That's the only reason I'm condoning any future shenanigans."

He grins sheepishly at her. I watch them for a moment. Their relationship seems so much better than Nora and her parents' even if he only has his mom here to visit with him. "Do you want to join us?" Hayden asks me.

"Oh." I look around and then back at him. I'm not really working today. The adult volunteers are here and all the campers are hanging out with their families. "It's Family Day. I probably shouldn't."

"But you don't have family to hang out with, right?" Hayden says. "Your mom and Dave are busy talking to all the other families. Join us. I was going to take Mom hiking on Songbird Path."

"I don't want to intrude," I argue, but I already want to say yes. I'm no longer nervous about meeting his mom. She's just as relaxed as Hayden.

"Nonsense, Paisley," Ms. Bennett says, her voice warm. "I want to get to know this girl who has my son smiling so big. I need to know the secret."

I catch Hayden's gaze and his lips curve even wider. It's easy to be happy at Camp Starling, though. But part of me wants to believe he's also smiling because of me.

✺

For the rest of the day, I am a designated third wheel, but it's not as bad as it sounds. It's actually kind of wonderful.

Hayden, his mom, and I go hiking. We kayak across Blue Lake and picnic with hot dogs and bags of chips in the sunshine. Hayden's mom embarrasses him sweetly with stories of his childhood, and he really does sound like he was a handful.

I think this is the first Family Day at Camp Starling where I actually got to participate and experience the family part. My mom and dad were always so busy on this day, and I was left to mingle and spy. I never minded because my mom has always been there for me when I needed her. She's never missed one of my school events. If anything, she's a little too present.

But today is nice. Also wonderful is the way Hayden keeps sneaking smiles at me when his mom isn't looking. There's a twinkle in his eyes that reminds me of last night's kiss. It's a small secret between us. Except it's not just our secret. Nora was there. She saw us. She knows.

"I've got to go," Hayden's mom finally says. "I'm working the night shift tonight."

Hayden's expression turns serious. "You're working? You should have spent your day sleeping instead of here visiting with me. You'll be tired."

She's at least two inches shorter than him, so she reaches up to pull his head down and kiss his forehead. "I spent my day exactly the way I wanted to. I've missed you this week. There was no way I was not coming here to hang out for a few hours. Plus, I got to meet your girlfriend." She looks at me.

My mouth drops and my gaze darts to Hayden's. We haven't used that word to describe one another. I've never been anyone's girlfriend before in my life.

"Yeah," Hayden says. "I'm glad you came, Mom. And that

161

you and Pais were able to meet." He doesn't deny the G-word. In fact, if I'm hearing him correctly, he just confirmed it.

Fireworks explode inside my chest cavity, all bright and neon-colored. Hayden's mom leans toward me and gives me a giant hug that feels warmer than the sun on my bare shoulders. "It was so nice to meet you, Paisley. Try to make my son behave, will you?" She pulls back and casts Hayden a teasing look.

"I'll do my best, Ms. Bennett," I promise.

We walk her to the camp's exit and watch her leave. Then Hayden turns to me.

"You okay with what I said?" he asks.

I tilt my head. "What did you say exactly?" I remember, of course. I just want to hear it again. To confirm that I wasn't misunderstanding.

"Well, I didn't say anything, exactly. My mom did, but I didn't disagree. She thinks you're my girlfriend."

"Yeah, I kind of got that impression." I roll my lips together, my eyes lifting to meet his. "Is that . . . what I am?"

"It's what I want you to be," he says. "I like you."

My heart is exploding. "I like you too. But—"

"But you're moving." He nods. "I know. You're not gone yet, though. We can figure it out when it gets here."

I've always been a planner. If I have a paper due at the end of the quarter, I start working on it the first day it's assigned. We have one more week of camp, though, and I can't imagine being here and not being with Hayden. One week of amazing is better than nothing, right?

"I've never had a boyfriend before," I tell him. "I'm not sure I'll be any good at being a girlfriend."

Hayden reaches for my hand and holds it. "All you have to do is be yourself."

✵

I'm walking on clouds as I enter Chickadee Cabin later that night. One week of camp down and Family Day was a success. Meeting Hayden's mom was also a success, and now I'm his girlfriend. I'm really not looking forward to telling Nora that—if she ever talks to me again.

"You're smiling pretty big," Simone notes. "Good day?" she asks with a knowing look in her eyes.

I sit beside her on the bottom bunk. "I hung out with Hayden and his mom for most of it."

"You two are getting serious, huh?" she asks.

I nibble at my lower lip. "I'm officially his girlfriend."

"Whoa. Awesome. Is Nora still upset with you?"

I nod. "I'm pretty sure."

Simone blows out a breath. "Well, if she's truly your friend, she'll get over it."

"I hope so."

The other campers are all lying on their bunks with their iPhones and electronics because this is the only time of the day when it's allowed. None of them are tuned in to a single word that Simone and I are saying.

"Are you enjoying Camp Starling so far?" I ask.

"It's like a parent-free vacation. I plan to save all my money during the year to come back every summer from now on. It was a huge deal for me to even ask my parents about coming here. They said no at first. They always say no to things that I want." Simone shakes her head. "But this was important to me. Sometimes you just have to stand up for yourself and demand to be heard, right?"

I blink at this thirteen-year-old girl who is schooling me on how to live. Instead of demanding to be heard like Simone, I have pretended like everything is okay and, instead, devised some childish plan to get what I want. Nora is right. If I'm not being honest about how I feel, then I'm not being honest at all.

I've tried to talk to my mom, but she always shuts me down and I just let her. Maybe it's because I don't want to hurt her feelings. We've been through so much together since my dad died. My mom was fragile after we lost him. I tiptoed around her emotions and tried to be the best daughter I could to make up for the fact that it was just us. I was all she had. I thought if I made all As and never got into trouble, I would be enough.

The thing is, I'm tired of shying away from my feelings just because voicing them might be uncomfortable for others. I want to use my voice. I want to be heard. I don't want to go with the flow. I want to resist. Persist. Make waves.

I stand with resolution and head toward the door.

"Where are you going?" Simone asks. Her voice lowers. "Are you meeting someone?"

I shake my head. Not this time. "I need to talk to my mom." And this conversation has waited long enough. I know my mom loves Dave and she's excited about a fresh start for us, but has she even considered that we don't need a fresh start? That I don't want one. Yes, memories are hard, but they're also wonderful, and the hardest thing would be losing them.

I walk down the path in darkness, which I know is breaking the rules. A month ago, I never would have left the cabin based on that fact alone, but here I am, out after curfew for the second time this week. That's not exactly a positive thing, being willing to break the rules. But being willing to tell my mom how I feel even if I know it might hurt her, that's new. Standing up for what I believe . . . that's new too.

When I get to Eagle Cabin, I pull a steadying breath into my lungs and close my eyes for a beat. Then I open them, lift my hand, and knock three times.

My mom comes to the door within a minute's time. "Paisley." Her lips part in surprise and she looks beyond me as if to ask if I walked all this way alone.

"It's just me," I confirm. "I need to talk to you."

"I saw you several times today. I'll see you in the morning. This couldn't wait?"

I shake my head, but I don't say anything right this second because I suddenly feel the swell of tears in my eyes. They're sad and angry, hurt and overwhelmed. If Simone can demand to be heard at thirteen, I can do this at sixteen. "I don't want to move, Mom. I don't want to sell Camp Starling. I need this place. The other kids need it too. I thought you felt the same way, but you're just willing to give it all up for some guy." I suck in a breath as hot tears wash over my cheeks. My chest is heaving. "Dave is nothing like Dad. And Wyoming? I'm sure it's a great state and all, but we don't belong there, Mom. We belong here."

"Oh, Paisley." My mom pulls me into her arms, holding me for a long moment. For the first time in forever, I feel like maybe things will be all right. That maybe this was all that was needed. I just needed to be completely open and honest with her. And now that she knows how I feel, everything can be fixed. She pulls back, smooths my hair from my face, and pats my back. "I know it's hard and scary."

A ball of dread coats my stomach. "Mom, you love your job. You can't just leave it."

"I have loved being a principal, yes, but I'm tired of being in charge, Paisley. The thought of being back in the classroom is exhilarating for me. It's what I want. Change is scary, but it's exciting too." She offers a reassuring smile, but I don't feel reassured. "And you'll make new friends. You can still keep up with your old ones here. We'll find a way. You'll see."

"You're not hearing me. I don't want to leave!" I demand, forcing the words out loudly. She needs to hear me this time. "This camp wasn't just Dad's heart. It's mine. How can you just sell it? You would never have even thought of doing that before Dave." My voice borders on yelling.

"Paisley Grace Manning," my mom snaps. "You need to calm down right now."

"And you need to think before it's too late." I have never spoken back to my mom like this in my whole life. "You and Dave are complete opposites. He's not even good at camping.

He's awful at it. You two get along now, but just wait until the honeymoon period is over. Then you'll see that he's not the one for you. You'll see that following him to Wyoming is a huge mistake."

"Honey, this wasn't a rash decision for me. Dave has been thinking about moving to his hometown for a while. He was waiting for the summer break. The more of a possibility that became, the more I realized that I didn't want to say goodbye to him. I think a fresh start in a new town will be exciting. For both of us."

"Well, I don't. And selling Camp Starling is the worst idea ever. Whose idea was it? His?"

"Mine, actually," my mom says. "You have no idea how much work goes into keeping Camp Starling afloat. Without your dad, it's become a burden that I'm not sure I can handle anymore."

I can feel the hope draining out of me like the last grains of sand in an hourglass. "I'm getting older, though. I can help out. I'm sixteen. I have a driver's license. I can get a part-time job. Whatever you need me to do, I'll do it."

"What I need you to do is accept my decision. I love Dave. I want to move with him. I want to sell this camp. It's time. It's not up for discussion, Paisley. I'm sorry." She reaches for me, but I pull away.

"None of this would be happening if you had never met Dave. I wish he'd never come into our lives!"

"Paisley Grace, that's enough!" my mom warns.

I notice now that Dave is watching our argument from

the bathroom doorway. Eagle Cabin is equipped with its own bathroom and tiny kitchen, which I sometimes forget. I realize that Dave has heard every word I just said. His usual smile is gone, replaced by a straight line. The rosy color of his face seems to have faded as well. The twinkle of his eyes is gone.

There's no time for guilt, though. I'm on a mission. I return my attention to my mom, prepared to continue making my case. "Mom . . ."

She holds up a hand. "I said that's enough. I don't want to hear another word out of your mouth right now. Since when are you so disrespectful? I didn't raise you this way."

"Yeah? Well, I'm not the only one who's changed. You used to actually care how I felt." My gaze bounces between her and Dave. "Forget it." I turn to leave. There's no use in pleading my case to my mother. She's not hearing what I'm saying anyway. She's not budging. It's already too late to change her mind.

CHAPTER SIXTEEN

Camp Time: Monday. July 25.

"She's still not talking to you, huh?" Hayden asks as he sits beside me at one of the picnic tables, his lunch tray touching mine.

I glance over and furrow my brow.

"You were searching the crowd of campers. I'm right here so you're obviously not looking for me." He offers me a lopsided grin that digs small dimples in his cheeks.

"Sorry. Yeah, Nora is still mad." I swirl one of my French fries in my glob of ketchup.

"So go find her and make up. I'm not going anywhere."

I glance over at him. "You make it sound so easy."

"It should be. All you have to do is tell her that, if dating me is really so upsetting to her, then you'll let me go."

My mouth drops. I shake my head. "What? No. I'm not saying that."

"You wouldn't mean it, of course. But I'm guessing she

would appreciate the gesture. Trust me, all Nora needs is to know that you'd be willing to give me up. Then she'll see that she'd be the selfish one to ask you to do that. She'll say she never liked me anyway and tell you to keep me. To which you'll reluctantly agree, and voila, everything will be better."

I blink at him. "It's scary how good you are at that."

"I guess I used to be pretty good at getting into trouble and digging my way out of it."

"Used to?" I ask, a playful lilt to my words.

He picks up his sandwich, holding it between two hands. "Go on, offer to sacrifice me and get your best friend back. I'll wait right here."

I lean over and kiss his dimpled cheek. "Thank you," I whisper as hope unfurls inside me. "You're the best boyfriend I've ever had."

He side-eyes me. "The only one you've ever had, right?"

"Yep."

He chuckles quietly and bites into his sandwich.

I stand and grab my own tray, looking around for Nora. I spot her all the way on the other side of the Birdfeeder. Emma and Tish are sitting on opposite sides of her. I pull in a breath, filling my lungs with as much air as they'll hold. My mom is upset with me today too. So is Dave. I need my best friend right now, more than ever.

When I'm almost at their picnic table, Nora looks up and her green eyes brighten at first. Then they dull and she lifts her chin wordlessly.

"Um, hi," I say, looking at her and then Emma and Tish.

Emma and Tish smile back at me. They aren't picking sides, which I appreciate.

"Look, I don't want to fight, Nora," I say quickly. "If you don't want me to see Hayden, then I won't," I tell her, taking Hayden's advice.

She looks at me, chin still lifted high. "Okay," she says, with a shoulder shrug.

The breath whooshes out of me. "What?"

Her eyes slightly narrow. "Okay. I don't want you to date him."

I put my tray down on the table in front of her before I drop it and take a seat. "But why not?"

"Because I don't." She shrugs again, the movement jerky. "I don't think he's right for you, that's all. You act differently when you're with him. You ignore me."

I shake my head. "No, I don't."

The corners of her mouth twitch as she frowns. "So what you just said when you walked over. About not seeing Hayden if I didn't want you to. That was just another of your lies. One of many this summer, huh, Paisley?" She lifts a brow. She's not going to make this easy on me.

I blow out a breath. It comes out shaky like a roller-coaster cart coming to a jerky halt on its track. "Complete honesty?"

Nora nods. "Preferably."

I pin her with my gaze, hoping she'll understand. "I like Hayden. A lot."

Something shifts in the way Nora is looking at me, but she doesn't reply at first.

"Okay, someone fill us in on what's going on," Emma says. "I feel like I'm missing something."

I look at Tish and Emma, realizing Nora hasn't told them what happened yet. I thought for sure she would have. "Hayden and I kissed on Saturday night down by the lake. After dark."

Nora continues to frown. "You snuck out after curfew. That's so unlike you, Paisley."

I nod again. "I know. I'm doing a lot of things that aren't like me these days."

"You must really like him to break curfew," Nora says.

I roll my lips together. "I've never really felt this way about anyone before. And when you started to show interest in him, I got angry because you've never had a hard time getting a guy to notice you." I point to myself. "Guys never notice me. Not really. I'm just the girl with red hair. Or the principal's daughter. Hayden is different, though. Of anyone, he's the least likely person to want to be with me because of who my mom is. But he doesn't care. He even likes my mom."

"Wow," Emma says.

"Wow," Tisha agrees.

Nora doesn't say anything for a long moment. "I didn't really think you were that into him. I mean, if you're into him enough to break one of the camp's rules, that's a pretty huge deal for you."

I grimace. "Yep. I also broke curfew last night to walk to Mom's cabin and tell her what I really think about this move they're planning and about selling the camp."

"And?"

"And she heard me, but she didn't listen."

Nora's rigid posture softens. "I'm sorry about what I said the other night. I don't want to lose my best friend."

"I'm sorry too." I exhale softly, feeling like a heavy weight has been lifted off my chest. "So we're still best friends? Even though I have a boyfriend?"

Nora smiles. "I can't believe you're going out with someone. And you kissed him. Was it a good kiss?"

I melt a little at the memory. "Not that I have anything to compare it to, but I can't imagine that there's ever been a better kiss in the history of first kisses." I sigh. "Anyway, I'm glad we're all friends again. Because if I'm moving away, I don't want us to be on bad terms. And I think I am moving." My heart falls like a lead balloon into the pit of my stomach. "My mom isn't changing her mind. This is happening, whether I like it or not."

"But what about you and Hayden?" Nora asks with a frown.

There was some small part of me that thought maybe Hayden and I would turn out like my mom and dad. They were first loves who met at summer camp too. They saw each other every year as they grew up until one day they were grown. Then my dad proposed, my mom said yes, and the rest is Manning history.

One summer camp does not equal a happily ever after for me and Hayden, though. I know that in my head, but my heart can't help but hope that maybe we'll find a way despite the distance. It's a silly fantasy. We've only had one first kiss.

I sigh. "Maybe we'll FaceTime or Zoom. My Aunt Jenny

and Uncle Leon still live here, so we'll come back every now and then. Maybe I can see Hayden then."

"Thinking long-term already?" Nora asks. Even though we just made up, there's a slight judgmental tone to her voice.

"If long-term means past this summer camp, then yes," I say.

She rolls her lips together as if she's holding in whatever it is she wants to say. I wait for it, though, because Nora never holds anything back. "Paisley, he's your first boyfriend. Don't you think you're getting a little too serious too fast?" Her eyes narrow. "I know you. You're probably already thinking about how you'll be in college soon and how maybe you'll go somewhere close to Hayden."

I inwardly bristle. Why does Nora think she always knows what's best for me? I have a brain of my own, although admittedly I have been more of a follower in our friendship until this summer. "I can think for myself, Nora."

Her lips part and her green eyes widen a touch. Her breath seems to whoosh out of her as she exhales. "I just don't want you to get hurt, that's all. Your first boyfriend will always break your heart, no matter what. It's inevitable."

I wonder again what happened between her and Jacob. He was kind of her first real boyfriend last summer. Did he break her heart? "My mom married her first boyfriend," I remind Nora. "Sometimes it works out." Then I shake my head. "Anyway, I'm not foolish enough to think I'm going to marry Hayden or anything like that. I'm just saying, maybe me and Hayden can make it work for a little while. I like him and he likes me, and as long as that's true, we can at least try."

Nora offers what might be a sincere smile. "Well, then I'm happy for you."

My defenses lower a notch. "Really?"

"Mm-hmm. It's about time you had a boyfriend. Even if he's not Jacob, who I was completely wrong about. You two are too much alike to be good for one another. Hayden's a much better match for you."

"I'm glad we're good again." I lean over the picnic table to give her a hug. Then all four of us are hugging. It's a perfect camp moment until we hear a commotion coming from the lake. We break away from the embrace and hurry in the direction of all the campers pointing from shore. They aren't allowed in the water yet. It's lunchtime. Water activities are restricted for thirty minutes after eating.

When I arrive at the water's edge, I see a bright yellow kayak tipped over in the middle of the lake. I make out a blurry image of Dave in the water, holding on to the side. I realize he's okay about the same time that everyone else seems to. The frightened gasps turn to laughter and pointing. Then I notice that even my mom is laughing from where she stands a little ways down the shore. One can't really blame her. Dave looks ridiculous out there wearing a bright orange life vest and holding on to his kayak for dear life.

"I thought Dave had gotten pretty good at paddling. Did you rig his kayak or something?" Nora asks, jokingly. "Because if you did, I'm impressed."

"Of course not. I would never do something like that," I say, even though I have done my share of harm to him this summer.

"Why is he even out there right now anyway?" Nora asks. "He just ate. He'll get a swimmer's cramp."

This is true. And Dave isn't exactly athletic.

I start to walk toward one of the bright yellow kayaks reserved for counselors.

"Where are you going?" Nora calls after me.

"To get him. Someone needs to." The lifeguards are on lunch right now. Dave can only hold on for so long and a swimmer's cramp is a real thing. He has a life vest on, of course, so I don't think he's in danger—not really. Even so, I head out to his rescue.

Dave focuses on me as I paddle out to him. Paisley to the rescue. Only, I don't feel heroic right now. I kind of feel rotten because of how I've been to him lately. If he weren't dating my mom and if he weren't the reason we're set to move, I might actually like Dave. In fact, I'm sure I would.

"Need help?" I ask when my kayak is right next to his.

"It was taking on water. I'm too heavy. It won't hold me." He's not really looking directly into my eyes, which only adds to the layers of guilt in my gut. He heard me the other night when I went to see my mom. He might have heard me better than she did.

"Climb in," I tell him. "We'll attach your kayak to this one and pull it back. You'll have to help me paddle though."

A small smile flickers on Dave's mouth. "Teamwork."

I resist telling him that we aren't a team. If this were a game, I'd be playing against him.

Dave latches onto the side of my kayak and prepares to pull himself aboard.

"W-wait." I whirl to face him. "You're going to—" My warning comes too late. My kayak tips over and throws me into the water. I go under for a moment and bop back to the water's surface, using my hands to claw my wet hair from my eyes.

"Paisley? Are you—are you all right?" Dave asks.

When the water is out of my eyes, I blink him into view. "No, I am not all right!" I practically growl. Nice guy or not, he's incompetent when it comes to all things camping. I tip the kayak right side up again and glare at him. "You get in first this time. I know how to get in a kayak without turning it over."

Dave frowns. It takes him several attempts to board the kayak. Once he's on, he reaches out a hand that I ignore. Then I hoist myself into the front of our vessel. I'm drenched and there's a chill running through my body.

I take a shuddery breath and turn back to Dave. "Look, I'm sorry about the other night, okay? I didn't know you were there."

"Paisley, I'm glad I was there. Don't ever apologize for being open and honest. I want to know how you're feeling."

I swallow, struggling with my current emotions as I face forward. "Yeah, well, my mom certainly doesn't," I mutter.

"Do you want me to talk to her?" Dave asks.

I plunge my paddle into the water at my side. "She's my

mom. She should be listening to me, not you. You're an outsider," I say, wishing I didn't sound like such a brat.

"I completely agree." Dave's hand finds my shoulder as he sits behind me. "I know you don't want my advice. I know you don't even want me around."

I don't say anything. Why does Dave have to be such a great guy, though? Why can't he have some quality about him that's unredeemable?

"But you should try again with your mom. The worst thing you can do is shut down on her. Open communication is important."

I flick my gaze back to meet Dave's, fully prepared to say something horrible to him. Instead, I just gesture at his paddle. "You ready?"

"Oh. Yeah." He lifts his paddle as well.

I wait for him to say it. I know he wants to, but his lips are pressed into a thick line on his sunburned face. So I say it instead as a kind of peace offering. "Teamwork."

※

Even though I rescued Dave from the water, there's a rumor going around that I'm the one who sabotaged his kayak. I think it started when someone overheard Nora ask me when we were standing onshore if I did it. You know how rumors go. One person overhears a snippet of something, misinterprets what was said, and passes it on.

Oh, and after the kayak disaster, Dave was pelted with a

tennis ball while walking past the girl campers. It was clearly an accident, and I wasn't even in proximity. Even so, the whispers around camp are that I threw it. Tisha told me this because one of her campers told her in passing.

I see the eyes on me as I walk by. I've gone from good girl to suspected criminal in one afternoon.

"So did you do it?" Maddie asks. She's been bucking my authority the entire time she's been here at Camp Starling. Of course she would think this silly rumor was true.

"Do what?" I echo back.

"You know, put the hole in his kayak," she says. "It was obviously put there intentionally. And Dave takes that kayak out every day after lunch. Everyone knows that." Her eyes narrow.

I'm a counselor. I'm supposed to be someone people look up to here at Camp Starling. A role model. The campers aren't supposed to suspect me of horrible things that I would never, ever consider.

Well. I mean, I would fantasize about doing something like that, but I would never act on those thoughts. I would only write about such things in my camper's journal. My brain skips like a needle on one of my dad's old vinyl records. I remember writing something eerily similar to what happened to Dave this afternoon.

Just this afternoon, I was fantasizing about putting Mr. Cheez-It himself on a rigged kayak in the middle of Blue Lake. In my fantasy, he struggles to keep it balanced and eventually just tips over. Splash.

179

My entire body freezes and a wave of panic crashes over me. I actually did write about Dave's kayak capsizing. And maybe I even mentioned the possibility of a flyaway ball coming Dave's way. It's almost too much of a coincidence.

I turn and start running as fast as my feet will carry me, flip-flops flapping against my heels as I race back toward Chickadee Cabin. I have to find my journal and make sure it's still there. I have a sinking suspicion I won't find it, though. That it'll be gone. There's a knot of dread in my stomach, weighing me down as I run. I fear that someone has found my journal and they're taking all the things I only thought about doing to Dave and making them come true.

I fling open the door of Chickadee Cabin, heart racing. Then I hurry over to my bunk and lift the mattress to look for my journal. It holds all my deepest thoughts and desires. I tell my journal everything, but only because no one else is ever supposed to get their hands on it or read the words written on those pages. It's private.

Please be there, please be there.

I'm holding my breath to the point that I feel like I might pass out. As I search with my eyes, I also run my hand along the far back of the mattress, just in case it got pushed farther back than I can see. I don't see it. I don't feel it. It's not here.

Finally, I sit back on my heels and pull in a breath. Then I press my hands to my face. I. Am. In. So. Much. Trouble.

CHAPTER SEVENTEEN

Camp Time: Tuesday. July 26.

I wake early the next morning and make Campers' Breakfast with Aunt Jenny, Uncle Leon, Hayden, and Nora. Dave is surprisingly MIA, and I wonder if he's upset about all the mishaps from yesterday. They weren't my fault and I even feel like Dave and I kind of made a small truce out on the lake. I still feel guilty about what's happening to him, though, because I wrote those things that are happening to him now in my camper's journal. Someone has gotten ahold of those thoughts and they're bringing them to life. That has to be what's going on.

"You're deep in thought over there this morning." Uncle Leon gives my shoulder a poke. "What's going on, Birdie?"

I flip a pancake—not as high or as entertaining as Dave does—and look over at him. "Just wondering where Dave is."

"Oh, that's nice," Aunt Jenny says. "So you two are finally getting along?"

I don't answer that question because what can I say? No, we're not exactly getting along, and I'm potentially the reason for all his problems right now. I haven't told anyone about my missing journal, though, because then I'd have to admit that I thought up all those horrible ideas in relation to Dave, which would make me out to be a horrible human being.

I blink and realize that everyone is staring at me again, concern knitted in the little crevices between their eyes. "Stop staring at me, okay? I'm fine. Really. I'm just in a week-two daze." That's a real thing at camp. Week two is when you've been in the sun too long, missed enough sleep from staying up late, pushed your body beyond its limits, and you're walking around in a fog.

"Ah. A camp daze. That explains it," Aunt Jenny says with a nod as she continues to work on Campers' Breakfast, filling bowls and dishes with delicious food. The aroma hangs thick in the air.

Finally, Dave waddles toward us. Yes, waddles. He's moving stiffly as if he doesn't want to bend his joints.

"Oh!" Aunt Jenny says. "What happened to you?"

Dave is less than his usual jolly self. He's coated in a light pink cream from head to toe. "I have poison ivy. It seems one of the campers thought it might be funny to put a few leaves in my bunk."

Aunt Jenny gasps loudly.

"I don't know how long the leaves had been there," Dave says. "I didn't even feel them under my blanket. But I'm allergic so a few leaves might as well have been an entire vine." He looks at me. "Your mom went out in the night to get me some calamine lotion."

I grimace, sincerely regretful for his situation. "That's awful." Especially after the day he had yesterday. I faintly remember writing something about putting poison ivy leaves in Dave's bunk in my camper's journal.

I hope Dave doesn't brush up against poison ivy today (insert sarcasm).

Ugh. This is not good. What else did I write?

"Maybe you should just go home, buddy," Uncle Leon suggests. "I mean, you're moving in two weeks. Sticking it out another week here might derail those plans."

We all turn back and look at Dave.

He shakes his head and then grimaces as if that simple movement was painful. "No, I'm staying. Ellen goes on and on about this camp and how much this place has always meant to her. What will she think if I can't even make it two weeks?"

"If it means so much to her, why would she sell it?" I ask. I can't seem to help myself.

Dave looks at me. "I don't know. In fact, I've tried to persuade her to keep the camp. I know how much it means to your family. Your mom makes her own decisions, though. She's tough. That's one of the things I admire about her. And about you."

I ignore the warmth that tries to close in around my heart. I

183

don't want to like Dave. He's the enemy. He has been wiggling past my defenses, though. Knowing that he grew up without the advantages I have, like camp experiences, has made me less judgmental. He also listens to me, which is a plus considering my own mother doesn't.

"Anyway, I want to stick it out here at camp for your mom," Dave tells me. "I want to prove to her that I can be a true camper."

He doesn't look like a camper, though. He's tie-dyed, sunburned, and covered in pale pink lotion and bug bites. He looks miserable. We all just stare at him until the bird call goes off. Then we scurry back to life, ready to feed the campers as they head our way.

The next few hours are a blur. Hayden gives another arts and crafts session. This time the campers all make friendship bracelets to give to one another. It's kind of cool, especially considering that both Hayden and Nora gave me the ones they made.

After arts and crafts, the counselors take the campers to the lake and Meghan, Maria, and Jacob review lifesaving techniques in the water. You know, what to do if you see someone struggling. Then the campers take turns pretending to go under while another camper swims out to bring them back to shore.

At some point, Jacob steps up beside me. At first, I think it's Hayden, but Hayden isn't participating in swim-rescue skills. He's still undoing his graffiti on the cabins. His handiwork has left a slight green hue that won't come off, so he and

Mom decided that painting the whole cabin brown might be the best option.

"Hey, Jacob," I say, smiling over at him.

"Hey. I haven't gotten much of a chance to talk to you. Not as much as I wanted, at least." He shifts around looking nervous. "Are you enjoying being a counselor this summer?"

"It's not as easy as I expected, but yeah. I'm loving every minute. You?" I ask.

He shrugs. "My cabin is pretty cool. The group tends to stay up too late talking. I guess I can sleep when we all go home, though, right?"

I laugh softly. "I turn the lights out at nine-thirty and we have a rule. If you talk, you have to make everyone's beds the next morning. It works like a charm."

Jacob's eyes widen subtly. "Wow. You're tough."

"My old camp counselor used to have that rule. I just borrowed it."

"Maybe I'll borrow it from you." He nudges me with his elbow. The touch is unexpected. Maybe he hasn't noticed that I'm with Hayden. Nora kind of thought Jacob had a thing for me last week. Maybe he still does.

I take a small step away and show off the purple-and-gray friendship bracelet on my wrist. "Hayden's class was fun, huh? He made this bracelet for me."

Jacob looks down at it, his smile faltering a touch. "Hayden's bracelet. Nice." His gaze lifts to mine. "I haven't given the one I made to anyone yet. I was saving it."

I wonder if he was saving it for me. I hope not. I was never really into Jacob, even though I guess on paper we make more sense than me and Hayden. "You'll figure it out," I say. "Maybe you can give it to Nora."

Jacob looks surprised and lets out a small laugh. "I'm not sure she'd want my bracelet."

"Why not? You two were close last summer," I say as the wind bats my hair around my face. I swipe the flyaways behind my ear. "What happened between you two anyway?" I ask.

Jacob shrugs. "I guess she got bored with me. I don't really know. I was a bit heartbroken when she dumped me."

"For no reason?" I ask. Then I look away. "Sorry if I'm being too nosy."

Jacob shakes his head. "I don't know exactly what happened. I'm pretty sure she liked me as much as I liked her. I kind of think that was the problem."

"What do you mean?" I ask.

"I don't know. You know Nora's parents don't get along. I think some part of her is scared to fall for someone. Like maybe her idea of what a relationship looks like is two people arguing and crying." He looks down at his feet. "And we were just too . . . I don't know, happy."

"That actually makes a lot of sense," I say. Then I gesture to the friendship bracelet on his wrist. "Maybe you could change her idea of what romance looks like."

"Maybe." Jacob takes a few retreating steps. "Well, I better get back to the water. Just in case one of the swimmers pretending to sink actually starts struggling for real."

I offer a smile. "Same. Talk to you later?"

"Yeah, see you around, Paisley," he says.

I watch him walk away. Out of habit, I look around for Hayden, even though I know exactly where he is. I just miss him. At least I have his bracelet on my wrist. Nora's too. I doubt that will be any comfort when I'm a million miles away this fall, though.

⁂

At lunchtime, Hayden still isn't around. I sit at the table with the girls of Chickadee Cabin. Simone and Tabitha have gotten close. They whisper between each other while the rest of us talk. Then after we finish eating, we head over to a ropes course behind the cabins. I catch a glimpse of Hayden painting as we walk by, but he doesn't see me. He's too engulfed in his work. Dave is helping Hayden now, even though I'm sure he's miserable and itchy.

Poor Dave.

My brain freezes like when you bite into freezing-cold ice cream. I can't believe I just thought that. Dave is growing on me whether I want him to or not.

The campers complete the ropes course and Chickadee Cabin earns a blue ribbon for finishing first.

"Poison ivy, huh?" Maddie says, stepping up beside me while Tabitha and Simone navigate a rope web. "That's a pretty brutal prank. Whoever did that has no right being a counselor here."

I turn and narrow my eyes. "What makes you think it was a counselor?"

Maddie shrugs and watches Tabitha reach the top of the

web. "Well, I mean, whoever did it would have to get inside Falcon Cabin. Hayden is sharing a cabin with Dave, right?"

I thought Maddie was going to blame me, but she's suggesting Hayden. That idea never even occurred to me. "Hayden wouldn't do that to Dave."

"Hmm," Maddie says. She looks at me. "Would you?"

My jaw drops. "Maddie, I don't know what you have against me, but I'm doing my best here, okay? I would never hurt Dave intentionally or anyone else for that matter. I'm here to help."

Maddie folds her arms over her chest. After a moment, she says, "It's not you, okay? It wasn't my choice to come to camp. I don't want to be here."

Could have fooled me. "What's wrong with camp?"

Maddie slides her gaze over to mine. "It's just a way for my parents to get rid of me. This is the third camp I've been to this summer. I'm camp-hopping."

I had no idea. "Wow. I love camp, but too much of a good thing is never good," I say, empathizing.

"For what it's worth, this is the best one so far." Maddie shrugs. "And you're a pretty decent counselor."

I smile. "Thanks. That's worth a lot." Maddie's approval feels like a tiny triumph. Like a blue ribbon just for me.

⁂

I don't get a chance to talk to Hayden until dinner, when he slides in next to me, his plate touching mine.

"Hey, you," he says.

Just the sound of his voice makes little flesh bumps rise on my arms. I didn't realize how much I needed to see him right now. I'm used to being with him throughout the day, but he's been MIA most of this one. "Hey."

"You okay?" he asks.

We've only officially been boyfriend and girlfriend for a couple of days, but already he seems to know me. "Yeah. It's just been busy. I'm exhausted."

"Yeah, me too." In my peripheral vision I can see Hayden using his fork to play with his food. "I doubt our day was as cumbersome as Dave's, though. He looks bad. Who would do these awful things to him?"

I feel myself folding forward over my own plate, weighed down by my own guilt. Not that I did those things yesterday. Whoever did crossed a line that I would never allow myself to go beyond.

"Paisley?" Hayden is watching me, his brown eyes narrowed.

"Yeah?"

"Please tell me it wasn't you who did all that stuff to Dave yesterday," he finally says, his expression serious.

I feel my back go rod straight. "What? Are you seriously asking if I nearly killed Dave by capsizing his kayak?"

"Come on, Pais, that stunt didn't almost kill Dave. The poison ivy was pretty brutal, though," Hayden says.

My mouth is gaping open. Suddenly I want to burst into tears. "I know everyone else is thinking I'm the culprit right now, but you're my boyfriend. You're supposed to be on my side."

"I am on your side," he says softly. "But we've been trying

to sabotage Dave since camp started. Our mission was to make him as miserable as possible." Hayden hesitates. "Short of hurting him. That was kind of an unwritten rule."

"I can't believe this. Mission Matchbreaker was *your* suggestion to begin with!" I say, my voice rising an octave. "Maybe you're the one who did those things to Dave yesterday," I say, remembering Maddie's assumption. She's right. Hayden did have access to Dave's bunk. "I would actually expect these behaviors from someone like you."

Hurt flashes in Hayden's eyes. He sets his fork down and stares at his tray for a long moment. "Someone like me?" he repeats in the form of a question, but he doesn't look at me.

"Well, you are the one with the delinquent background. That's the whole reason you're even here, isn't it?" I say. "If anyone should be accusing anyone of these crimes, it's me accusing you." I point a finger. "You and Dave are both in Falcon Cabin. . . . Oh, that's right, though. You're too cool to sleep inside."

Hayden shakes his head. "I asked if you were behind these recent pranks out of concern for you, Pais. Nothing else." He visibly swallows. "I can't believe you'd expect those behaviors from *someone like me,* though. If that's what you think of me, why are you even with me?"

"I could ask you the same. If you think I'm horrible enough to do those things to Dave, why are you with me?" I ask.

"I guess I'm not." Hayden looks at me for a moment. Then he picks up his tray and stands.

Reflexively, I reach for his arm. "Wait. What's that supposed to mean? Where are you going?"

"I'm not hungry anymore. And I'm feeling like I need a little fresh air."

Considering that we're outside right now, I'm taking that to mean he needs air that isn't shared with me. Did we just break up? "Well, I need air right now too," I call after him. He doesn't stop walking.

I can't decide if I'm more mad or if I feel more guilty. Both, I guess. How dare he even think I would do those things to Dave.

I look around, breathless, my chest heaving like a fish that's flopped up on the shore.

"Hey, Ms. Ellen is looking for you," a camper tells me.

I blink her into focus. Her name is Jasmine, I think.

"Oh? Where is she?" I ask.

Jasmine points. "Down there. I know she's your mom and all, but I think you might be in trouble or something," she says with a slight grimace. "She didn't look too happy when I saw her."

My breaths turn shallow. "What?"

"Maybe it's because of those things you did to Mr. Dave." Jasmine's growing grimace shows off her full set of braces.

My lips part, but I don't have any words. All the people who are supposed to think the best of me are currently thinking the worst. Instead of responding to Jasmine, I stand up, grab my tray, and toss it into the garbage as I head in the opposite direction of where Jasmine told me my mom was looking for me.

Darkness settles in around me, but I don't move from the fallen tree that I've been sitting on for at least an hour now. The sun has set and the moon is high in the sky, which means I'm officially late getting back to Chickadee Cabin. Tabitha will take the lead with the campers. If Camp Starling were staying open, she would make a great counselor next year.

Me? After this stunt I'm pulling, I would be banned from ever being a counselor again. Even so, I stay put. Once you break one rule, breaking another is easy. Once you disappoint one person, disappointing the rest isn't so bad. Everyone at camp already thinks I'm an awful person, including my own boyfriend and my mom. I might as well prove them all right and do something rebellious. Maybe I'll stay here all night.

The sounds of cicadas and other nighttime creatures grows louder as the darkness thickens around me, casting long shadows like something out of a scary movie. I close my eyes and take several deep breaths. I'm not even sure what my plan is. Waiting until they send a search party is probably not the best idea. That would get me grounded for life. I imagine my mom is being alerted right about now that I'm not in my cabin. Everyone is likely worried. I'm not the type to run away, but then again, I'm not the type to purposely hurt someone and yet everyone assumed that I had.

A coyote's howl sends me shooting to my feet. Okay, this is crazy. Time to head back to camp. I'll find my mom and talk to her. That's the new plan. I'll explain that I'm not the one sabotaging Dave. At least not over the last couple days. Then I'll confess that I did write about a couple of those things in my camper's journal that someone else stole from beneath my bunk.

Honesty is the best policy. That was always my dad's advice. Even if it gets me in more trouble than I've ever been in in my entire life.

I exit the woods and step into moonlight, expecting to see a formation of people looking for me. Instead, the camp is like a ghost town. Everyone seems to be in their cabins for the night. I make my way back toward Chickadee Cabin just waiting for someone to call out, *"There she is! I found her!"* But no one does.

I pass Chickadee Cabin and keep walking, deciding to continue with my plan to find my mom and tell her everything. I know I just went to her cabin the other night and after the big display I put on, she is definitely suspecting me of doing those things to Dave. And while that hurts my feelings, I also understand. If I were her, I would suspect me too. Emphasis on *if I were her.* I'm still mad at Hayden for thinking it was me. I didn't make a huge display with him the other night like I did with my mom. I haven't given him any reason to peg me as the bad guy here.

When I reach my mom's cabin, I take a moment. I will be rational and controlled this time, I tell myself. Then I lift my hand to knock, but stop when I hear loud voices coming from inside. I recognize one voice as my mom's. She's nearly yelling, which is so unlike her that I lower my hand and take a tiny step backward. The other voice belongs to Dave. He's not yelling, but his voice is stern.

Are they arguing? That's hard to believe because they always get along perfectly. Dave is always so happy except for these last couple days when he hasn't been. Is that why they're fighting? Are they arguing about what's happening at camp? About me?

I lean in closer to the door to hear what's being said.

"Have you even told her that you have a buyer for the camp?" I hear Dave ask.

My breath catches. A buyer for the camp? Already? The For Sale sign hasn't even gone up yet. I thought I had more time to convince my mom that selling Camp Starling was a bad idea.

"No wonder she's acting out," Dave continues. "You're keeping Paisley in the dark, Ellen. She's not a child anymore."

"Sixteen is hardly grown," my mom snaps back. "She's a teenager and teens act foolishly. The things she's done to you this past week just shows how much of a child she still is."

"She's not the only one acting childishly," Dave says.

My mouth drops open. I can't believe he just said that. I can't believe he's standing up for me.

"What's that supposed to mean?" My mom's voice is rising with every word. I know if she was talking to me in that tone right now, I'd be cowering.

"It means, you need to talk to your daughter," Dave says. His voice is calm. "She's not happy."

"She'll get over it," my mom insists.

"Probably. But I can't be the wedge between you two. I won't."

There's a long silence and I wonder if my mom is crying. Then I realize that I have tears running down my cheeks too. I take a step backward and nearly stumble over my feet. Then I turn and start running as far and as fast as I can. I'm not even sure where I'm going until I arrive at Falcon Cabin. I know Hayden doesn't sleep inside. He sleeps around back in a hammock suspended between two tall pine trees.

As I approach, he sits up and looks at me. "What are you doing here?"

I struggle to catch my breath. "I . . . I . . . didn't know where else to go. I was at my mom's cabin and I heard her and Dave arguing inside. Dave said that there's already a buyer for the camp," I say breathlessly as tears press behind my eyes. "It's all been for nothing. All of it. I'm still going to lose what's most important to me, and Mom and Dave might not even stay together."

Hayden says nothing. Maybe he's processing what I just said. I'm still processing it myself.

"I can't believe this is happening." I lift a hand to my forehead.

Hayden exhales loudly. "Is that all you came here to tell me?"

My mouth drops open. "Isn't that enough? Why aren't you upset?"

He looks up at the stars. "I am upset, just not about that." The chilly tone of his voice hits me right in the middle of my chest.

That's right. I forgot. Last Hayden and I talked, we were

both mad with one another. "Can we just get past that little argument from before because this is big, Hayden?" My voice quakes.

"What's big about it? Your mom told you that she was going to sell the camp. Maybe it's not all about Dave, like you think. Maybe it's about her too. And didn't you want your mom and Dave to break up, Paisley?" he asks. "Or do you even know what you want? Because you seem to be confused about everything. What you think about people. What you think about yourself and this camp. And me. Honestly, I'm pretty confused too because I thought I knew you. I thought you were the girl who had your act together. You were Paisley Manning. You knew who you were and you always did the right thing. You were the exact opposite of me, and that's why I thought you were so special."

"Thought?" I say.

"I've been asking myself why a girl like you would ever want to be with a guy like me?" He shakes his head. "But now I'm asking myself if I ever even knew who you were at all. All I know is that a lot of people have made me feel like a bad seed in my life. Like a nobody, a failure, a loser. I guess I expected to be treated like that from those people, but I didn't expect you to make me feel that way."

I swallow painfully. "Hayden, what I said earlier . . ." I shake my head.

He hops off the hammock and collects his blanket, his movements quick and choppy.

"Where are you going?" I ask.

"Into my cabin." He laughs, but the sound comes out dry and humorless. "I told you that the reason I didn't sleep in there is because I was afraid they might reject me. But that's one good thing that came out of you and me being together. Being rejected by anyone else will never hurt as bad as being rejected by you. So thanks for that, Pais. I guess I owe you in that sense," he says. Then he turns his back to me and walks away, leaving me standing there, dumbfounded, and wondering what just happened.

CHAPTER EIGHTEEN

Camp Time: Wednesday. July 27.

My mom doesn't come to breakfast so I head to her cabin afterward to check on her. When I knock, it takes forever for her to answer the door.

"Mom?" I ask, because she doesn't quite look like herself. No smile. Her hair is unbrushed, probably her teeth too, and her clothes are wrinkled as if she slept in them. "Mom, are you okay?"

"Mm-hmm." She nods unconvincingly, rubbing her hands over her face. "I must have slept in."

My mom never oversleeps. She's a morning bird like me, always eager to get the day rolling. I step inside her cabin and close the door behind me as she turns her back to me and walks over to a long mirror. She reaches for a brush on the table next to it and starts to pull it through her long brown locks. "Did I miss breakfast?" she asks.

The argument I heard from this very cabin is still fresh on my mind. It replayed in my thoughts all night, keeping me from sleep. "You did. So did Dave," I say.

From the mirror's reflection, I see my mom flinch. "I think Dave left early this morning," she tells me. "You were right, Birdie. I don't think camp is really his thing."

This should be music to my ears, but somehow it's not. "I don't know. He was starting to catch on," I lie. He really wasn't. If anything, he was getting worse at it. Mom never seemed to notice, though. She had love goggles on and maybe I had on loathe goggles.

"He tried his best, but the odds were against him on this one." She looks at me for a moment. "And maybe you were too?" she says.

My mouth falls open to protest, but how can I? I have been against Dave the entire time.

Mom's eyes lower for a moment. She looks so sad that I can hardly breathe. "Birdie, you know I only want what's best for you, right?"

"Yeah," I say.

She walks over and sits on her bed. "This move was something I thought I needed. Running this camp hasn't been easy since your father died. Your aunt and uncle help as much as they can, but as much as I love Camp Starling, the responsibility of keeping this place afloat is too much. If this place isn't rented a majority of the year, I'm out of pocket for the costs of running it. If something goes wrong, it's on me to fix it. Between running the high school and this camp, I haven't had any time for fun. For me. Meeting Dave made me realize that there's more to life than work. I want more for myself. And for you."

I wonder if the move has been called off. If so, I should be jumping for joy. How can I, though, when my mom looks so crushed? "Will Dave come back before the end of camp?" I ask.

Mom picks up a brush and walks back over to the long mirror on the wall. She pulls her hair into a low-hanging pony-tail that falls on her yellow T-shirt. "No. I don't think so." Her gaze connects with mine through the reflection. "I don't think he's returning," she says quietly. I suspect that she's not just talking about camp. Maybe she's talking about forever. I'm too overwhelmed to ask, though. The way my mom looks right now, I think she'd start crying if she had to spell out her breakup with Dave. The last thing I want to do is make my mom break down. She's so tough. So strong. She's always been my hero, just like my dad. I don't always treat her like one though because, well, she's here. I guess I take for granted that she always will be.

"Mom, I'm really sorry," I say, choking on my words.

She looks down again. I haven't actually seen her cry since the year after Dad died. Part of me had wondered if there was a lifetime cap on tears and she'd surpassed it. "Well, camp goes on, right?" She forces a smile, which is almost worse than seeing her cry. It's shaky and fragile. It's a lie and it's all my doing.

"Is there anything I can do?" I'm pretty much willing to do anything in this moment.

She sighs and turns to me. "I think you've done enough, Paisley."

The breath stills in my chest, and I have no doubt she knows what I did. Even if I didn't do those last few things that sealed Dave's fate.

There's another knock on the cabin door. My mom lights up for a brief second. Instinctively, I know she's hoping it's Dave on the other side. But when she opens the door, it's just Aunt Jenny.

"Hi, you two." Aunt Jenny looks between us, her gaze worried. "I was just coming to see if everything was all right."

"Everything's fine," my mom says.

Everything is not fine, though. I'm not as tough as Mom. I can't hold in my tears and force a smile like her. So instead, I walk out of the cabin, leaving my mom and Aunt Jenny to chat. I walk fast, looking for a place to duck and hide, and wipe away my tears in private.

✺

After lunch, my friends and I stand on the lakeshore watching the campers enjoy free swim in the water. We have on visors to shield our faces, sunglasses, and whistles in case we need to get someone's attention fast. Our eyes are pinned to the water, even though our conversation is absorbed in my drama.

"It was just a fight. Hayden will come around," Nora assures me.

I nod as I listen. There are only three full days of camp left.

Usually I would already start to feel nostalgic and sad about the impending goodbye, but this camp is turning into a disaster for me. I'm just ready to go home, but then once I get there it'll be time to pack up and leave. Unless Mom and Dave truly did break up last night. It was more than just an argument. Same with me and Hayden.

The few times I saw him today, he was with the other guy counselors, which surprised me. Hayden has been kind of a loner since he got to Camp Starling. He slept in the cabin last night, though. This morning I've seen him hanging around Jacob and the others. They were laughing and acting like fast pals. That's good, I guess. Those guys are nice and Hayden should have friends. He's wrong about everyone rejecting him, even if that's how he feels I treated him.

"Earth to Paisley," Emma says.

I blink and find Nora, Emma, Meghan, Maria, and Tisha all watching me.

Nora leans in to give me a closer look. "She has the classic brokenhearted, dazed and confused look. She needs chocolate and the Hallmark Channel stat."

They all nod as if they understand exactly what she means about the brokenhearted daze, and they probably do. I'm the last one to have a boyfriend and to experience a breakup. Hayden and I weren't even together for all that long. Should it really hurt this bad after such short a time? Because it does. It feels like someone has injected poison into my heart and it's dying a slow death inside me. And when I see Hayden making new friends, laughing and enjoying himself like he doesn't even care that we've unraveled as a couple, it hurts worse.

"Hi, guys." Simone approaches us. She has a towel draped around her shoulders and her hair is sopping wet. She hasn't been as much of my shadow over the last twenty-four hours, and I can only assume it's because I'm not so much her hero now that everyone suspects I'm the one who made Dave's life miserable. Dave is the sweetheart of camp. He's like the adorable, nerdy, lovable uncle who always has kind words and candy in his pockets. Kind of like my real-life Uncle Leon.

Simone gives us all a wide, beaming smile that's almost contagious as she stands in front of us. Her confidence over the last week of being here at Camp Starling has blossomed and it's amazing to see.

"Hi, Simone." I smile back at her. "Are you having fun in the water?"

She nods quickly and then looks around as if trying to find someone. "I haven't seen your mom or Dave today," she notes, her gaze landing back on me.

It's kind of an odd thing to note because I doubt she usually sees them both most days before lunchtime. There are lots of adults and volunteers and junior counselors like me around. My mom is always busy, and Dave, well, he's always finding himself out of some kind of mishap.

"Do you need their help with something?" I ask Simone. "I can call my mom if you do. Or maybe it's something I can help with."

She looks at me and shakes her head quickly. "No." Then

she nibbles at her lower lip as if she has a little secret that she's not telling. "I was just wondering if something happened, that's all. They're both MIA." She offers a little shrug and ducks her head, looking out at the lake. "Well, I better get back to swimming with my friends. I just wanted to say hi." She doesn't quite meet my gaze when she turns back to me, and I get a strange Spidey sense as I watch her jog back toward the water.

"That was a weird convo," Nora remarks beside me.

"It was, wasn't it?" Simone's interest in my mom and Dave has my mind working overtime, making connections that I don't really want to make. Am I just being paranoid? Simone is one of my cabinmates. She could have seen me writing in my journal. She could have snooped. She's definitely had this hero thing with me ever since I pulled her out of the water, like she's wanted to return the favor.

I gasp and clap a hand to my mouth. All my friends turn to stare at me.

"What is it?" Emma asks.

My gaze moves to Simone. She's back in the water again, seemingly having the time of her life. Could it be? Is she the one? I turn to my friends. "I think Simone might have stolen my camper's journal. She might be the one who did all the horrible things to Dave. On my behalf."

"Simone?" Nora repeats, in disbelief. "She's like twelve."

"Thirteen," I say.

"Why would she do those things to Dave?" Meghan asks.

"Because I saved her life. Kind of. And she wants to repay

me. And if she's the one who took my journal, she's read some of my mental rants where I just want to make Dave as miserable as possible." I pull in a breath. "Can you all cover the water?"

They agree.

"What are you going to do?" Nora asks as I turn to leave.

"I'm going to search Simone's things," I say.

"You can't do that," Emma says. "You can't search someone's stuff without cause."

I lift a brow. The old Paisley would agree. But my gut is telling me that Simone is the one who took my journal and that I'll find it in her belongings. I'm sure her intentions were golden, but everything is in disarray and it's time to sort it all out. There's only three days left of Camp Starling this summer and forevermore. If we're going to end, we need to do so on a high note.

※

I jog back to Chickadee Cabin and slip inside, looking around to make sure no one sees me. Everyone is on the lake, though. Going in others' bags is a huge no-no, as stated on the first day of camp. In just over a week and a half, I've become a rebel, but I have a good cause. If Simone did these things for me, then I need to have a heart-to-heart with her because I was wrong to even think those things or write them in my journal. I've been wrong about a lot lately.

I pause as I stand over Simone's stuff. Then I take a breath, and reach my hand into her trunk to feel around, finding nothing at first. I keep moving my hand to different spots and then my hand hits something hard. A book. Or more specifically, a purple leather-bound camper's journal with a tree and a bird embossed on the front.

My heart kicks and I pull it out to confirm that's really what I've found. So it *was* Simone who took it. She's the troublemaker. I close my eyes and let out a breath, hugging my journal to my midsection. I can't tell on her. I won't. Which means I'm stuck with the bad rap. How am I going to fix all this?

The cabin door opens and I whirl, prepared to explain what I'm doing snooping through Simone's stuff. Then my heart kicks wildly. "Oh. It's you."

Hayden narrows those dark eyes at me.

I swallow. "This isn't how it looks."

Hayden shakes his head. "I'm not trying to bust you, Pais. I just saw you leave the lake and followed."

"Why?"

"I wanted to tell you something. Or give you something, actually." He closes the cabin door and steps toward me, handing me a folded piece of paper. It reminds me of the one he handed me last week at the beginning of camp. And again the other night before our first kiss.

"What's this?" I ask, looking up.

"Open it."

I put the journal I'm holding down on the bed beside me. Then I carefully unfold the paper, taking my time. Just like his first note to me, it simply reads *I'm sorry* in neat block letters. Instead of a single rose drawn at the bottom this time, he's drawn a dozen.

"You're sorry? For what?" I ask, looking up at him.

"For overreacting." Hayden looks serious. "Not gonna lie. The things you said hurt. They just made me realize that I haven't proven myself to you yet. But I will. I don't want to be the kid who's always in trouble. I want to be the guy who's in the principal's office because I'm doing good things."

I smile back at him. "I'm sorry too. You didn't deserve my accusations." I look down at my journal and back up at Hayden. "I know it wasn't you who did those things to Dave. It was Simone."

"One of the campers?" Hayden asks. "Is that the girl you saved in the lake?"

"Yes, but it was my journal that did this," I tell Hayden, gesturing at my camper's journal. "Simone has been using it. Everything that's happened was my idea. I wrote it in my private thoughts. What am I going to do?" I plop down on my bunk. "Everything is a mess. I'm pretty sure Dave is gone for good and everyone thinks it's my fault. I guess it kind of is because Simone did all of this for me. I'm a horrible camp counselor. And a horrible daughter too. All I wanted was to stay in Seabrook." I blow out a breath.

"Slow down, okay?" Hayden sits on the other side of me. "We'll fix this."

"We?" I look over at him. "You're willing to help me after how I treated you?"

"You can't get rid of me that easily, Pais." He bumps his shoulder to mine. "What do we need to do?"

I think for a moment. "Well, I guess we start by somehow getting my mom and Dave back on speaking terms again." I feel the corners of my mouth lift as an idea unfolds. "I guess now, instead of matchbreakers, you and I need to become matchmakers."

CHAPTER NINETEEN

Camp Time: Wednesday evening. July 27.

I'm waiting in the cabin when all the campers arrive after swimming. They need to shower off before dinner and nightly events at the Birdfeeder.

"Simone, can we talk?" I ask.

Simone looks at me sitting on my bunk. "Yeah. Of course."

"Maybe we can go for a walk?" I look at Tabitha. "Can you be cabin leader while I'm gone?"

Tabitha nods. "Sure."

"Thanks." I stand and head out of the cabin, hoping that Simone will follow me. When we're a couple feet from the cabin, I stop walking and turn to wait for her. She's still in a swimsuit and shorts with her towel draped over her shoulders.

"Everything okay?" she asks, looking worried.

"Not so much. Let's go to the lake." I head down the stone steps, leading her away from listening ears. Once we're out of earshot range from the others, I turn to her. "I know you took my camper's journal. I know you're the one who's been doing those things to Dave."

Simone nearly stumbles over a stone.

I quickly reach out to break her fall, hoping she doesn't feel indebted to me yet again. That's kind of what started this whole mess. Although, I have to take a big chunk of the blame too. If I wasn't so selfish, only thinking of what I needed, wanted, I wouldn't have written those things in my journal. I never would have entertained the idea of breaking Mom and Dave up. "Why did you do those things, Simone?"

She looks at me, suddenly looking young and scared. "I just wanted to help you the way you helped me, that's all. I heard you talking to your friends about what was going on and I saw you writing in that journal of yours. So I took it. I know it was wrong, but when I read it . . ." She shrugs. "I didn't want to hurt Dave. I just wanted him to leave camp so you could be happy. And now he's gone." Simone flashes a shaky victory grin.

"But my mom is miserable and so am I. The thing about journals is that you write your inner thoughts in there, and while it's good to get them out somewhere, sometimes it's best not to let them spill out into your real life." We reach the lake and I drop into a crisscross seated position, patting the ground beside me. Simone sits too. I look out on the water and watch for a moment as a gull sweeps and dips toward the water. "It's just been me and my mom for a long time since my dad died. I guess I didn't realize my mom was lonely because

210

she had me. But I can't fill every area in her life that needs filling. Dave makes her happy, and after all we've been through, she deserves that." I look at Simone.

Simone's eyes are wide and apologetic. "I'm really sorry, Paisley. I was only trying to help."

"I know," I say. "But now I'm asking for your help for real."

"Anything. I'll do whatever you need me to."

The matchmaker plan that Hayden and I came up with in the cabin might not work. That's why we need to talk to Aunt Jenny and Uncle Leon. If we have their backing, we've got a chance. That's our thinking, at least. "I'll let you know, okay? There are a few other pieces that have to fall into place first."

Simone picks at some blades of grass beside her. "Just say the word. I'm here for whatever."

I blow out a breath, hoping that I can undo all my wishes that accidentally came true over the last few days. Maybe wishing on fire embers is luckier than I thought. I wish I would've made better wishes. Better choices.

As Simone and I head back to the cabins, Hayden is waiting for me.

"Did you talk to Uncle Leon?" I ask.

He nods. "He and your aunt are on board. Mission Match-maker is a go."

"Really?" I grin at Hayden, finding him just as adorable as ever. I'm also regretful that I messed things up so much with him. He was my first boyfriend. Did I screw things up so badly that we can't repair what we had? Does it even matter?

Because if this matchmaker plan works, I'm still moving to Wyoming.

"Yep. Your aunt and uncle gave us their permission to leave camp."

"Great," I say. "Meet in one hour?"

Maybe it's my imagination, half longing, half still being caught up in the fantasy of first love, but I think I see something twinkle in Hayden's eyes. The stars aren't out yet, so maybe he still has feelings for me. Maybe one misstep doesn't lead one completely off path.

"Sounds good. The Birdfeeder?" he asks.

"Don't be late," I say.

He laughs quietly, eyes still twinkling and those adorable dimples digging into his cheeks. "If you're there, I'll be early."

***

An hour later, Hayden is already waiting for me at the Birdfeeder when I walk up to meet him.

"You ready?" he asks.

I nod even though I'm so nervous that I can't stop fidgeting. "Dave might be pretty mad at me," I say. "I have no idea what's going through his head right now."

"That's why you and I are going to see him together. To explain everything." Hayden offers me his hand.

I look at it for a moment. I'm still not quite sure where we stand. Are we friends? More? I take his hand and he gives mine a small squeeze.

"I'm driving," he says. "Your uncle gave me the go-ahead as long as I promised to drive the speed limit the entire way there and back."

I grin. "You do have a license, right?"

"Of course I do. And I'll have you know that I'm an excellent driver. You are completely safe with me." He leads me through the camp to where the parking lot is. I feel completely safe with him too. And I know Dave is a great guy. No matter if he's upset with me, he'll still hear us out. I owe him an explanation. And I owe it to my mom to fix what I've royally messed up this summer.

When we get to the parking lot, there are three cars, a truck, and one motorcycle with a canvas covering it.

"Which one is yours?" I ask. "Please tell me it's not the motorcycle, because my uncle would kill you."

Hayden waggles his brows and my stomach drops for a second. Then he laughs. "Just kidding. I'm not old enough to have a motorcycle license. I've looked into it. The dinged-up Toyota is mine."

I expel a breath. "Phew. You get to live."

"That's good because I want to see this whole mission with you through to the end." He walks around to the passenger door, unlocks it, and opens it for me. Would he do that if we were just friends?

I dip into the seat and he closes the door behind me. Then I watch as he jogs around and gets behind the steering wheel.

"You're sure we shouldn't call first?" I ask nervously.

"I think the element of surprise will work in our favor," Hayden says. "If Dave knows we're coming over, he could get worked up for whatever reason. It's best if he's caught off guard and only has a chance to listen at first." Hayden cranks his car and pulls out of the parking lot.

"What if he's not home?" I ask.

"Then we call," Hayden says.

"What if—"

Hayden slides his gaze over. "Relax, Pais. We'll be there in thirty minutes. We don't need a Plan B, C, or D unless we're sure that Plan A is a bust."

"Right. You're right." I wring my hands in my lap. "And Plan A is to knock on Dave's door and be honest."

"Just tell him how sorry you are and how miserable your mom is without him," Hayden suggests.

I pull in a breath and then turn to look at Hayden. "Thanks for coming with me. I wouldn't want to do this alone."

"You probably could have convinced Nora to tag along with you."

"But it wouldn't be the same. I'm glad it's you."

Hayden looks at me again. Not for too long because he's driving. And he really is a good driver. My Uncle Leon would be pleased. "You're welcome. I'm glad to be your partner in crime."

I laugh softly. "Or crime undoing. I just hope Dave loves my mom as much as I think he does. I hope he's willing to fight for what he and Mom have and not throw it away over some stupid argument that was all my fault."

Hayden opens and closes his fingers around the steering wheel. He's quiet for a moment, but then finally says, "When

I was younger, and me and my brother, Raidon, argued, my mom would force us to sit together on this oversize recliner in our living room. It was torture." He slides a hand through his hair, gaze directed on the road outside the windshield.

This is only Hayden's fourth mention of having a brother. I know he lives with his mom and that his dad is MIA. "You don't talk about Raidon a lot. Is he older or younger than you?"

Hayden doesn't answer immediately, and I feel this invisible pressure close in around us. "Mom called us Irish twins. We were eleven months apart so a lot of people thought we were actual twins."

My brain is still trying to solve the mystery. "Did your dad take Raidon with him when he left?"

"No, my dad left after Raidon died." Hayden says it as normally as one might say they had a ham sandwich for lunch with lettuce and tomato, rye bread, no pickles.

My heart sinks. "I'm so sorry, Hayden. I didn't know," I say quietly.

"How would you?" He pulls in a quick breath. "I was eight and he was nine when it happened. My dad ran a stop sign and the whole world stopped after that. For a while at least." He glances over and his eyes have a little shine to them. He visibly swallows, making his Adam's apple shift up and down. "When you first told me about your dad, I realized that's why you always felt so familiar to me, even though we're universes apart. We've both lost people who were pretty much our whole worlds."

Hayden's truth hits me like a stack of bricks. "I know

exactly what you're talking about. Even when I thought we had nothing in common, I always felt like I somehow knew you. Like we were friends even when you were the last person I'd ever want to hang with."

He laughs, which eases the heavy tension in the air between us.

"Is that why your dad left?"

Hayden lifts a shoulder. "Mom and I didn't get to pack up and leave the pain and grief behind us. We stuck around and worked through it. I mean, yeah, I'm a bit of a punk. Or I was until you."

My heart does this triple-beat thing that makes my thoughts swirl around in my head. I can't think straight for a moment. "I'm sorry about Raidon. And about your dad too." I reach out and grab his hand, giving it a small squeeze. If we weren't driving, I'd give him a huge hug.

"Thanks," he says. "I don't really talk about Raidon to others anymore."

"I'm glad you talked about him to me," I say quietly.

His gaze slides to meet mine for a millisecond. "Me too."

We drive in silence for a moment after that. Then I realize that Hayden has pulled onto Dave's street. Dave only lives about five minutes from my house. Mom could have run into him at any time, but she had to find him on a dating website. What are the odds?

Hayden drives all the way to the end and turns into Dave's driveway. He cuts the engine in front of a small brick ranch-style home. There's a For Sale sign in the front yard because Dave is moving in a couple weeks, with or without us.

"Dave's truck is here so it appears that Plan A will suffice." Hayden looks at me and offers his hand across the center console. "I'm pretty sure he loves your mom as much as you think, Pais. So let's go convince him to come back to camp."

CHAPTER TWENTY

Dave looks like the walking dead.

I wave as he peers from inside his house at us standing on his porch.

"What are you doing here? Is everything okay?" he asks. He's wearing a Seabrook High School T-shirt with stains down the front. Just a guess, but I'd say he's been drowning his sorrows in chocolate ice cream. "Is your mom all right?"

"Oh, yeah. She's fine," I say. "Well, I mean, she's not fine. She looks about as bad as you do, which is pretty awful."

Hayden elbows me softly.

I grimace. "Um, sorry. Can we come in?"

Dave opens the door wider, gesturing us inside his home. I've been in Dave's house a few times before, but I never stayed for very long. It was usually when I came with my mom to get or to do something. "Have a seat." He motions toward his brown suede couch while he takes the recliner beside it. Once we're all seated, he looks at us expectantly.

When I say that Dave appears like a zombie, what I mean is he looks like he hasn't slept in a month. I know he only left camp twenty hours ago so it hasn't been that long. I doubt he slept well the night he bunked with poison ivy either. The poor guy has had it rough, no thanks to me. "So, I came here because I need to tell you something. To confess."

Dave doesn't look surprised by this. But of course he doesn't. That's why he and my mom probably broke up to begin with. Like everyone else, Dave probably thinks I'm the one who rigged his kayak and put poison ivy leaves in his bed. The one who pitched that rogue tennis ball in his direction.

"Okay," Dave says. "If you have something to get off your chest, I'm all ears."

"All those things that happened to you at camp this week and last are my fault," I say.

I note the tiny look of surprise in Dave's eyes. Maybe I was wrong about what he thought. "You did all that stuff, Paisley?" Hurt lines his words.

"No." I shake my head quickly. "I didn't literally do those things. Not the ones that happened this week, at least." Last week's mischief is a different story.

Now Dave looks confused. He casts a look at Hayden as if pleading for a little help.

Hayden just reaches for my hand and squeezes. I like the way he does that. It's like a hug for the hand, a gentle nudge to keep going. Don't turn back. Be strong. Persevere.

"I wanted you and my mom to break up, though." My voice comes out shaky. "Because if you broke up, then we wouldn't have to move to Wyoming or sell Camp Starling. Hayden and I tried to make you miserable last week so that you would leave. And we thought maybe if you were miserable enough and left, my mom would see that you didn't belong with us."

Dave flinches softly and looks at Hayden. "Hayden?"

"Nothing against you," Hayden explains. "I was just trying to help Pais. It seemed like a good idea at the time." Hayden lowers his head. "Sorry, Dave."

"I did put honey in your sunblock last week," I confess. "But I only wanted to attract bugs. Not bees."

"I see," Dave says a bit disappointedly.

"But all the stuff that happened to you this week—the kayak, the flyaway ball, and the poison ivy—I didn't do those things," I say quickly. "I wrote about wanting to rig your kayak in my camper's journal, but I would never actually go that far. I couldn't. Someone took my journal." I spare Simone's name.

"But you wanted those things to happen to me?" Dave asks with a shake of his head. "I stood up for you, Paisley. When your mom said she'd heard rumors that maybe you'd put the poison ivy in my bed, I defended you. She thought maybe it was true and she wanted to bring you to her cabin to question you, but I told her no. I told her you might not like me very much, but that you were her daughter and you were better than that."

"You did?" Now I'm the surprised one.

"I know we have a lot of room to grow, Paisley, but to wish things like that on me . . . You must really hate me to do that."

"That's not true." My eyes are burning. "I don't hate you. I don't like moving. I don't like selling the camp. I don't like change," I say as more tears fill my eyes. "I just want things to stay the way they are. Or, at least, that's what I thought I wanted." I feel Hayden's palm against mine. "Now I realize that things can't stay the same now that you've come into our lives. If you leave without us, my mom will be devastated. I wasn't thinking about her or you. I was only thinking about myself."

Dave looks at me for a long moment, seeming to process all that I've told him. "I'm glad you told me. It's also reassuring that you could only think those things and not actually do them to me. That proves me right about you."

"Is that why you and my mom broke up?" I ask.

"Your mom thought you were doing those things to me and I didn't." Hurt flashes in his eyes. "Your mom cares about you too much to force this new life on you if you don't want it. To force me on you, if you don't want me. She said she loved me, but she couldn't go through with something that was going to turn you into someone she didn't recognize." Dave blows out a breath. "I don't want that either. You're a good kid, Paisley. The world can change. Life can change. But you shouldn't change who you are. Ever."

A tear slips down my cheek. My emotions are gushing, like the dam that's supposed to hold them in has sprung a leak. "You're not my dad," I say, chin quivering. "My dad was amazing. He was my hero and I miss him every single day." Hayden's hand holds mine tightly. "And if I had to choose a boyfriend for my mom, I don't think I would have chosen you," I say honestly.

Dave listens quietly.

"But now that I know you," I continue, "now that you've come into my life, I can't imagine a better choice for my mom. Or for me." I swallow thickly. "You have to come back to camp, Dave. You have to fight for my mom. You have to make up."

Dave's eyes are smiling and making little lines veer off at the corners. "You're sure that's what you want?"

I nod without hesitation. "Change can be a good thing." Those aren't my aunt's words. Those are mine now because I believe them. "So, Hayden and I have a plan. And my aunt and uncle too. It's called Mission Matchmaker. If you're game for winning my mom back, we'd like to help."

"Can't I just go back to camp and have a talk with her?" Dave asks.

To this, I smile. "Yes. But it's all about timing in romance." And I need to talk to my mom first. I need her to know that it's okay. That I'll be okay. I lean forward and look at Dave. "Here's the plan."

⁂

When we leave Dave's house, Hayden drives us back to camp. We're mostly quiet, spent from our confessional with Dave. There's also the knowing between us that if Dave can woo my mom back into his good graces tomorrow, I'll be moving to Wyoming. When Hayden finally reaches the parking lot of Camp Starling, we get out and walk back toward the Birdfeeder.

"You're one of those people, you know," Hayden says.

"One of what people?" I turn my head to glance at him. In the moonlight, his skin seems a bright contrast against his dark hair. The color of his eyes, a bright coppery brown, seems to stand out.

"The kind that changes a person whether they want to be changed or not. That's exactly what happened to me."

"Sorry?" It comes out as a question because I'm not sure if this is a bad thing or not.

"Stop apologizing. I'm the one who should be telling you I'm sorry, Pais. I guess I'm a little defensive after all these years. I'm always waiting for people to think the worst of me. You didn't deserve that."

"I did, though. The things I said to you . . ."

Hayden reaches for my hand as we walk under the stars. I know I keep bringing up the starry night, but it's romantic. A shock of electricity rides through my nerves, rewiring my heart. "If this matchmaking mission of ours works, you're moving this summer."

I don't breathe.

"If it doesn't, I guess you'll be staying. It's hard to root for us to win tomorrow because that's also rooting for us to lose. If that makes sense."

"Yeah. I understand what you mean."

He looks up at the stars. "What are the odds we'll see another falling star tonight?"

"Not likely," I say on a tiny laugh.

He looks down at me. "What are the odds we'll kiss again?"

I roll my lips together, heart stuck somewhere between my chest and my throat. "The odds are pretty good, I'd say."

He smiles, dimples digging in his cheeks. "Good to know. I'll walk you to your cabin."

My legs feel a little shaky. I doubt I'll be able to breathe or think the entire walk back for anticipating the kiss that is likely to happen under the starry night sky.

"Whatever happens tomorrow . . . ," Hayden says, but he doesn't finish the sentence. Maybe he doesn't need to. Maybe we just have to figure it out as we go along.

❋

As I lie in my bunk later that night, after a good-night kiss that makes my small world grow larger, I pull my camper's journal out from beneath my bunk, where I returned it after talking to Simone. I hesitate to write in it, after having my deepest thoughts invaded, but Simone has promised to never touch my journal again. I think once I'm back to my real home, I'm going to get a diary with a lock and a key, just for added security.

I pull out my purple gel pen, suck in a deep breath while collecting my thoughts, and begin to write.

Dear Journal,
  The first kiss was a sky full of stars. The
second one was an entire universe. The goal has
shifted from doing anything to stay in Seabrook, to

putting myself and my mom back on track to move to Wyoming with Dave.

Yeah, I want to stay, more than anything. I want to keep seeing Hayden. I just found him and I like him an impossible amount. I didn't even know I could like someone this way. It feels like magic that he likes me too, because I've had crushes before that never gave me a second glance. When Hayden looks deep into my eyes, though, I feel like I'm the only person in the whole world. If that's the way Dave makes my mom feel, who am I to ruin it?

So tomorrow is game on. It's Have-a-Ball Day here at Camp Starling. My dad came up with that theme. Tomorrow is all about every ball sport imaginable. We put up volleyball nets, Ping-Pong tables, basketball poles, everything. This year, tomorrow is also about getting Mom and Dave back together, where they belong. We'll have to wait until dark, of course. Because . . . stars.

CHAPTER TWENTY-ONE

Camp Time: Thursday morning. July 28.

Have-a-Ball Day was not my dad's best camp idea. Ball sports have always kind of freaked me out. It might have something to do with my slow reflexes or my tendency to freeze like a deer in headlights when faced with a volleyball, tennis ball, soccer ball, etc., coming at my face. The campers seem to be enjoying themselves, though. Everyone has been assigned to a group for today, and they start in one ball sport but switch after an hour.

"I'm so glad I'm a counselor this year," I say more to myself than Nora, who is standing beside me.

She laughs. "So you don't have to play?"

"No black eyes for me this time," I confirm.

"You've only had a black eye from a ball twice that I remember." She taps a pointer finger to her chin.

"But a football once hit me in the hip. That left a shiner and it counts," I say.

She shakes her head. "I can't believe this place is shutting down. Can't your mom just keep it and come back over the summers?"

I sigh. "We had a heart-to-heart yesterday morning. Apparently, the camp is a lot of responsibility. Mom rents the camp out to various groups during the year. She has to manage upkeep and maintenance." I shrug a shoulder. "I guess I didn't realize it was such a burden on her. It's time-consuming and costly. If she doesn't book the campground and cabins a certain number of weeks per year, she can't cover the bills."

Nora adjusts the ball cap on her head. "I had no idea."

"I didn't know the half of it either. I've just been living in my own little bubble, thinking everything was perfect."

Nora hums softly. "That's how I felt when my parents decided to get a divorce. Even though they argued all the time, I kind of assumed that was normal. I was happy so I figured they must be too."

"Yeah," I say. "I've always kind of been so proud of being a straight-A student who never gets in trouble. But that didn't mean I was perfect. If someone would have given me a test on my mom and how she was doing, I would have failed. I've been a little self-centered and didn't even know it."

"I'm still self-centered," Nora says. "I know it, but I guess you've inspired me to maybe try to be less that way. You're taking the lead and I'm following this time." Her smile turns into a frown. "What will I do next school year without you?"

"You have other friends."

"Yeah, but none who would put up with all my flaws and

attitude and spoiledness the way you do. I'll never have another friend like you, Paisley."

"Well, you don't need another one like me because I'm not
dying," I say, trying to lighten the mood. "And maybe you can
come to Wyoming next summer to see me."

Nora doesn't look enthused. "Or you can come here and
stay with me. We can get into all kinds of shenanigans. And
you can see Hayden."

I'm so glad she's not crushing on him anymore. She got
over him fast, which means she must not have even liked him
all that much. He was just the chosen one to spend her attention on this summer. Nora needs a chosen one every summer.

Speaking of crushes, Hayden walks over and stands beside
me. He bumps his shoulder against mine and my heart skips
around helplessly in my chest.

"You two are kind of cute together," Nora says.

"If there's anything cute about us, it's all Pais." Hayden
glances over at me.

I hear Nora say "Aww," but I'm too flustered to react. I
want to tell Hayden that's not true. That he's so cute, so smart,
so everything I never knew I wanted in a first boyfriend. Instead, I just smile and wish we were alone so I could kiss him.

"Hey, guys!" someone calls behind us.

We all turn as Dave comes walking over. In broad daylight.
And he's wearing one of his tie-dyed camp T-shirts.

"What are you doing here?" I ask, walking toward him,
slightly panicked.

He looks at me like I have two heads. "You invited me

228

here last night. I'm here to make up with your mom. Mission Matchmaker, remember?"

"Yeah, of course I do, but if she sees you now, you'll ruin the surprise," I say, panicking.

"I wanted to talk to you first." Dave rubs a hand along the back of his neck.

I really hope he hasn't changed his mind about wanting to get back together with Mom. "We talked things out last night," I tell him. "I'm okay with you and my mom. I'll be okay with the move too."

Dave pulls in a breath. It lifts his chest a couple inches in the air. "Good, good. It's just, you know that your mom and I have been discussing marriage."

"Mm-hmm." I look around to make sure my mom is nowhere in sight. This is supposed to be a surprise.

"Well," Dave says, "after camp this week, I was planning on giving her a ring."

My gaze cuts to his and my mouth falls open. "A diamond ring?" I clarify.

Dave's face is red and not from the stacked sunburns he's gotten over the last week and a half. He reaches into his pocket and pulls out a small black box. I have a feeling I know what's inside. Slowly, Dave lifts the lid and reveals a ring with a circular diamond that glimmers under the bright sun. It's simple, but sometimes the best things are.

"Wow," I say, unable to take my eyes off it. Tiny rainbows of color wink at me as he moves the box slightly.

"It was my grandmother's," Dave tells me, putting the lid

back on and shoving it into his pocket. "I wanted to ask your permission first. I don't want to do anything you're not ready for, Paisley. This is about me and your mom, but it's also about me and you. That's the way it's gotta be if we're going to make this work, right?"

After a moment, Hayden clears his throat beside me. I guess I've been quiet for too long.

"Right," I finally say. "Yeah." I smile to myself, surprised that I'm not a bit freaked out. "You're going to propose tonight?" I ask.

"I was thinking about it. Sounds like you all are setting the stage for us. It'll be perfect timing for me, don't you think?"

"It'll be a night she'll never forget." I swallow thickly. "You should definitely ask my mom tonight, Dave. There'll be candlelight and stars. It'll be amazing."

Dave narrows his eyes. "So I have your blessing?"

"You're technically supposed to get the blessing from my mom's dad," I say. "But that's a bit old-fashioned."

Dave nods. "And it's your blessing I really want."

I'm shocked and completely humbled. "Yes. I want you to ask her."

Dave grins. Then he shakes his hands down by his side. From the corner of my eye I see Aunt Jenny rushing toward us. She's looking around too, no doubt to make sure my mom isn't going to see Dave before the big surprise—which just got a little bit—or a lot—bigger.

"Dave!" Aunt Jenny says. "Come on, let's get you fixed up for tonight." She gives me a wink. Part of the plan is sprucing

Dave up from his usual long shorts and oversize tie-dyed T-shirt. Mission Matchmaker involves a makeover for Dave. He and my Uncle Leon are roughly the same size.

"Fixed up, how? Please tell me this doesn't involve poison ivy or calamine lotion," Dave teases.

Always teasing. And you know what, it doesn't really annoy me as much anymore.

"Just a suit and tie," I tell him. "Trust me. You're going to look like a million bucks."

"But we better get you somewhere out of sight," Aunt Jenny says, taking Dave's arm. It's still bumpy and red from the poison-ivy fiasco.

I stay to continue supervising the campers. Nora branches off to go help with one of the games. I think she's really just making herself scarce so I can be alone with Hayden. I watch as she joins Jacob nearby.

Hayden reaches for my hand and holds it. "No turning back now. Mission Matchmaker is a go. And assuming your mom says yes, you're going to have a stepdad in your future." I squeeze his hand and then look out on the lake.

"She'll say yes. She'd be crazy not to. And I actually think my dad would be happy to know my mom has found someone else to make her happy. I think he'd like Dave."

Hayden squeezes my hand back. "Do you think he would have liked me? Or would he have thought I was some punk kid who sprayed green paint all over his cabins?"

I take a second to think about this. "I guess that's one way that he and Dave are kind of alike. I think my dad would have thought that was a punk move, spray-painting the cabins, but he probably would have insisted you join us at Camp Starling, just like Dave."

As ball sports go on all around us, we just talk. About my dad and his brother. The future. Hayden wants to go to art school. I want to study wildlife. Maybe I'll run a camp one day too. The more Hayden opens up to me, the more he surprises me at every turn. I fall a little more with every shared look and soft kiss. He's in the middle of telling me about his dog back home when I hear someone shout, "Heads up!"

I turn in the direction of the voice too late and stumble back as a soccer ball hits me square in the face. If my left eye were the goal, that kicker would have scored.

Hayden steadies me while I clutch my eye and groan.

"Oww!"

"You okay?" Hayden asks.

I crack my unaffected eye to look at him. "If there's such a thing as karma, it just hit me. Ice. I need ice."

He grimaces. "Yeah, that's going to be a shiner for sure."

"It wouldn't be camp without one. Did I mention that I don't like Have-a-Ball Day?"

This makes him smile. "I thought you loved everything about Camp Starling."

"Except that." I remove my hand slowly. "I need to wear armor on this camp day. I'm like a ball magnet."

Hayden gives my hand a tug. "Let's go to the first-aid station and get you some ice. And get you as far away from the ball sports as possible. Besides, if karma was behind that rogue ball, it's coming after me next."

Camp Time: Thursday night. July 28.

It's firefly o'clock. That's what my dad used to call it when the fireflies start lighting up. The moon is even visible now.

With the help of my aunt Jenny and Simone, we've set up a picnic table by the lake. Aunt Jenny brought a beautiful white tablecloth from home. Simone places it on and I add a small vase of fresh wildflowers, courtesy of Hayden, who picked them earlier down by the woods.

Simone taps a finger to her lip. "Hmm. It's too bad we can't play a little music. To set the mood."

I look at her thoughtfully and then pull out my cellphone. "I have the perfect playlist." I bring up my music app and a soft tune begins to hum through the air just as Dave heads toward us. He's wearing a black suit and a canary yellow tie.

He holds his arms out to his sides. "Well. How do I look?" he asks.

I take a moment to assess him. The calamine lotion is gone. The sunburn has faded. There are a lot of words that I can use to describe Dave, but the most prominent is "Nice."

Dave lowers his arms. "I passed your aunt and Hayden with the food on the way down here. They've outdone themselves."

The menu tonight is fresh fish from a nearby market and roasted and seasoned vegetables. Simone and I already prepared the sweet tea and also a dessert—assuming Mom allows things to progress to dessert.

"What do you want me to do?" Dave asks.

Simone pulls out a chair. "Sit here," she says.

"And leave the rest to us," I add.

"All that's left is for me to go get Mom." I turn and head toward Eagle Cabin. Hayden offered to come with me, but I want to do this alone. There's something I need to tell her before her romantic dinner with Dave.

I pull in a breath and knock on the door of Eagle Cabin. When she opens it, her mouth drops and her eyes round.

"Paisley! What happened?" she exclaims.

I have no clue what she's talking about at first—I'm too focused on the night's events—but then I remember my bruised eye. "Oh. Yeah. A soccer ball. I have to admit, I won't miss the annual Have-a-Ball Day."

Mom smiles at me as her shoulders relax by her side. "Well, I haven't put the camp up for sale just yet. Who knows? Maybe your luck will change and you'll get your wish to stay in Seabrook."

I pull in a breath and blow it out. "That's why I came to talk to you, Mom. I need to apologize for being such a brat lately. It wasn't fair for me to make you or Dave feel guilty about your plans to move. I'm really sorry."

"You don't have to be sorry." My mom clears her throat and then narrows her eyes. "Do you?"

"I didn't tip his kayak or put poison ivy in his bed, if that's what you're asking. But the things that happened to him were partly my fault." I roll my lips together. "Then I realized that, yes, our family was fine before Dave, but it won't be fine if I force him out. You'll be heartbroken and miserable, and I'll feel guilty and responsible. There's no going back to the way things were."

My mom shakes her head. "That's the thing about life, Birdie. It moves forward, no going back, no matter how much we want it to."

She's right. I don't know how often I've wished I could go back to when my dad was here. When our family was complete. "I also realized that I don't dislike Dave," I tell her. "I actually kind of like him."

"Well, Dave and I are on a little bit of a break right now," my mom says as tears flood her eyes.

"But you don't want to be. And I'm sure he doesn't either. He's crazy about you, Mom."

She shrugs. "You are the most important person in my life. I need to apologize to you as well if I made you feel differently. I always want to know your thoughts and opinions. They matter. *You* matter. If being with Dave makes you miserable—"

I hold up my hand and stop her mid-sentence. "That's what I'm trying to tell you. I was wrong. And all I know is you and Dave have to make up. Tonight."

She blinks away her tears. "Tonight? He's not even here."

"Actually, he is. And he's waiting for you right now."

"What?" Her eyes widen.

I drop my gaze to look at what she's wearing—a yellow shirt and olive green shorts. That won't do. "So you should probably change for dinner."

"Dinner?" she asks.

"And since this is camp and I'm sure you didn't pack anything nice, Aunt Jenny is lending you a dress."

"A dress?" My mom looks completely baffled. Who ever heard of wearing a dress at camp? "Paisley, what's going on?"

"I already told you. You and Dave are making up. You're having dinner tonight, and in two weeks, as planned, we're moving to Wyoming. Maybe we can't go back, but we can fix our mistakes. And tonight, I'm fixing mine."

CHAPTER TWENTY-TWO

Simone and I play hostess for my mom and Dave's meal, serving their food and lighting the candle at the center of their table.

My mom looks gorgeous! I mean, a little black dress and lipstick go a long way. Plus, she is smiling bigger than I've seen in forever. Dave cleans up nicely in a suit and tie too. I wish I could stay to watch their dinner unfold and see Dave propose. *Gah*, I just hope he doesn't fumble the ring or something like that. The man isn't exactly graceful, but he loves my mom. That's as clear as tonight's sky.

Simone turns to me as we leave on the shore. "I'm going back to Chickadee Cabin," she says. "But you're staying here."

I furrow my brow. I'm the one making the night's plans. What does she know that I don't? "What?"

Simone points toward the Birdfeeder. "Hayden is waiting for you over there. I've been instructed to send you in that direction. I'll make sure the lights go out in our cabin at nine-thirty."

I feel a little flutter in my chest. "Why does Hayden want me to meet him over there?"

Simone shrugs, but the smile on her face tells me she knows exactly the reason. "Guess you'll have to walk over there and find out." She turns to head down the path toward the girls' cabins.

"Simone?"

"Yeah?" She turns back to me.

"Thanks."

"You're welcome."

I watch her leave and then set my sights on the Birdfeeder. I can't see Hayden or what he might be doing from here so I start to walk, hoping my mom and Dave are having a good time. As I draw closer to the Birdfeeder, I see Hayden sitting at a picnic table. There are two plates of food. One in front of him and another at the spot across from him. At the center of the table, there's a candle with a small flame flickering in the slight breeze. He turns to look at me and his eyes seem to light up.

I swallow. "What's all this?"

Hayden stands and gestures at the empty spot. "It's a candlelight dinner for two. For us."

He's wearing a T-shirt that has a picture of a tux on it. I slide onto the bench and sit, glancing down at the meal. It's the exact meal that my mom and Dave are enjoying right now. "This looks delicious. Thank you for doing this."

Hayden sits again and looks across the table at me. "I figured we hadn't officially had a first date yet, so . . ."

"First and last date," I say, swallowing for a moment. To-night is bittersweet. "Assuming tonight goes as planned."

"Let's not think of what happens after tonight, okay? Let's just enjoy the moment. And the stars." He winks at me.

I look up. "Did you arrange any shooting stars for to-night?" I ask, tipping my head as I return my gaze to his.

He chuckles. "Nah. I didn't want to become predictable or anything."

This makes me laugh. "You are anything but predictable, Hayden Bennett." I pick up my fork.

"I could say the same about you, Pais. You're full of sur-prises. The good kind."

It's the best first date a girl could ever want. Complete with heart flutters, stolen breaths, and dreamy eye gazes. I hope Mom and Dave are having half as much romance as me and Hayden. If they are, then there's no way my mom will say no to Dave's proposal.

Hayden and I are in the middle of dessert when we hear a woman's squeal coming from the direction of the lake where Mom and Dave are sitting. We look at each other, eyes wide. "Was that a happy squeal or should we run to help your mom?" Hayden asks.

"I think it was a happy noise. I think she just said yes to Dave." Tears sting my eyes.

"Are those happy tears or sad ones?" Hayden asks, reach-ing for my hand.

I pull in a breath, wondering at my answer. "Both."

Dear Journal,

Mom said yes My life is about to change in so many ways. It won't be easy, but I'll be okay.

That's all for tonight. I'm too tired to think or wonder about all the unknowns in my future. I'll think and wonder about them all tomorrow. One thing I know for sure, my matchbreaker days are over. Matchmaking is a lot more fun.

I leave my purple gel pen in my journal, close it, and shove it beneath my bunk. Then I force my breaths to come out slow and easy. I need to remain calm. I'm a camp counselor, after all, even if I'm afraid I haven't set the best example. There are some things I wish I would have done differently. And now with only one full day left, it seems like it's too late to redeem myself.

"Paisley?" Simone's voice whispers to me in the darkness.

I open my eyes. "Hmm?"

"I'm really sorry for taking your journal." I hear her shallow breaths and suspect she's on the verge of tears too.

"You've already apologized. I've forgiven you."

"I know, but I'm worried that I messed things up for you. You've been so nice to me."

I sit up in my bunk and stare across the cabin into the darkness, willing my eyes to adjust. I see Simone on her bottom bunk across the room. I walk over and sit down next to her so we don't wake the others up.

"It's okay, Simone. Why are you crying?"

She shrugs. "I don't know. Camp is almost over and I'm

not ready to leave, I guess. I've had such a great time here. Once I return home to Clifton, I'm worried I'll just go back to being the shy girl with no friends. I have friends now."

I wrap my arm around her. "You won't go back. You are new and improved, and more confident. You are a Starling, and don't you forget it."

Simone sucks in a shaky breath. She sniffles and nods. "I'm a Starling," she repeats.

"I'm a Starling," Maddie says from the bunk nearby.

I look up and smile. Then I hear several other girls say the same thing.

"We are Chickadee Cabin Starlings," I add, "and that's a whole new beast."

The girls all repeat after me. Then we laugh, filling the cabin air with the sounds that camp should be made of. We talk well into the night, exchanging stories, hopes, dreams, fears. It's the end of two weeks, but it feels like we're just getting started. Like we're suddenly a sisterhood. The Chickadee Cabin Sisterhood.

"I'm going to miss you all," I say when I'm finally back in my bunk, my head sunk into my pillow. The girls all promised to return next summer, but I kept my mouth shut. The fact that this is Camp Starling's last hurrah is still a secret to the campers. I wonder if Simone knows since she read my journal, or if she somehow missed that little detail. If she knows, she hasn't spread the word. For tonight, these girls are all sleeping well on the hope that they can reunite here same time next summer. I don't want to take that away from them.

Camp Time: Friday morning. July 29.

I arrive to Campers' Breakfast, where Mom and Dave have already started preparing the food. Dave is making large stacks of pancakes alongside my Uncle Leon. Mom is smiling while cooking alongside Aunt Jenny.

I stop and watch, taking in the scene from afar before they notice me. It appears that my mom and Dave have made up and that things are back to normal. As I walked down the stone path, I had wondered if I'd be in trouble from all my admissions. But if they made up and got engaged, maybe not. Maybe everyone is just so happy that all is forgotten.

"Hey." Hayden comes beside me, leaning in close so that his face is next to my ear. His breath warms my cheek. "What's going on?"

I swallow past the rush of endorphins I get at being this close to him. "Mission Matchmaker was a huge success." I turn to him, finding my face closer to his than I expected. His brown eyes have golden flecks from the sun this morning.

He smiles at me, hesitating a moment before stepping back. It's not a good time for a kiss with my family in eyeshot range. I want to kiss him, though. For one, I want to celebrate yesterday's wins. For two, I'm feeling our time together start to diminish and I don't want to waste a second. I want to memorize his face, his smile, the way his hand feels holding mine. I want to memorize his kiss so that when I'm all alone and miserable in Wyoming, I can at least lie in bed and think of that.

"Are we going to help them with breakfast or not?" he asks.

"They haven't seen us yet. Maybe we should just sneak off and skip. There's a secret stash of granola bars if they run out of food," I say.

Hayden grins. "You were so adamantly against that for Campers' Breakfast last week."

"Yeah, well, things change."

He smiles and reaches for my hand. "Okay, come on. We better hurry before we get spotted." We turn and jog down the path.

"You are a bad influence," I say on a laugh.

"Wait. Not helping with breakfast was totally your idea just now." He stops and turns to me.

"I still blame you." I laugh as I continue in the direction of the lake. It's early. The campers are still in their cabins. They haven't woken yet and when they do, they'll be heading down to the Bird Bath and then the Birdfeeder. They know the drill. "Wanna go for a swim?"

"Now? You're not in a suit," he notes.

"So? I'm in shorts and a shirt. It's good enough. What do you say?"

Hayden lifts a brow. "Isn't it against the rules to swim alone?"

Since when does Hayden care about rules? "We're not alone. We have each other." Without waiting, I jog ahead toward the water, kicking off my shoes and leaving them on the shore.

"You're crazy, Pais."

I turn back and tilt my head. "That's kind of music to my ears. I have always been too normal. Too goody-two-shoes. Too—"

"Stop right there." He heads toward me, kicking off his graffitied shoes to rest beside mine and then joining me with his feet in the water. "Everything you've ever been was amazing. But it's okay to want to be different too."

I tip my head back to look up at him. "Yeah. I think my dad would have really liked you."

"What about you? Do you like me?" he asks, his voice low, just for me.

I step toward him. "Mm-hmm. So are you going to swim with me or not?"

He glances past me toward the water. "Today's the boys against the girls, right?"

"Yep."

One corner of his mouth kicks up and I see that familiar mischievous spark light his eyes. I turn and start running because I know exactly what he's thinking before he says it— and, counselor or not, there's no way I'm losing any of the games today.

※

At midday my mom steps up beside me and waves her left hand in front of me, showing off her diamond ring.

"I'm happy for you and Dave," I tell her for the twentieth time today.

"Do you mean that?" she asks.

I lean in and give her a huge hug. "Of course I do, Mom. Dave is a great guy."

She looks pleased. She's also beaming like someone turned a flashlight on inside her. The light is radiating out. "Thank you, Birdie. That means a lot to me." She watches the water where the campers are currently racing kayaks. It's the boys against the girls today in competition for the Starling Trophy. Last year the boys won, but so far today, the girls are ruling by a long shot.

"I'm so lucky to have you for a daughter."

"How can you say that after what I did? I have been awful lately, especially to Dave."

My mom puts her arm around me and pulls me in. "What kind of talk is that? You're my daughter. Your dad's daughter. And Dave is looking forward to having you as his stepdaughter one day."

"He really is a saint after all he's been through these last two weeks."

My mom squeezes me tightly against her side. "I'm sorry that you have to leave your friends, your school, your boyfriend." She side-eyes me and I feel my cheeks burn. "We'll return to visit your aunt and uncle, though. You can see Hayden and Nora. All of your friends."

"I know."

"And you'll make new friends. And meet new boys."

I don't respond to that. Hayden is my first boyfriend and I really can't imagine ever feeling the same way about anyone. I know that's probably me being dramatic, but it's how I feel.

Cheers ring out on the lake as the girls secure the victory for the current task.

"This really has been a great camp. Maybe the best ever," I say, surprising myself. I didn't think it would be possible to think that last week, but it's true. Things happen fast on camp time. Feelings changed, relationships changed, and so did I.

"And it's not over yet." My mom tugs me against her once more. "We still have the big end-of-camp bonfire tonight. We'll celebrate the winners of the day. I also have a special announcement."

"Other than the fact that you're marrying Dave?" I ask.

"Yep. There's more." She winks at me from the side.

I'm pretty sure I know what the announcement is. Mom is planning to tell everyone that Camp Starling is closing. That this summer was the last before the proverbial doors shut forever.

At least it'll be a relief not to have to keep that under wraps. I'm tired of keeping secrets. They always come out in the end.

☀

The last task of the Camp Starling Guys and Girls Day is the ropes course. For the first time in Camp Starling history, the campers gathered and consulted with my mom, Dave, Aunt Jenny, and Uncle Leon to flip the tables on us counselors.

It's still the guys against the girls, but instead of campers, it's the counselors who are competing against each other!

"Uh-oh. Your competitive streak is showing," Nora teases as we congregate in front of the course.

The rules of this task are easy. We make a line and when the horn sounds, the first persons in line—one guy and one girl—take off, navigating the ropes course as fast as they can. When they reach the end, they sound the buzzer for the next person to get started. The first team to go through, whether it be the guys or girls, wins the task.

The guys and girls are currently tied for the day, so it all comes down to this.

"Paisley, you're last in line," Nora says, bossy as usual.

I fold my arms over my chest. "Why?"

"Because you're the most competitive. You'll do whatever it takes to pick up any slack if needed. And that's what we need. We need to win," she says.

I smile at Nora. Bossy or not, she's always been a good friend. She's a great leader too. "Okay. I'll be last. You go first. Let's win this."

Nora takes her place at the front of the line. She's partnered alongside Jacob, which hardly seems fair. Jacob is a football player. He's fast and determined. Nora casts him a hard glare. "I'm not going easy on you, Jacob," she calls to him.

To this, he laughs. "I wouldn't expect you to, Nora."

Jacob is a good guy. Hayden is the one for me, though. Speaking of, guess who is at the end of the guys' line, set to go against me on the ropes course?

"I won't be cutting you any slack either," I tell Hayden.

"I wouldn't want you to, Pais." He winks at me and then we all face forward. My heart kicks into gear. Nora is right. These end-of-camp challenges have always excited me. I've missed the head-to-head competitions this year, but it looks like I'll still get my chance. I turn my attention to the girls of Chickadee Cabin, who are holding a sign that reads *You Go Girls!* Simone waves at me. I wave back, and then my mom's voice comes over the megaphone.

"Everyone ready?" she asks. "The Starling Guys and Girls Challenge comes down to this final event. Good luck to all!" The campers break into cheers. Then my mom counts down. "On your mark, get set"—she gestures to Dave and he blows the horn—"go!"

Nora takes off running. So does Jacob. They come to the spiderweb course, which is one of my faves. There's a red ring beyond the web. The two have to make their way through the web without touching it and retrieve one of the rings. Then they drop it on an orange cone beyond the course and hit the buzzer for the next teammate to come through and do the same.

Nora has an edge to this task because she's smaller than Jacob. It'll be easier for her to get through. If either of them touches the web, they don't get that point for the task. And the spider eats them—in theory.

I hold my breath alongside Meghan, Maria, and Emma. Tisha is next up so her gaze is set on moving as soon as the buzzer sounds. She'll be up against Dom.

Nora gets the point against Jacob.

Tisha plows into the web, nimble and determined. She wins the point.

Meghan loses her point to Ricardo, even though they've been talking and they're totally into one another as camp crushes go.

Maria loses her point too, but Emma comes out on top.

Then it's time for me and Hayden to race. The buzzer goes off and I dash toward the web. Boyfriend or not, this is about my team, and I intend to win this point for the girls of Chickadee Cabin. I dip, lunge, and roll. Then I wrap my fingers around the red ring and carry it to the orange cone, slamming it on with both hands.

"Tie!" my mom calls into her megaphone. I glance over and realize Hayden dropped his ring at the same time as me. "One point to both the guys and girls for that one!"

Hayden grins. A tie is better than a loss, but I'll be getting that next point for my girls.

After the spiderweb course, we go through the Alligator River, where we cross narrow boards and try not to fall off into Alligator River, which is just grass and imagination. The girls end that task eight to nine. The guys are in a slight lead.

The last course is a series of things. First the counselors must commando-crawl under a stretch of horizontal ropes. Then climb the cargo net up to a rope bridge, cross it, and wait for the next team member. When the last one reaches that spot, there's a huge victory bell to ring. I'm determined that I'll be the one to ring that bell!

Dave sounds the buzzer and the counselors get to work while the campers cheer us on.

When it's my turn, I drop to my belly and commando-crawl. Then I climb the cargo net. I'm already breathing hard. I'm not even thinking about Hayden, who is going through this on the opposite course. My mind is only on winning. If this is my last year at Camp Starling, I want to ring that bell for once. I reach the platform and then hurry onto the rope bridge as it sways beneath my feet. Have I mentioned that I don't like heights?

There's no time for fear, though. I keep my focus forward on my friends who have already crossed. They're cheering me on. *Right foot, left foot, Right, Left*. I reach the opposite platform and stumble over my feet to grab the string that will ring the bell. The chime punctures the air BEFORE the boys' chime!

Suddenly Nora's arms are wrapped tightly around me. Then Maria's, Meghan's, Emma's, and Tisha's. There's hugs and tears and lots of laughter.

"We won, right?" I finally ask.

"Winning isn't everything," Emma chides. "But we definitely kicked the guys' butts."

We all laugh some more. It's a good camp moment. One of the best, and I'll never forget it—ever.

CHAPTER TWENTY-THREE

Camp Time: Friday night. The last night.

Later that night, the traditional end-of-camp campfire is ablaze and the campers' excited chatter and laughter fills the air. I'm sitting with Nora, Emma, Tisha, Meghan, and Maria, but I'm not saying much. Instead, I'm scanning the crowd for Hayden. He's been gone for a long time, ever since the games finished. Part of me wonders if he's upset about the loss, but that's not Hayden's style. I seriously doubt he cares about winning or losing.

"You're okay with the move now?" Emma asks.

I blow out a breath. "Actually, yes. I'm not okay with losing you all, but we'll keep in touch."

"This big announcement your mom is making. Is that the big secret about closing down Camp Starling?" Nora asks me.

"I think so." That's still one thing I'm not quite okay with. This place was my dad's heart and soul. Losing it will take a little piece of that away from me as well. But I understand that my mom doesn't feel like she has a choice. It's a financial burden on her that she doesn't want to keep carrying. It's too much to maintain, especially if we're moving so far away. "I'll always have the memories." That's the mantra I keep telling myself over and over. Writing it in my camper's journal again and again.

My friends look deflated. I know how they feel.

"Has anyone seen Hayden?" I ask. "He's been MIA since the games."

They all shake their heads and look around as if he's there and I'm just not seeing him.

"I'm sure he's somewhere around here," Nora says. "He's crazy about you. No way he left."

"I know." Although the thought has occurred to me. Maybe he's not good at goodbye. Maybe he's one of those people who disappears to avoid it. The thought that I might not see him again before I leave makes me nervous.

Nora stands to leave. "Um, speaking of guys. I'm going to head over and talk to Jacob." Her cheeks bloom pink. I'm pretty sure Nora and Jacob mended whatever differences they had from last summer and they're together again. I'm happy for her. "If I see Hayden, I'll tell him you're looking for him."

"Thanks."

My mind wanders as Emma, Tisha, Meghan, and Maria all share different camp stories from their cabins. Then they slowly break off and return to their campers. I head over to be with the girls of Chickadee Cabin as well, still looking for Hayden. He's nowhere to be found when my mom finally steps up to the group for her big announcement. My insides freeze. I already know the news, but hearing it announced will make it real. The For Sale sign will go up on Monday. The camp will be sold. Dad's camp. My camp.

Where is Hayden when I need him most?

"Good evening, Camp Starling! And congratulations to the girl campers and the victors of the day!"

The girl campers cheer impossibly loud. I cheer as well, although a bit robotically. I'm all cheered out and now I feel the sting of anxiety over what Mom is about to say. I listen as she talks about the last two weeks and all the things we've shared. She gives some version of this same speech every year. I know it by heart. My dad used to be the one who gave it, his voice loud and booming. His energy contagious, even at the tail of two long weeks.

My eyes fill with tears. I swallow hard, reminding myself that I'll always have the memories. Change is okay. Then I feel Simone's arm wrap around my shoulders and squeeze me in a side hug. I look up and she gives me a small smile.

"You okay?" she whispers.

I nod, feeling like she's the one swimming out to rescue me this time as I'm drowning in Blue Lake. "Yeah."

"So, now for a huge announcement!" My mom is smiling so hard. Why does she look thrilled about what she's about to tell us? She should look as devastated as I feel. "It is with a heavy heart that I am stepping down as the owner and director of Camp Starling. I have loved my time here, but a new adventure awaits me and my family in Wyoming." She gestures for my Uncle Leon and Aunt Jenny to come up and stand beside her on the small stage.

I feel my posture straighten because that makes no sense to me. What's going on?

"But," my mom says, "the fantastic news is that Camp Starling is not closing its doors. Leon and Jenny Levins, who you all know and love, are purchasing this place and taking over. Camp Starling will be back next summer and the one after that."

I'm barely breathing. I can't believe my ears. My mom's eyes connect with mine through the crowd and tears spill down my cheeks. She's crying too. She hands her microphone to Uncle Leon and they start talking about how excited they are to run the camp, while my mom makes her way to me. When she reaches me, she wraps her arms around me tightly and we hug for a long time.

"And they've invited you back to be a camp counselor next summer," she says, once she pulls away. "And Nora, Emma, Tisha, Meghan, and Maria too."

I wait, breath bated. This is the best news, but . . .

My mom gives me a knowing look. "And they've invited Hayden as well."

❋

I'm both walking on air and also harboring a heavy pit in my stomach later that night as I lie in my bunk with my journal. Camp Starling is saved. I'll return next year to work here with my friends. My dad's dream will live on. I would be over the moon right now except I haven't seen Hayden in hours.

Maybe he did leave without saying goodbye. He had his car in the parking lot. It'd be easy for him to just drive away. At this point, camp is pretty much over. He's served the time for his crime. The thought that he would go so early leaves me feeling hollowed out.

I heave a sigh and then freeze when I hear something rustling outside my window. I roll onto my side and listen. Then before my mind even catches up, I'm sitting up, sliding on my flip-flops, and tapping Simone's shoulder.

"What are you doing?" she asks.

"There's a noise outside. I'm going to investigate."

She frowns at me, eyes barely open. "Investigating things that go bump in the night might not be the best idea."

"It'll be fine. Watch the cabin for me?"

Her frown deepens. "Okay. But if you're not back in thirty minutes, I'm sending a search party."

"Thank you." I hurry out of the cabin, pulling the door shut and looking around at the same time. Then I hear a *psst*.

I whirl on my heel and there Hayden is. He hasn't disappeared for good.

"Where have you been?" I ask, stepping toward him. "I've been worried."

"I'm sorry about that." It's hard to be upset when he's smiling. He has the most contagious smile. "I have a surprise for you. It took longer than I thought it would. I didn't mean to scare you."

"A surprise? For me?" My insides melt like a sliver of butter on top of hot pancakes. I look around again. "What is it?"

"We're going to have to take a little walk to get there. Don't worry. Your mom and Dave have already said it was okay."

"They did?" I ask, shocked.

"Yeah, well." He shrugs. "I figure if you get caught breaking curfew because of me, I might not be invited back here next year after all. I don't want to risk that."

I smile. "So you heard?"

"It's great news." He tips his head to the side, gesturing for me to follow him. Then he reaches for my hand and we walk along the stone path, his palm against mine.

"Are we going to the Birdfeeder?" I ask after a stretch of silence. It's not an uncomfortable silence. On the contrary, every moment with Hayden is comfy like a flannel shirt on a chilly summer's night.

"It's just a little farther," he says. "I hope you like it."

I squeeze his hand. "I'm sure I will."

We reach the Birdfeeder. I don't see anything special at first.

"Okay, close your eyes. I know you're a bit of a rebel these days, but no peeking please."

I giggle softly and use my hands to cover my eyes. "I wouldn't dare ruin your surprise."

"I'm going to lead you, okay? Do you trust me?" he asks.

I nod. "Of course I do."

He places his hands on my shoulders and maneuvers me onward. I step awkwardly, stumbling a couple times, but he catches me. "Almost there."

After another moment, I ask, "Are you ready to show me yet?"

We stop walking. "Let me first say that this is a work in progress. I'm not finished, okay?"

"Okay." My curiosity is so high that I can hardly stand the anticipation.

I hear him take an audible breath behind me. Then he steps to my left side. "Okay, Pais. Open your eyes."

I remove my hands and open my eyes, blinking my surroundings into focus. We're standing around the back of the Birdfeeder where there's a storage building. Leaning against it is a giant piece of wood that Hayden has used to make the brightest, most beautiful graffiti mural I've ever seen. There are dozens of different types of birds spray-painted all over the wood. Seagulls, sparrows, blue jays, cardinals. And right there on a tree limb, front and center in the picture, is a tiny bird sitting next to a falcon.

It's hard to breathe for a moment. I can't find any words. The picture is so beautiful and meaningful.

"Your uncle gave me the piece of wood. He's going to hang it in the Birdfeeder once I'm done," Hayden tells me. "The chickadee is you. See how I put a little hint of red in its hair?"

I grin, feeling the sting of happy tears behind my eyes. "She's beautiful."

"Just like you." He points at the bird sitting on the tree limb beside the chickadee. "The falcon is—"

"You," I say.

"What gave it away?" he teases.

"Oh, I don't know. You were in Falcon Cabin for one. Plus, it's wearing Converse shoes that someone has drawn all over." I turn to him as my eyes well up with tears. I swipe them off quickly.

"Got any interesting facts about falcons?" he asks, teasing me.

I laugh. "Well, actually . . . ," I trail off.

Hayden chuckles. "Go on. You know you want to."

"The male falcons usually impress their mates with their aerobatic flying skills. Lots of swoops, loops, and dives." I look at the mural in front of me. "What you've done here is the equivalent of swoops, loops, and dives. This is the most amazing surprise I've ever had, Hayden. Well, in addition to my aunt and uncle buying the camp. Today has just been . . ." I shake my head as more tears spring up. "Thank you. I love it."

Hayden looks down for a moment. Then he looks back at the picture and points. "The mockingbird is for my brother Raidon. He always loved to tease me so . . . I wanted to include him if that's okay."

I look at the tiny bird he painted into the picture. It's wearing a Yankees ball cap, which I'm guessing is sentimental. "It's more than okay. I can't wait to see this hanging in the Birdfeeder next summer. And I can't wait to do this all over again."

He steps closer to me. "Minus all the shenanigans with breaking up and making up."

"Minus all that." I tip my face up to his and look at him. "If you're going to kiss me, you better do it quickly. Simone said she'd send a search party if I'm not back in thirty minutes."

Hayden takes my hand, running his thumb over the back for a moment. Then he dips his face to mine. The kiss is brief, his lips brushing over mine as softly as the wind across my bare arms. Then he leads me back to Chickadee Cabin. Tomorrow all the campers will go home, back to life as normal. My life will never be the same, though, and I don't want it to be anymore. Everything works out in the end. Not that this is The End. It's just the beginning of a new adventure. And the beginning of my and Hayden's love story.

"You'll return next summer, right?" I ask. "You'll be here with me?"

He stares into my eyes and I can't look away even if I wanted to. "As long as you still want me, I will be. Once a Starling, always a Starling, right?"

I nod. "Always."

ACKNOWLEDGMENTS

A million thanks to everyone who helped make this book possible. Writing a young adult novel was a new adventure for me. It was exciting, but also intimidating, to say the least. I am so grateful to Wendy Loggia for giving me the chance to step into a new genre and for her guidance during edits for this book. I am also grateful to Hannah Hill and Alison Romig for helping me to mold this book into the very best version it can be.

I also want to send shout-outs to Jacqueline Li, the talented cover artist for this book. I couldn't possibly love this cover more!

Thank you to my amazing agent, Sarah Younger, for all that you do, whether it be pitching, reading, advising, or just lending an ear. I am so fortunate to have you as an agent and a friend.

Much love and thanks goes out to my #GirlsNightWrite ladies, especially Tif Marcelo for encouraging me to write this book and for being one of my first readers. You are an amazing author, and I'm so lucky to have you as a friend. Thank you to Rachel Lacey for being my critique partner, even though this book was a change from what I normally send over. I couldn't do this writer journey without you!

Last but never least, I want to acknowledge and thank my

family. Thank you, Sonny, for helping me work through this plot and for always giving me the time I need to write. Thank you to my children, who are patient and understanding when it comes to my job as an author. You are what inspires me most in the world. I love you all!

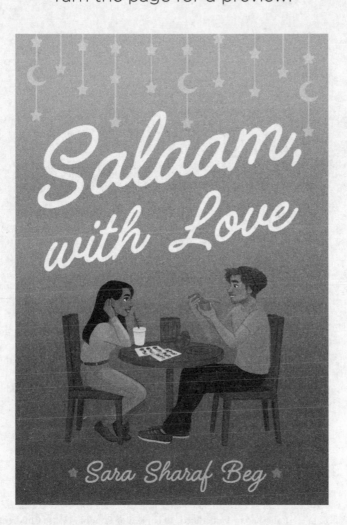

one

I was rocking out to the radio in my room when my mom walked in. I froze, one foot behind me, and reached up to pull my earbuds out as my mom watched me with a bemused expression.

"Dua, come into the kitchen. Your father and I have something to tell you," she said, the Urdu words flowing like poetry from her lips. "And please stop jumping around like an electrocuted penguin," she added, closing the door behind her.

"Electrocuted penguin," I muttered as I put the earbuds away. Actually, I'd been called worse when it came to my dancing.

"What's . . ." My voice trailed off as I walked into the kitchen and saw the looks on my parents' faces. "What happened?" My heart hammered in my chest. Was this about my music again?

"We'll explain," Mom said gently. "Sit down, please."

I bit my lip. If music hadn't been on their minds, I didn't want to bring it up and cause an argument. Instead, I asked, "Did someone die?"

Dad shook his head. "No, alhamdulillah—all praise is due to God. You remember Uncle Yusuf and his family?"

Dad had seven brothers; keeping all their names and faces straight in my head was almost impossible unless a cup of coffee sat at the bottom of my stomach first. "Yeah, of course. His family visited Dada and Daadi in Pakistan at the same time as us five years ago."

"Dua," Mom said, as if I hadn't even spoken, "as you know, Ramadan starts in a week."

"Yeah," I agreed, my brow furrowed as I leaned forward, waiting for her to finish. I wasn't even sure I *wanted* to hear what else she had to say. "And?"

"Well, Yusuf invited us to come and stay with them for Ramadan," Dad said, a smile breaking out on his face, his teeth startlingly white against his tanned skin. "And we're going to take him up on it."

For a minute, all I could do was blink at him, my mind suddenly blank. Of all the things I expected him to say, this had been nowhere on the list. Once my brain processed his words, I said, "What? Wait . . . *what?*"

"We are going to stay at your uncle Yusuf's for Ramadan," Mom repeated, slowly this time, enunciating each syllable. "Now, please, be happy; we haven't seen them in years."

I would've jumped out of my seat if I hadn't already been in danger of falling off of it. "Exactly! I haven't seen or even talked to Uncle Yusuf or my cousins in five years; that's a long time. How am I supposed to connect with them? What are we going to talk about?"

"There's so much you have in common with your cousins. Your heritage, your faith," Dad reminded me.

I barely held in a snort. Heritage, sure. Faith? Not so much. I knew enough about Islam from what Mom and Dad had taught me growing up, from years of weekends spent at the dining table while they read from the Qur'an or books on prophetic tradition. But Uncle Yusuf and his family were on another level. My cousins grew up going to Sunday school where volunteers would teach them the Qur'an and Islamic history every week. They had Muslim friends from the moment they were born, all the way through university. Compared to them, I wasn't a *bad* Muslim, but the differences in our experiences were huge. Ramadan wouldn't be a quiet, private affair in their household the way it was in my small family.

Like Dad, Uncle Yusuf was a doctor—pediatrics for Dad, cardiology for Uncle Yusuf. Unlike Dad, when Uncle Yusuf wasn't seeing a patient, he was often found attending or listening to Islamic conferences and lectures. A phone call from him meant getting a free lesson on the importance of waking up on time for fajr, the morning prayer. In comparison, I preferred my parents' occasional complaint about my lack of focus during worship.

Sure, my uncle meant well and was kind, generous, and soft-spoken, but I could only take so much preaching before it got on my nerves. I knew enough; I didn't need every moment to become another teaching opportunity. How would I live for a month with him and his family?

"And how do you connect with strangers?" Dad went on, oblivious to the thoughts spinning in my mind. "Just go up and talk to them, but it's even better because they're your family. They'll accept you no matter what.

"You'll be applying for college soon and Mahnoor just finished her bachelor's. I'm sure she'd love to answer any questions you have about college life and the application process."

I didn't respond, recalling the last time I'd attempted to bring up my thoughts about "college life" and the major I wanted. A slight heaviness settled in my stomach, just as it had that evening. As soon as the word *music* left my mouth, Dad had gotten a confused look on his face while Mom chuckled—assuming I was joking. I hadn't had the guts to bring it up again.

"Aren't you Facebook friends with Mahnoor?" Mom asked, reminding me of the dangers of being friends with your parents on social media. Even when you only added them because they wouldn't stop crying that their only child is ashamed of them.

"Yeah, but she's almost never online," I answered. From what I remembered, she'd always been a little on the antisocial side. Plus, I almost never use Facebook anymore. "I think the last time I talked to her was a year ago."

"When she got engaged?" Mom asked, thinking back.

"Right, I reached out to congratulate her, and then we only talked for a few minutes because she was studying for the LSATs." I wasn't exaggerating either. We'd talked for two minutes, and in that time all I'd gotten in was *Hi, I'm so happy for you*, and *bye*. Not that we would have had a lot to say to each other anyway.

"You're cousins, sweetheart. No matter how much time passes, you can always pick up right where you left off. That's what happens when you share blood."

I gnawed on my lower lip as I studied my parents' faces. My mom, with her light brown hair and warm, amber eyes, a smile that could get me to do anything, even the chores I hated the most. My dad, with his thousand-watt grin, merry dark brown eyes, and jet-black hair cropped short and going gray at the temples. I was an even mix of both of them, with my skin tone somewhere between my mom's light complexion and my dad's olive coloring, my eyes an exact match with my mom's, my hair as black and thick as my dad's, and a nose like someone stuck a pear in the middle of my face (I wasn't sure where the nose had come from).

They were being gentle with me, trying to allow me to accept their decision maturely rather than pushing it on me. Not unlike their approach to the options they posited for my future: business, prelaw, or premed. Still, I knew them too well to think that I had any real say in what was going to happen. Family had always been important to Dad, and once Mom made a decision, there was no turning her away from it.

"I can't get out of this, can I?" I asked anyway, slumping in my chair.

"No," my mom said, stopping to kiss me on the head as she got up and left to start packing. "Have your suitcase ready by tomorrow morning, honey. We leave in the evening."

I sat up straight. "You're not even giving me forty-eight hours' notice when you make plans now? I'm your only child—why the lack of communication?"

"We just told you. How much more notice do you need? We're going for a visit. You're not getting married and moving away. You don't have to pack the whole house," Dad said, not getting it, as usual.

I sighed. I just wanted to be consulted for once, to feel like I actually had a voice. "I'm not saying I'm going to New York kicking and screaming, but you could've at least told me earlier. Kat and I had plans for the rest of summer vacation. Now I have to let her down, and we don't have time to hang out before I leave. And what about my birthday? It falls during Ramadan this year, so we're not going to be able to celebrate it together."

"Just celebrate it when we get back," Mom said calmly. "It's only a matter of a few days."

Clenching my jaw, I mulled that over. Kat was more than my best friend; she was my constant companion. We'd played in sandboxes and learned to ride our bikes together. We talked about everything, were always together, always a team. Now our plans were ruined. To my parents, it was only a month, but I felt robbed. Kat knew how to make me forget the stress of trying to deal with everything that came with being different, not just from my non–Pakistani American, non-Muslim classmates and friends, but also from my own family, Uncle Yusuf and my cousins included. Whenever that familiar feeling of not fitting in started to set in, Kat knew how to make me feel better.

"You can invite her for dinner tonight. Your mom's making chicken karahi. Kat loves it, right?" Dad said, like he couldn't get what I was making such a big deal out of. "Try to be happy about this, Dua. I haven't seen my brother in years, and we used to be even closer than you and Kat are now. If you're excited, then Kat will be excited for you too. A month away from your best friend isn't going to kill you." He paused, looking thoughtful, as if he wasn't sure if he should continue or not. "Besides, Kat's a nice girl, but she's not Muslim. There are some things about the way we live that she just can't relate to. You've spent your whole life in this little town, and it's high time you made some Muslim friends."

This wasn't the first time I'd heard this, but it was the first time Dad seemed to be genuinely regretful about it. We'd moved to Burkeville, Virginia, when I was a toddler because of Dad's residency and stayed on because he'd received an offer he couldn't pass up. While Dad had always intended to move closer to his brothers one day, or at least where there were more Muslims or Pakistanis, that day always got put off for one reason or another.

My education. Mom's budding, home-based catering service (anyone craving chicken tikka masala within a fifty-mile radius would be out of luck if we moved). So, Dad put off moving indefinitely. He'd spent almost half his life away from his family. In comparison, one month wasn't much to ask.

"It's not that there's something wrong with your friends now," Dad said softly, almost desperate that I not take his words the wrong way, "but you'll see, it's a little different. You actually belong, unified in a group by our love of God."

I understood what he was saying. It made sense, but I *had* to stop this mini-lecture before it turned into something you might see on Lifetime. "Okay, Dad. I'll call her to come over tonight and start packing right after." I even tried to smile despite the growing knot of dread in my stomach. "I make no promises that I'll enjoy this trip, but I'll keep the complaining to a minimum."

"Good. Ingratitude is displeasing to God," he said, bending to kiss me on the head before going after my mother.

I stared like he'd suddenly turned into a two-headed calf. How were *those* words supposed to encourage me about a trip I didn't want to go on? "God help me," I muttered, plopping my head down on the table.

☾

"New York?" Kat shrieked, almost rupturing my eardrums. "You're going to New York and you're *complaining* about it?" Her eyes were as big as tennis balls, her chicken karahi and roti forgotten.

I stared at her, wondering how her jaw hadn't cracked, she was grinning so hard. "How are you not upset? We were supposed to hang out together this summer. We made plans to go out to the state park, go hiking. My parents didn't care about that."

Her perpetual smile finally slipped. "Yeah, our plans . . . Honestly, I can't remember a time when we've been apart for that long. Don't forget about me while you're exploring New York."

She said it like she was joking, but she looked away, and I could see the tiny bit of skin between her brows wrinkling. She was trying not to cry.

"Oh, Kat." I pulled her close, squeezing her in a hug. "I'm sorry. I'll make it up to you when I get back, I promise. Besides, I don't think there'll be much exploring involved. Everyone's going to be fasting, so we won't have a lot of energy to go out often. Plus, Uncle Yusuf is more conservative than Dad, so I don't really know what day-to-day life is going to look like there." I paused for a moment. "It's going to be so weird for me; I've met Uncle Yusuf and his family five times in my whole life, and now I'm going to live with them for a month. How am I supposed to adjust to that? How am I supposed to relate to *them*?"

She held back a sniffle. "You're overthinking it. It might be weird for you at first because you're not used to having that many people around. Take it one day at a time, and when it gets tough, imagine I'm there with you, like a guardian angel."

"Yeah, I guess you're right," I replied half-heartedly. I wasn't Kat; I wasn't close to my extended family. I was happiest at home where it was just me.

She wiped away a tear. "Of course I'm right." She reached for my hand. "I'm happy for you, though. Really. It sucks about our plans, but honestly, how much are you going to miss? There are only so many things to do in Burkeville, and we'll do them when you get back. Right?"

I squeezed her hand. "Definitely."

She squeezed back. "Come on, I'll help you pack."

Dragging me to my room, she pulled some clothes from my closet and flung them on the bed. Graphic T-shirts with references from my favorite TV shows and movies. Long-sleeved blouses. Jeans.

"Okay, now let's talk about the important thing here." She turned, draping a scarf about my shoulders, checking its hue against my skin. "You have a guy cousin there only a couple of years older than us, right?"

It took a moment to get out of my own thoughts. "Um, yeah. It's not long enough to cover my hair during prayer. I should have some longer ones in the back."

"Yeah, yeah, sure." She whisked it away. "So, your cousin, What's-His-Face, is he hot?"

"Ibrahim, and he's not your type." I glanced down at the long, pale blue scarf in her hands. "That should work."

"Not my type, my butt. If he breathes, he's my type." Kat draped the scarf over my head, checking the length.

"Dua!"

I turned toward my mother's voice, the scarf haphazardly wrapped about my head.

"I brought this in for you," she said, pushing an old suitcase toward me. "Hurry up and get packing." Waves of light brown hair fell from her messy bun, her eyes wide as she perused the mess on my bed. "Where are your shalwar kameez?"

"My closet." Seeing as we never had much occasion to wear

traditional Pakistani outfits, I only had three, all presents from previous Eid holidays.

"Pack them," Mom said, opening the suitcase and folding my jeans into neat stacks. "We might have some dinners to go to. Yusuf and Sadia know quite a few people. If you need them, you can borrow some of mine; I'll pack extra."

"Okay," I agreed, already pulling them from my closet. I folded the matching scarves first, then the trousers, and then, very carefully, the richly colored and embroidered kameez tunics.

Kat grabbed my jewelry box off the dresser and, in a smaller compartment of my suitcase, added a few pieces to pair with the beautiful clothes. "Hey, what about this?" she asked, pulling a gold teeka headpiece from the box, a gift from my grandma on our last trip to Pakistan. "It's so pretty!" She held it up to her own forehead and posed, pouting, the gold beads shimmering against her skin.

Mom smiled brightly. "It looks beautiful on you."

I felt a little twinge, seeing the light in Mom's eyes as she watched Kat twirl before the mirror. Despite admiring the teeka, I'd never been half as excited to try it on. Sure, it was pretty, but I never had much occasion to wear it. If not for myself, I could've worn it for Mom, to make her smile.

We'd always been the only Pakistani family in town, though that never stopped my parents from trying to keep the culture alive at home. I'd worn shalwar kameez every Eid since birth. I'd sit with Mom as she watched Pakistani dramas. Dad was always listening to old Pakistani songs. Yet somehow, Kat seemed more connected to my culture, more willing to embrace my parents' customs and values, than I was.

At home, we only spoke in English on Mondays. The rest of

the weekdays, we spoke in Urdu, and on weekends, Punjabi. Even though we visited Pakistan infrequently, they wanted me to speak and understand both languages easily, so I wouldn't have trouble talking to my grandparents and relatives still living there.

In a way, I understood. If I'd lived half my life elsewhere, I'd want to remember that culture too. Maybe that was part of the reason for this trip: the desire for a stronger connection to our heritage, our family. Dad and Uncle Yusuf weren't far apart in age, so they'd been close as children. Dad must be feeling nostalgic, and I knew Mom, who talked to Aunt Sadia often, longed for friends like the ones she'd had at college in Lahore. She was friendly with all the women in our neighborhood, but they didn't have the comfort of shared experiences and customs.

"So?" Kat said, finally taking the teeka off, her hand hovering over the open suitcase. "Are you taking it?"

I smiled lightly. "Yeah, why not? Maybe I'll wear it on Eid."

"Where's your tasbeeh?" Mom asked. "Don't forget to bring that too."

I glanced around the room. There it was on the windowsill, by my electronic keyboard. I stretched over the length of the keyboard as I reached for the string of black beads, and just as the tassel was within my grasp, my other hand landed firmly on the keys. A single high note rang out, beautiful, but lonely in its solitude. The tasbeeh slipped from my fingers as I caressed the keys. They seemed to hum with anticipation just beneath my fingertips.

"Dua, hurry up!"

"Can I take my keyboard?" The question was out before the thought fully formed, my tongue quicker than my brain.

Mom paused, her forehead wrinkling, eyes slightly narrowing.

"There isn't room in the car, and I don't think there will be in their house either. Besides, are you going to focus on Ramadan or your music?"

Why can't it be both? I wondered.

Mom didn't wait for an answer. As far as she was concerned, the conversation had ended before it began. "Finish your packing; you don't want to forget anything."

I jerked my hands away from the keys, my fingertips tingling. I did as I was told. Although I was careful not to look at the keyboard again, the air hung heavy, thick with the promise of melody.

narrow passageway between two buildings and Curtis heard him give a yell of frustration. *'Hell, it's a dead end!'*

Curtis chuckled to himself and slowed his pace. When he reached the corner of the passageway, he paused.

'You in there, Hudson?' he called. 'Reckon you are.'

There was a pause, then came an answer. 'Curtis? That you?'

'You know damn well it's me,' Curtis said. 'Now just move into the light where I can see you. An' keep your hands away from your guns.'

'I ain't armed, Curtis,' Drew shouted. 'Look!'

Curtis moved carefully into the passageway. He could see Drew at the end, up against some crates that stood against the back of a building, hands in the air, moonlight silvering his pale face. But the kid seemed to be telling the truth. There was no gunbelt around his waist.

Emboldened, Curtis began walking slowly towards him, six-gun drawn.

'You ran out on me, kid,' he said. 'Nobody does that to Curtis Jordan.'

'I-I thought you were dead, Curt. Honest I did!'

Curtis gave a mirthless laugh. 'Takes more'n a babyfaced deputy to finish me off. Point is, you've got my money, kid. Now that ain't fair, is it?'

'No, Curt. But we can put that right. I'll get it for you, soon as you like.'

Curtis was within ten yards of him, eyes and ears alert. And at that moment he sensed rather than saw movement to Drew's left, between the crates. A second later, he heard the explosion of gunfire. Instinctively he dropped to the ground, firing at the muzzle flash at the same time — *one, two three*!

He heard an agonized cry of pain, but the sniper fired again so that Curtis was forced to roll away, scramble to his feet and hot-foot it back to the open end of the passageway, firing over his shoulder.

Drew yanked one of the crates clear of the wall behind him revealing a small door which led into the building. Frantically, he wrestled with the door handle as another exchange of gunfire sounded behind him. At last he was able to push the door open. He went through, followed moments later by the staggering figure of Clayton Chandler, blood pouring from a wound in his thigh.

'Wait!' Clayton yelled, collapsing on the floor. 'Bolt the door before we head for the front of the building!'

Reluctantly, Drew turned back. He slammed the door and shoved home the bolts that were at the top and the bottom of it.

'Help me!' Clayton said. 'Give me your arm.'

As encouragement, he lifted his Colt and pointed it at the kid.

'Sure, sure, Clayton!' Drew said. 'I was gonna help you.'

He was sick with disappointment at Curtis's escape and doubly fearful now that the gunslinger knew for sure that he, Drew, was in town.

It took them more than half an hour to make their way to the back doors of Opal's House and make the climb up to Lottie's room without drawing attention to themselves. Thankfully, because of the late hour, the saloon was nearly empty except for a table of late-night card-players in one corner and a drunk slumped over the bar. The barkeep saw them making their way up the stairs but decided it was more prudent to pretend that he hadn't.

Lottie was asleep, but woke instantly when her door opened. The two men half-fell into the room, one with his blood-soaked pants' leg, the other white-faced with shock and the strain of hauling his partner for more than a mile through the backstreets, forever looking over his shoulder and expecting to see Curtis Jordan bearing down on them.

'He needs a doctor,' Drew said. 'We need to hole up for a few more days until he's better.'

'*So I see.*'

The voice came from the open

doorway behind him, and Drew turned to see the elephantine form of Opal Harris standing there, arms crossed over a floral wrap, fluffy mules on her feet. She wore a crooked smile on her face.

'Doctors cost money, Drew,' she said. 'Our silence costs even more. Right, Lottie?'

'Right,' Lottie said.

Drew groaned.

⋆ ⋆ ⋆

After the shooting in the passageway, Curtis tried to find the front entrance to the building through which Drew Hudson and his ally had escaped. He eventually tracked it down by the blood-stains outside it, but the trail of these petered out within a few yards, the injured man somehow having managed to stanch the flow.

Now Curtis was back in his room at the Bib'n Tucker, cursing his luck and speculating about who Hudson's helper had been. One thing Curtis *was* sure about. He'd been tricked into going down that passageway by Hudson's cry of 'dead end'. It had been a con. The kid had *known* there was an escape route through the building at the end, and he had known his accomplice was waiting ready to bushwhack Curtis. He had offered himself up as bait. It had been risky, but effective. Although the mystery helper getting hurt wouldn't have been part of the plan.

But who was he? A gunman Drew Hudson had hired, having learned Curtis was in town and looking for him? It was the only explanation Curtis could think of.

He went across to the window of his room and looked out. The street below was as deserted now as it was at two o'clock in the morning. Directly opposite was the Opal's House saloon and a couple of cathouses. Further along were two more smaller saloons. Was Drew Hudson holed up in one of those? He wasn't in the Prime Hotel, Curtis knew that, having checked. Nor in any of the other three smaller hotels. There were rooming-houses, of course, but they were at the other end of town. Maybe, Curtis thought, over the next couple of days, he should check those, too.

He moved away from the window and threw himself down on the bed. 'You can run, Hudson,' he muttered to himself. 'But you won't get away.'

22

Thirty-six hours later, the stage stopped outside the Prime Hotel where, the driver guessed, most of his five passengers would be putting up for the night, if not longer.

Danny waited until the others had disembarked before easing himself from his seat and stepping out into the early-afternoon sun. His back hurt like hell after the bumps and jerks of the journey, and he still had only half his normal stamina.

Latimer's Main Street had a central plaza. Strung out opposite the Prime Hotel was another, smaller hotel, a real estate office, a bank, a general stores and a saloon.

And the sheriff's office. This was a low-roofed building with an alleyway running along one side of it.

After a hot bath in his room at the

hotel, Danny paid a visit to the local lawman. He identified himself and explained his reasons for being in town.

'Kinda outside your jurisdiction, aren't you, Deputy Ridge?' the sheriff said.

'I've got personal reasons for catchin' the varmints, too,' Danny said.

'Curtis Jordan, you say?' Sheriff Sam Lewis stroked his greying moustache, then ran his tongue over tobacco-stained teeth. 'Heard the name, of course. Like you say, one of the Cotton gang. And Wolf Cotton's dead?'

'That's right,' Danny said. 'Ab Cooper, too. A fourth man also got away, name of Drew Hudson. Reckon he might be in town, too.'

'Hudson? You could be right. There's a young woman with the name of Hudson helping out at Bella Gower's Eating House, a relative of hers apparently. Only been here a short time.'

'Workin' at the Eatin' House, you say?'

Lewis nodded. 'Don't know anything about the brother. Could be the young man who's been haunting the saloons and cathouses. He arrived about the same time. Staying at the Prime Hotel, last I heard.'

'That's where I'm stayin',' Danny said. 'Guess I'll check with the hotel clerk. Drew Hudson's somebody I want to find, and he's also my best lead to Jordan.'

'Because Jordan will be looking for him, that right?'

'Certain to be, seein' as Hudson ran off with the loot from the bank raid.'

'You got any solid *proof* that these two gentlemen were involved in the raid?'

'Hudson's horse,' Danny said. 'It's got distinctive white markin's, an' several witnesses in Suta Springs saw him ridin' off on it. He's sold it, but the livery man he sold it to could testify.'

'His horse,' Lewis said, looking dubious. 'Flimsy kind of evidence for a court of law. What about Jordan? Anybody identify him?'

Danny shook his head. 'But we know he was a member of Wolf Cotton's gang.'

'But we don't know — can't *prove* — he took part in the raid. So unless we can catch him doing something unlawful here in Latimer, there's not a lot I can do to help you, Deputy Ridge.'

Danny stared at the other man for a full minute before turning on his heel and stalking out of the office.

Sheriff Lewis sighed. 'Reckon that's one dissatisfied customer,' he said to no one in particular.

★ ★ ★

'Mr Hudson checked out a few days ago,' the clerk at the Prime Hotel informed Danny. He was in his fifties with thinning grey hair and a hooked nose.

'Did he say where he was goin'?'

The clerk shook his head. 'I'm afraid not.'

Danny left the hotel and headed towards the Eating House. It seemed Sheriff Lewis was not going to be much help, even if Danny did identify and locate Curtis Jordan. Proof of Jordan's complicity in the bank raid — proof that would satisfy a court of law — would be almost impossible to find, unless he could get this Drew Hudson to admit his own part in the robbery and then name Curtis Jordan as the other raider. Was that likely? Danny had severe doubts.

★ ★ ★

Late afternoon, and the café was almost empty except for a couple of old-timers drinking coffee and bragging to each other about their wartime adventures, each knowing the other was lying more than a little. They looked across at Danny but ignored him almost immediately.

Kate was alone in the kitchen, her aunt upstairs taking a nap before coming down to cook suppers.

Kate was cleaning vegetables when Danny came in, selected a table and sat down. She left the kitchen to take his order.

'Coffee,' Danny told her. 'Please.' He gave her a friendly smile.

She moved away, then came back with the coffee pot and a mug.

'Passing through?' she asked, making polite conversation. She was sure she hadn't seen this young man in the café before.

'Depends on whether I find the person I'm lookin' for,' Danny said.

Kate's hand jerked and she slopped coffee over the edge of the mug. 'Sorry!' she said quickly. 'Wh-who are you trying to find?'

'In the first instance, a fella by the name of Drew Hudson.' He glanced at her. 'Reckon you know him. Reckon you're his sister.'

Kate's face clouded over. 'Yes,' she admitted. 'But I can't tell you where to find him.'

'That's too bad. How about Curtis Jordan?'

Kate swallowed. 'Are you a lawman?'

'Deputy from Suta Springs,' Danny informed her. 'Lookin' for the men who

169

robbed the Suta Springs bank, the two that are still alive, that is. Two innocent people died in the raid. The bank manager and a young woman expectin' her first child.'

Kate's mouth dropped open and her face blanched. 'Drew . . . killed a woman?'

Danny shook his head. 'Curtis Jordan,' he said.

Relief flooded through her. It was bad enough that her brother had killed a man. Killing a pregnant woman too would have sickened her. 'How did it happen?' she asked.

Danny explained.

'Dear God!' Kate said, when he'd finished. 'What a terrible tragedy.' She glanced over her shoulder at the two old-timers, but they were still gabbing. 'Well, I can tell you Curtis Jordan's almost certainly still in town. He's looking for Drew.'

'Because of the money your brother ran away with,' Danny said.

She nodded. 'Yes.'

Kate considered for a moment. If she

helped this man find Curtis Jordan before Jordan found and killed Drew, maybe she and Aunt Bella could work something out with the law.

'If I help you, will you help Drew?'

'Can't promise anythin' like that,' Danny replied. 'Your brother killed a man.'

'I know,' Kate said, quietly.

'Jordan killed two men before finally getting away from Suta Springs,' Danny told her. 'He's gonna hang, so the law's keen to get him. So maybe if Drew helps identify him as the other raider, it might save your brother from hangin' too. Might get him a lighter prison sentence. First, though, I need to find Jordan, an' I don't even know what he looks like. His picture ain't on no law dodger. Can you describe him?'

'I can do better than that,' she said. 'I can draw you a picture of him. From memory.'

Danny grinned. '*Can* you now?'

23

Clayton Chandler's thigh wound was healing, but movement was still difficult. The doc had done a good job, but had told Clayton it would be several days before he could walk properly, never mind ride.

Clayton had told Drew that it was now up to him to eliminate Curtis Jordan. For one thing, the plan he'd worked out entailed climbing on to a roof, something completely beyond Clayton at the present time.

From Lottie's window, he had pinpointed a place of concealment where a sniper could watch the entrance to the Bib'n Tucker and not be seen by passers-by or anyone coming out. The hiding-place was the flat roof of one of the cathouses, next to the Bib'n Tucker, but angled with the curve of the street, thus giving a clear view of the bar's batwings.

And tonight was the night he had urged Drew to do the deed.

'It's only a matter of time before somebody realizes somebody's hidin' out here in Lottie's room,' Clayton said. 'The barkeep was ready to tell me as soon as I slipped him a gold eagle. Suppose Curtis gets talkin' with him?'

'Opal's fixed the barkeep,' Drew said. 'Threatened him with losin' his job an' not gettin' another anywhere else around here. Opal's got that kind of influence in the red-light district.'

'Even so, we can't stay here for ever. It's drivin' Lottie crazy,' Clayton said.

Lottie was currently down in the bar, making herself 'available'. Opal had given her another room for entertaining 'clients', but all her clothes and other things were still in her old room.

So it had been decided. Tonight would be the night.

Drew waited until dark, then ventured out through the back door of the saloon. Half an hour earlier, he had seen Curtis enter the Bib 'n Tucker and, so far, not come out again.

Head down, Drew walked quickly across the street, Clayton's Winchester tucked under his arm. A narrow alleyway between the cathouse and the bar was cluttered with broken kegs which he used to boost himself on to the roof. He scrambled across it and stretched out on his stomach behind the fascia board, breathing heavily.

It was a dry night, but heavy cloud hid the moon, something Drew was grateful for. Of course, Curtis could have gone to bed, but it was early yet and Drew was gambling on the raider's appetite for women requiring gratification before he slept. Which meant emerging to enter one of the whorehouses, thus making himself a perfect target.

Drew thought about Kate and considered how she would feel about him killing Curtis to save himself. She had already distanced herself from the money — what was left of it. The big question was, would she go to the law?

Drew didn't think so. He was her kid brother, after all. But staying in Latimer wasn't an option any longer, so he had to move on as soon as he was sure Curtis could no longer track him down and kill him. And Kate would not go with him, he was certain of that. From now on, he was on his own.

But what was he to do about Clayton Chandler? He had no intention of sharing any part of what was left of the money from the bank raid. And he wasn't convinced Chandler was prepared to take less than the full amount or allow Drew to stay alive.

It was something to consider later, he decided, after Curtis Jordan was taken care of.

24

Thirty minutes earlier Sheriff Sam Lewis had been sitting at his desk wrestling with his conscience. He couldn't get that young whippersnapper of a deputy from Suta Springs out of his head. The kid had been angry when he'd left, Sam knew that. And even though what he'd told him was right — that without more proof that Curtis Jordan or Drew Hudson had taken part in the bank raid his hands were tied — he felt bad about it.

Sam pulled thoughtfully at the drooping ends of his moustache. The kid reminded him of himself when he'd been a young man. The same doggedness and determination mixed with idealism that he'd had as a young lawman. And he'd told Sam that he had a personal motive for pursuing the bank raiders.

It was at this exact moment that the young man in question stormed in clutching a sheet of paper, and with a purposeful expression on his face.

'OK, Sheriff,' he said, slamming the paper down on Sam's desk. 'Maybe this'll move you off your butt. Ever seen this man?'

Sam hid a smile. *Darned if the kid didn't have grit, too.* Without looking at the picture, and picking up from his desk a smoke that he'd built a few minutes earlier, he looked the young man in the eye.

'You're all fired up, kid,' he said, lighting his cigarette. 'Ease off a little and maybe I'll take a look. Tell me, what was your name again?'

The young man took a couple of deep breaths and forced himself to relax a little. 'Danny Ridge,' he said. 'Just take a look at the picture, will you, Sheriff? Please?'

Sam glanced down. He was silent for several moments, then he said, 'Might've seen this critter somewhere.'

'Where?' Danny asked. 'In town?'

Sam nodded. 'Down in the red-light district when I was doing my rounds last evening. Reckon it might've been in the Bib'n Tucker.'

'What's that? A whorehouse?'

'A bar.'

Danny gathered up the picture. 'Thanks,' he said, and turned to leave.

'Hold on there, young feller,' Sam said, easing himself out of his chair and picking up his hat. 'Prob'ly be a good idea if I came with you.'

'OK, let's be goin',' Danny said.

★   ★   ★

Deep in thought as he considered his future, Drew was unaware of the shadow appearing at the far edge of the roof. It was only at the last moment that he heard movement behind him. He swung round, trying to straighten his rifle, only to have it kicked from his hand followed by a punishing kick delivered to the side of his head,

178

knocking him almost senseless. More blows from the same boot took him on the nose and cheekbone, then sank into his stomach so that he retched and doubled up. Finally, he was dragged up into a sitting position to face his attacker.

'Evenin', Drew.' Curtis Jordan's crooked grin was close enough for Drew to smell the whiskey on his assailant's breath.

'How . . . ?' Drew gasped. Blood ran from his broken nose and his mouth, and he appeared to have double vision.

'Saw you cross the street, didn't I? Been keepin' an eye out for you from my room at the Bib'n Tucker. Figured you'd find your way to one of the whore-houses afore long. Happens you've been in that one for some time, seein' as I didn't eyeball you go in. Am I right?'

After a moment, Drew nodded.

'What happened to that hired gun-slinger of yours?' Curtis asked. 'The one I winged the other night? Not in any shape to climb on to roofs?' Curtis laughed. 'No, I figured not.'

Drew made no reply, his head feeling as if it was about to explode with the crushing pain.

'Yeah, well it don't matter. Caught up with you now, you thievin' bastard!'

'Like I said before, I thought you were dead, Curt,' Drew pleaded.

'*Hoped* I was, more like. Well, I ain't, an' now I'm gonna take my share of the money. Fact, I'm gonna take yours, too, how about that?' Curtis smiled again. 'Or I'm gonna kill you.'

'All of it, sure, Curt,' Drew mumbled. ' 'Course I spent a little of it, but what's left is yours.'

'How much? How much is left?'

Drew spat blood from between his loosened teeth. 'Well, now, I don't rightly know. Six or seven thousand.'

More like two or three.

'Judas! That all?' Curtis eyed him closely. 'You'd better not be lyin' to me, keepin' a share back for yourself.'

'No, truly, that's all there is,' Drew said. 'There weren't as much as Wolf were hopin' for in the first place, Curt.

Only about eight thousand.'

'Where're you keepin' it?'

Drew nodded across the street.

'At the *whorehouse*?' Curtis looked astonished.

'I've been stayin' there,' Drew said. 'Moved out of the hotel.'

'You stayin' with a lady?'

Drew nodded.

'OK, here's what you're gonna do,' Curtis said. 'You're gonna get the money an' bring it to the Bib'n Tucker. I'll be in the bar. You've got twenty minutes from the time you leave this roof. If you get any ideas about runnin' off, forget 'em.' He took a knife from his boot and waved it in front of Drew's face. 'Unless you want your sister to lose her pretty looks.'

Drew's stomach lurched. 'No! Please, leave Kate outa this, Curtis. You'll get the money.'

'Get goin',' Curtis told him 'I'll be waitin'.'

Curtis watched Drew climb down from the roof. Taking his time, he pulled a cheroot from his waistcoat pocket and lit it with a lucifer. He had no intention of leaving Drew alive once he'd got the money. He smiled to himself. He did kind of like the idea of taking that pretty sister of Drew's with him when he made tracks out of Latimer though. He entertained some pleasant thoughts of the soft, shapely flesh which lurked beneath the overall the girl had been wearing in the eating house.

25

Danny and Sheriff Lewis were twenty yards from the Bib'n Tucker when the lawman said, 'Maybe it would be best if we went in separately. Two of us together might make Jordan trigger-happy, 'specially if he works out who you are.'

'OK,' Danny said.

'So I'll go in first,' Sam said. 'Give me five minutes, then you join me at the bar. We'll front him together, assumin' he's in there.'

Danny nodded.

Gaspar Row was buzzing with noise and activity as cowboys, miners and assorted drifters sought the companionship of obliging ladies.

Danny stood on the boardwalk outside the Bib'n Tucker and watched Sheriff Lewis enter. He kept his eye on the street, half-expecting to see their quarry approaching from one direction or another. He had Kate Hudson's drawing of the outlaw clutched in one hand, and he glanced at it again to refresh his memory.

'Ugly bastard,' he thought.

Five minutes later, he followed the sheriff into the bar.

★   ★   ★

Several minutes earlier, Clayton Chandler had been watching the street from Lottie's bedroom window, hoping to see Curtis Jordan emerge from the Bib'n Tucker. But the sight that shocked Clayton to the core was the figure of *Danny Ridge* walking down the street with the local sheriff!

For several seconds the shock of seeing Danny alive stupefied Clayton. Hadn't he shot and killed the deputy only a few days ago? What was he, a cat with nine lives?

Clayton grabbed his gunbelt and strapped it on. He had to do something about Ridge before the deputy saw either Curtis or Drew. Also, it wouldn't do for Drew to take a potshot at Curtis now, should the gunslinger come out of the bar. Not with Danny Ridge standing there.

Clayton decided it would be too dangerous to shoot Ridge down from Lottie's window, nor would it be safe to do it in the street. Somehow he had to separate Ridge from the sheriff and get him into some quiet backstreet or alleyway.

But when he'd limped his way down to the boardwalk outside Opal's House, he was just in time to see Danny entering the Bib'n Tucker. Seconds later, Drew appeared from the alleyway alongside, and crossed the street. Clayton waylaid him when he reached the boardwalk.

'What're you doin'?' he wanted to know. 'Why ain't you up on the roof?'

' 'Cause Curtis is up there, or he was,' Drew answered.

'What!' Clayton grabbed Drew by the

shoulders. 'What the hell happened up there?'

'He took me by surprise,' Drew said. 'I gotta get him the bank money an' take it to him in the Bib'n Tucker, otherwise he's going to hurt Kate. I can't let that happen.'

'But you told me the money ain't in Lottie's room.'

'I — it ain't,' Drew said quickly. 'I just told Curtis it was. It's at the café. I plan to get my things an' go there right away.'

Clayton tried to think. 'Listen, maybe I can stall Curtis. Unless he's worked out it was me who shot at him when you lured him into the passageway the other night, he don't know I'm here. Maybe I can get close enough to kill him.' He glanced across at the Bib'n Tucker, but decided to say nothing to Drew about Danny Ridge. 'You go on back up to Lottie's room an' wait for me there.'

Drew looked doubtful. 'He gave me just twenty minutes to get back to him with the money, then he's goin' to go for Kate.'

'Quit worryin',' Clayton said. 'It'll be all right.'

He gave Drew a shove towards the Opal's House batwings. Then he started to cross the street.

★ ★ ★

Curtis had seen the local sheriff enter the Bib'n Tucker but had paid no mind to it until he'd spotted the young man who was hovering outside. Something told Curtis that the two men had come together but, for reasons of their own, were choosing to enter the bar separately. Not that there was any reason to suspect that their movements had anything to do with him, and yet . . .

Curtis had learned to trust his intuitions. He lived by the gun and that sixth sense of his, warning him of impending trouble, had saved his life more often than he could count.

He decided to stay put on the roof

for the time being.

At that moment he saw a man move off the boardwalk opposite, and make a beeline for the Bib'n Tucker. *Clayton Chandler*!

What in hell was he doing here? Had he joined forces with the law? No, he seemed to be working independently.

Even so, then Curtis knew it was himself the three men were seeking. For the first time in his life, he panicked. He drew, took aim quickly with his Peacemaker, and fired.

The shot was hurried and inaccurate. It missed Clayton by a hair's breath but was sufficient to send him running the rest of the way across the street and diving behind the safety of a drinking trough.

Curtis cursed.

At the sound of the shot, there were cries of alarm and people scattered trying to find cover. Within seconds the street was deserted.

Curtis's second shot clipped the edge of the drinking trough before Clayton returned fire with his own Peacemaker.

Then both the sheriff and the young *hombre* who'd followed him into the Bib'n Tucker appeared and, after taking cover and having a shouted conversation with Clayton behind the drinking trough, began firing up at the roof.

Curtis swore and rolled away from the fascia board above the bar. He needed to get down fast, otherwise he'd be trapped like a bear up a tree.

He scampered on all fours towards the alleyway, swung himself over the side of the roof and dropped on to one of the broken kegs below. From there, he bolted towards the darkness of the open ground behind the buildings in Gaspar Row.

Cursing his bad luck, he made a quick decision. If he was going on the run, it would be in the company of a lady. That way he'd have himself some life insurance and a reason for Drew to come after him. Hopefully with the money.

★ ★ ★

Drew Hudson, at the sound of the first shot, had run to the window of Lottie's bedroom and peered out. His eyes widened at what he saw.

'Judas! Curtis is takin' pot-shots at Chandler!'

Lottie, who had just returned to her room, joined him at the window.

'Over there!' he told her.

She saw the muzzle flashes coming from the roof opposite.

'What're you gonna do, Drew?' she said.

'I'm gettin' out of Latimer, that's what,' he answered. 'Hey! The sheriff and some other *hombre* have joined in the fight!' He laughed.

'How come — ?' Lottie began.

'Don't know,' Drew cut in. 'But maybe it'll be to my advantage. 'Specially if somebody kills that bastard Jordan. Look! He's headin' across the roof to the alley-way!'

They watched the shadowy figure

moving across the roof like a cat. Saw it drop down between the buildings before disappearing into the blackness.

Drew laughed. 'Don't reckon Curtis will be keepin' his appointment with me in the Bib'n Tucker after all.'

He finished gathering up his things, including checking the money belt under his shirt. Thank God Curtis hadn't found it when they were on the roof. He would have discovered that it was a lot emptier than when Drew and Kate had arrived in Latimer.

'What're you gonna do now, Drew?' Lottie asked.

'Get out of town fast,' he said.

'What about your sister?'

Drew was heading towards the door. He paused, remembering Curtis's knife and the threat . . . *unless you want your sister to lose her pretty looks*.

'Kate'll be comin' with me,' he said after a moment. 'She'll have to.'

'And Clayton Chandler?'

'Clayton Chandler can go to hell! 'Bye, Lottie. Thanks for everythin'.'

The door opened before he could reach it and suddenly Opal's frame was filling the doorway. She was smiling. 'You leavin'?' she said.

'Yeah, get out of my way, Opal.'

'Why the hurry?' Opal said. 'An' you ain't paid me your leavin' fee.'

'What'n hell are you talking' about, *leavin' fee*?'

'I charge — ' she began.

'You've had all the money you're gonna get outa me, Opal,' he told her. 'Now move!'

He hit her hard across the face with the back of his hand. She yelped and stepped back. About to speak, something of the desperation in Drew's eyes signalled danger to Opal and made her pause. Reluctantly, she moved out of his way, rubbing her sore cheek.

'Just don't come back!' she yelled after him, as he scrambled down the stairs.

He made no reply.

26

'Reckon he's gone?' Sheriff Sam Lewis shouted to Danny, who was crouching under the batwings of the Bib'n Tucker. The sheriff was squatting behind a buckboard across the street.

It had been quiet for several minutes now and there had been no movement from the roof where the shots had been coming from.

'Yeah, I reckon he has,' Danny shouted back.

Sam moved cautiously into the street, becoming more emboldened when there were no gunshots in his direction. Seconds later, Danny joined him.

Danny pointed towards the alley. 'Guess he made his escape through there. You reckon it was Curtis Jordan?'

'Who else would get nervous seeing you?' Sam said.

'But it weren't me he shot at to start

with. It was the other fella. Where is he, by the way? He was behind the drinkin' trough, but he ain't there now.'

'Must've used our return fire as cover to get away,' Sam said.

'Who was he? Did you see him?'

'Didn't see his face,' Danny said. 'Could've been Drew Hudson.'

Or even Clayton Chandler, he thought.

'So where's Jordan?' Danny said.

Sam Lewis shrugged. 'Could be anywhere by now, but we could start by checking his room at the Bib'n Tucker.'

'Doubt he'll go back there.'

'Then we check his horse at the livery. He'll probably want to get out of town fast.'

'Maybe he'll just steal a horse from a hitchin' rail somewhere,' Danny opined.

'Gotta check though,' Sam said. 'Come on. His room first.'

★ ★ ★

After slipping away from behind the drinking trough whilst the sheriff and

Danny Ridge kept Curtis busy, Clayton limped along the boardwalk until it was safe to cross the street and make his way back to Opal's House.

He went straight to Lottie's room.

'Where's Hudson?' he demanded.

'I-I don't know,' she said.

He was across the room in three strides and backhanded her across the mouth.

'Don't lie!' he told her. 'I ain't got time for games.' He took his six-shooter from its holster and pressed the barrel against Lottie's head. 'Tell me!'

'OK, OK!' she cried. 'He's gone to Bella Gower's eatin' house for his sister before Curtis gets there.'

'Curtis is kinda busy at the moment,' Clayton said.

'I don't think so,' Lottie said.

'He ain't still on the roof?' Clayton got to the window in time to see Danny and the sheriff enter the Bib'n Tucker. 'Damn, you're right,' he said. 'The shootin's stopped. He's got away.'

He gave Lottie a final look.

'Guess I'd better head for the café,' he said.

★ ★ ★

The barkeep directed Sam and Danny to Curtis Jordan's room and they took the stairs two at a time.

Flattening themselves against the wall either side of the door, Sam yelled, 'Jordan! Come on out with your hands up!'

Silence.

'What d'you reckon?' Danny whispered. 'Do we go in?'

Sam nodded, and turned the door handle.

Not locked, he mouthed. And with that, Danny pushed open the door and went in on a roll, six-shooter extended.

The room was empty.

Feeling something of a fool, Danny got to his feet. 'He ain't been back,' he said. 'Look, his things are still here.'

There was not much. A buckskin waistcoat and a denim shirt, both stuffed into a small, worn leather bag.

'He won't bother to come back for that, now that he knows we're after him,' Sam said. 'Come on, let's check the livery.'

As they made their way back down the stairs, Danny said, 'What about Drew Hudson? Won't Curtis be lookin' for him before he leaves town?'

'Might've seen him already,' Sam said. 'Might've killed him an' taken the bank money.'

'He's only been in town a short time,' Danny said.

'Chances are, Hudson's kept out of his way and Jordan hasn't been able to find him. In which case, what would he do to make sure Hudson would *come after him*?'

Sam stared at him. 'You thinking about the sister?'

Danny nodded. 'Reckon he'd want to take her with him as bait for Hudson.'

'Hell, you could be right.'

'You go to the livery and check on Jordan's horse,' Danny said. 'I'll go to the Eatin' House an' make sure Miss Hudson's OK. Meet me there.'

'OK,' Sam said. 'Be careful.'

*   *   *

Breathing heavily, after his non-stop run from Gaspar Row, Curtis almost collapsed against the door of Bella Gower's eating house. The last two diners were finishing up their suppers when he entered the building. The men looked up from their table and took in the drawn six-gun Curtis was holding. Instinctively, both men put their hands in the air.

'Don't shoot, mister,' one said.

'Get out!' Curtis told them. '*Move!*'

The two men got up fast, one of them knocking his chair backwards so that it crashed on to the floor.

The noise brought Bella from the kitchen. She watched the two diners make their hurried exits, then saw Curtis lock the door after them and pull down the raffia blinds on the door and windows. Her heart began to thump in her chest.

Curtis smiled his crooked smile. 'Guess you're closed for the night.

'Wh-what d'you want?' Bella stammered.

'That pretty little niece of yours. *Get her*!'

'N-no, I — '

Curtis fired a shot at the lamp hanging from the ceiling, plunging the room into darkness and leaving just the rectangle of light that leached from the kitchen doorway.

'Get in there!' Curtis shouted, waving his six-shooter towards the kitchen. 'Fast!'

Bella retreated and he followed her.

Curtis saw the terrified girl pressed against the wall when he followed the café-owner through the lighted doorway. She was holding a pile of plates in her hands and she immediately dropped them on the floor, where they smashed.

Curtis smiled again. 'Evenin', Miss Hudson.'

Kate's face paled. 'Please . . . ' she began.

Curtis holstered his gun and lifted a hand to stall her.

'You do 'xactly what I tell you, an' you'll be all right.' He turned to Bella. 'Now, you're gonna go to the livery an' pick up my horse, an' another for your niece here, then you're gonna come straight back with 'em.'

'I ain't leavin' her with you,' Bella said.

Curtis ignored her. 'You ain't gonna talk to anybody 'ceptin' the livery man, an' you can tell him what story you like. Just get the horses round to the back door here in five minutes or . . . ' He took his knife from his boot and moved quickly across to Kate. He hooked the knife under the bodice of her dress and sliced upwards so that the material of her dress and chemise parted neatly in the middle, the blade finishing under her chin.

'*Comprende?*'

Kate whimpered and clutched the

two halves of her dress, trying to cover herself.

'You filthy bastard!' Bella cried.

'The horses,' Curtis said. He moved the knife up under Kate's throat and grinned at Bella. 'You've got five minutes.'

'Don't hurt her!' Bella pleaded.

'*Go!*' he yelled.

27

Drew had arrived just in time to see Curtis pulling down the blinds at the front of Bella's café.

Drew cursed. He'd been just those few minutes too slow.

He stood on the opposite side of the street trying to decide what to do. He was still pondering this when the door opened and the portly figure of his aunt emerged. She half-ran in a direct line in the direction of the livery.

'Bella!' he called. 'What's happening?'

She stopped in her tracks and turned as he jogged across.

'Curtis Jordan's got your sister, that's what's happened, damn you!' Bella said. 'This is all your fault. If you've got the bank money, get in there an' bargain with the varmint. The money for Kate.'

'Where're you headin'?' he asked.

'The livery,' she said. 'I'm supposed to get his horse an' a spare for Kate. I'll stall as long as I can. Now, get goin'!'

'An' do what?' Drew asked. 'He's a killer, an' I ain't no gunhawk.'

'Just do *somethin*'!' Bella told him, and hurried on towards the livery.

Drew watched her go and tried to decide on his next move. Facing up to a hardened killer like Curtis Jordan wasn't an option as far as he was concerned. Not alone, anyway. He'd be dead meat in no time. Maybe if he got the sheriff and a few other men . . .

It was just then that Clayton Chandler came limping down the street. He spotted Drew, a carpetbag in one hand, about to move away from the café.

Moving as quickly he could, Clayton stepped into the other man's path.

'Hang on there, Drew,' he said.

Drew's shocked expression was quickly followed by a movement of his hand towards his holster. Anticipating the move, Clayton grabbed Drew's wrist and twisted his arm behind his back.

'Aaagh!' Drew tried to hit Clayton with the carpetbag but missed. 'Judas! You're breakin' my arm!'

'Then hold still,' Clayton told him. He removed his Peacemaker from its holster and pressed the barrel against Drew's neck. 'Listen to me. If you were thinkin' of visitin' your sister, you should know that Curtis Jordan is almost certainly with her, probably with a gun to her head.'

'I know that,' Drew said. 'Bella Gower just scuttled off to the livery to fetch a coupla horses for Curtis an' Kate to ride out of here.' He looked at Clayton, a hopeful gleam coming into his eye. 'Listen, maybe the two of us can get her out of there.'

Clayton's thoughts whirled. Maybe teaming up with Drew would give him the chance to kill both him and Curtis before Danny Ridge and the sheriff showed up. It would only be a matter of time before they, too, worked out that Curtis would have come to the café for a hostage.

'OK,' he said, removing the six-gun from Drew's throat. 'You concentrate on gettin' your sister out an' leave Curtis to me.'

Drew glanced at him, as if trying to read his mind. It was clear the youngster suspected a double-cross.

'One more thing,' Clayton said. 'If the sheriff and a coupla other men come lookin' for Curtis, you don't know me, OK? We just met, an' you asked me to help you, that's the story, OK?'

Puzzled, Drew nodded.

'Is there a back door to the café?' Clayton asked.

'Sure,' Drew said. 'But it'll be locked.' He gave a halfhearted chuckle. 'You won't have the key to *that* one, Clayton. It ain't the Suta Springs bank.'

Clayton ignored the jibe. 'We ain't goin' in,' he said. 'We're gonna wait for Curtis an' your sister to come out, then we make our move. Meantime, we wait in the shadows round the back 'cause I reckon they'll leave from there.'

28

Bella arrived at the livery, breathing heavily. Moving quickly didn't come easily to her these days.

The liveryman glanced in her direction. 'Hello,' he said. 'You wantin' somethin', Bella?' He looked at her more closely. 'Is somethin' wrong?'

She shook her head. 'Nothin', Oakie,' she said. 'Nothin's wrong.' It came out too quickly and she knew at once that the the liveryman didn't believe her.

Oakie Parks walked across to her. He was a tall, heavily muscled man with kindly blue eyes. 'So why're you lookin' like somethin's scared the pants off you?'

'Please! I can't talk right now,' she pleaded.

'So what've you come for?' Oakie asked, gently.

'Good question,' came a voice from

behind them both. It was Sam Lewis. 'Let me guess,' he said to Bella. 'You've come for Curtis Jordan's horse. Right, Bella?'

At that, Bella let out a sob, unable to control her emotions any longer. 'He's got my niece, holdin' her hostage, Sam. He's going to take her with him unless we can stop him.'

Oakie looked at the sheriff, alarmed but thinking quickly. 'We need some men to surround the café, Sam,' he said. 'Can you fix that — an' fast?'

'Sure can,' the sheriff said, and turned on his heel.

Oakie put a hand on Bella's arm. 'It'll be all right, we'll get her out.' But he sounded less than confident.

★　★　★

Danny saw the drawn blinds on the café. He also saw two men on the opposite side of the street watching the place. Danny walked over to them.

'Café closed early?' he said.

One of the men nodded. 'Fella came in totin' a gun,' he said. 'Me an' Charlie didn't wait to see what his problem was. We got the hell out fast.'

Danny scowled at them. 'An' left two unprotected women in there? What kinda men are you?'

Both men looked sheepish.

'We ain't no gunhawks, that's fer sure,' Charlie said. 'Weren't aimin' to get ourselves killed. We were goin' to get the sheriff, er — ain't that right, Lou?'

The other man nodded — too quickly. Danny didn't believe them, but there was no time to stand around arguing. Instead, he began to move towards the alleyway which would take him round the back of the café.

'Coupla fellas already round there,' Charlie told him.

Danny turned back towards them. 'Two men?'

'Yup,' Charlie said.

'One of 'em manhandled the other,' Lou said. 'Put a gun against his neck. Didn't hear what they were talkin' about, but the critter with the gun was in charge. The other fella did as he was told.'

'An' they went round the back of the café?' Danny said.

Both men nodded.

'OK,' Danny said. 'If the sheriff shows up any time soon, tell him what you've just told me. Then tell him I've gone round the back of the café to see if I can gain entry. Got that?'

Both men nodded again.

Danny moved quickly towards the alleyway, then approached the back of the café cautiously. He could hear low voices, but was unable to distinguish what was being said until he reached the end of the alleyway. To his surprise, he recognized the voice of Clayton Chandler.

He was about to step from the shadows of the alleyway and start asking questions when something Clayton said stopped him dead in his tracks.

'If you hadn't got trigger-happy, Drew, it wouldn't have all gone wrong,'

Clayton was saying, keeping his voice low. 'Wolf Cotton had it planned to be in an' out of the back door quiet as mice. That's why he got the key off me. 'Stead of that, you get jumpy an' kill the manager, an' all hell breaks loose. Consequence of which is a panicky getaway durin' which my brother's widow gets herself killed!'

'That weren't my fault,' Drew said in a half-whisper. 'Anyways, the stupid woman just stood there, in the middle of the street, without movin'. Askin' to get mown down, if'n you ask me.'

Clayton struck Drew across the mouth and nose. 'Don't say that!' he hissed. 'Don't talk about her like that!'

A stream of blood poured from Drew's nose and he tried to stem it with his neckerchief.

At which point Danny stepped out of the alleyway. 'No, don't talk about Julie Chandler like that, Hudson,' he said.

Both men whirled, and the shock which registered on Clayton's face was mixed with raw fear.

'Ridge,' he breathed. 'Right, you bastard!'

He made a hurried move for his pistol, but Danny was faster.

The first shot clipped Clayton high on one cheekbone, the second penetrated the side of his neck. Blood spurted and hs eyes were filled with a terrible agony.

'*Ellie . . . Julie . . . dear God . . . .*' he gurgled, fingers clawing at his neck.

Seconds later, he died.

Danny turned in time to see Drew reaching for his Colt. He fired two quick shots, his gun coughing smoke and lead. The two slugs took Drew in the middle of the stomach like a steam-hammer and in his shirt grew an ever-widening dark hole. He crashed backwards against the wall of the café, slid down and lay still.

29

At the sound of the shooting outside, Curtis spun towards the back door of the café, gun poised, waiting for someone to burst in. When nothing happened, he turned back to Kate.

'Where's your aunt? She's been gone more'n five minutes,' Curtis growled.

He began pacing up and down the kitchen.

Kate was squatting on her haunches in a corner, holding her torn dress together. Somehow, she had got her nerves under control and was trying to think quickly.

'Th-there may have been someone at the livery,' she said. 'She may have had to wait. She'll be back.'

Curtis looked out of the window next to the back door, cupping his hands around his eyes to keep out the interior lamplight. Almost immediately he jumped back. '*Someone's out there.*'

A split second later, there was a roar of a six-shooter and a bullet shattered the window, sending shards of glass flying in all directions. Curtis caught one on his cheek; instantly it drew blood.

'The bitch!' he cried. 'She's double-crossed us.'

'No!' Kate screamed. 'She wouldn't — '

Another bullet tore at the window surround, splintering the wood. Curtis saw the direction of the flame, fired back, then flattened himself against the wall. He waited. Was it just the one assailant? If so, who was he? The sheriff? Drew Hudson?

'You out there!' he shouted. 'Another shot, an' the girl gets a bullet. You hear that?'

'I hear!' came the reply a moment later.

★　★　★

Both Bella and Oakie heard the shooting, and Bella screamed. 'It came from the café! Oh, dear God!'

Oakie was already running from the building. 'Stay here, Bella,' he yelled over his shoulder.

As he came into the street, he saw four men with rifles running in his direction, headed by the sheriff.

Sam was yelling orders to them. 'Eddie, Josh, go round the back, but keep your heads down! Tab, Pete, position yourselves out front wherever you can find cover.'

The men scattered as they drew closer to the eating house, two taking off up a side street that would take them round to the back of the building. Two or three people had emerged from the saloon opposite the café and Sam yelled at them to get back inside and stay there.

He joined Oakie. 'He's penned in,' the sheriff told him. 'Danny's round the back. Jordan ain't goin' nowhere.'

'But what about the girl?' Oakie said. 'How're we gonna get her out safely?'

'Jordan's not likely to kill her whilst

there's still a chance of his using her as a ticket to get away,' Sam said. 'I'm going round the back to see what's happening with Danny. You stay out front, Oakie. Just find some cover, though.' He glanced towards the livery. 'Bella, stay the hell away from here!'

'Can't I do something'?' Bella pleaded. She had come out of the livery in spite of Oakie's warnings.

'Like what?' the sheriff said. 'Getting yourself shot? Get back to the livery.'

Reluctantly, Bella turned and headed back as Sam ran off.

Oakie positioned himself on the boardwalk at the side of the café. The man called Tab was flattened against the wall of the building the other side of the café door.

There were no more shots from the back of the building.

'What's his next move, d'you reckon?' Tab whispered. Oakie shook his head and gestured *who knows?* with his hands.

They waited.

Some minutes later Sam returned.

He came alongside Oakie. 'Two men dead,' he said in a low voice. 'One of them's Drew Hudson.'

Oakie sighed. 'Think his sister knows that?'

'Doubt it,' Sam said. 'There's another fella dead, too.' He looked puzzled. 'Danny seemed to know him, but didn't say. I don't understand that. When did he turn up?'

30

Curtis grabbed a handful of Kate's corn-coloured hair, dragged her out of the kitchen and into the darkened café, his Peacemaker at her back.

'You're gonna start talkin',' he told her. 'You're gonna say 'xactly what I tell you to say. Got it?'

She made a whimpering sound of assent.

'Good.' He slammed her against the drawn blind of the door. 'What's the sheriff's name?'

'I-I think it's Mr Lewis,' Kate said.

'Call him.' He pushed his pistol against her neck. 'Now.'

Kate swallowed, then cried out. 'Sheriff Lewis!'

Seconds later, Sam's reply came from close by. 'Miss Hudson, that you?'

'Tell him you're all right, but he's got to do as I say,' Curtis told her.

Kate repeated his order, her voice shaking.

'OK, Miss Hudson,' Sam replied.

Curtis unlocked the door and eased it open two or three inches. 'Sheriff, you hear me?' he shouted.

'I hear you,' Sam answered. 'You ain't gonna get away with this, Jordan. You harm a hair of that girl's head an' I'll — '

'Shut up, an' listen!' Curtis yelled. 'You do 'xactly what I tell you or I'll strip her buck naked and send her out with three bullets in her back! You got that?'

Silence. Then, '*I hear you*,' came from a voice filled with defeat.

'OK, you an' your men move out into the centre of the street where I can see 'em.'

He peered through the crack and watched as, one by one, the men moved into the middle of the street, the light from the streetlamps behind them turning them into black silhouettes.

Curtis could just make out faces at

windows in the saloon directly opposite but nobody looked about to venture outside. There were four horses at a hitching rail alongside the boardwalk.

'Drop your weapons!' Curtis yelled. 'Now!'

He watched as three of the four men dropped their rifles and Sam Lewis unbuckled his gun belt and allowed it to fall to the ground.

Curtis yanked the door open the rest of the way and pushed Kate out ahead of him, his gun at the back of her head.

'You!' he yelled at Oakie. 'Unhitch two of those horses behind you an' walk them across. Do it real slow, unless you want me to blow the girl's head off.'

Oakie moved towards the four horses like a man heading for his own funeral. He unhitched two of the animals and started walking back.

★   ★   ★

At the back of the café, Danny moved across to the shattered window and climbed through, careful to avoid the jagged glass. He cursed the light given out by the oil lamp hanging from the ceiling, craving the security of darkness, but moved quickly across the kitchen and into the darkness of the café dining room.

He could see Curtis's back through the open door. He could see the back of Kate Hudson's head close to the man's shoulder, and the gun Curtis was holding to the back of it. He heard the shouted order to the sheriff to get the two horses. Danny lifted his Peacemaker, drew a bead on the back of Curtis's head — then hesitated.

Would his shot trigger a reflex action from Jordan so that he fired his six-shooter, killing the girl?

The sheriff was coming back with the horses now. Danny knew he had to make a decision fast, or it would be too late.

'Jordan!' he yelled, moving into the open doorway.

A startled Curtis whirled round, releasing Kate but firing into the blackness of the café doorway in the one movement. At the same moment, Danny squeezed the trigger on his Peacemaker.

Both shots found their targets, but neither was fatal. Curtis's bullet creased Danny's thigh but did little damage, whereas the slug from Danny's gun caught Curtis's right shoulder, spinning him to the dusty street.

The exchange of shots sent Sam dropping to the ground to snatch up his holster and yank out his guns. But the two or three seconds it took to do this was time enough for Curtis Jordan to roll over on the ground and fire blindly in his direction.

Sam dived out of the line of fire, triggering his own weapons but without finding the moving target. Oakie released the two horses and grabbed Kate Hudson around the waist, pulling her away from the middle of the street and into the safety of the shadowed boardwalk.

Curtis scrambled to his feet and made a desperate run towards the café doorway, but another bullet from

Danny's Peacemaker took the raider in the base of his neck, and a second shot from Sam's iron blew the back of his head away.

★　★　★

Minutes later, figures were emerging from the saloon and other buildings along the street. Bella Gower was with Kate Hudson who was sitting, head in hands, on the boardwalk just yards from the café entrance. The older woman was doing her best to comfort her shocked and distraught niece.

A handful of men stood in a group, looking down at the prone body of Curtis Jordan and speaking in low voices.

Sam Lewis was round the back of the café with Danny staring down at the bodies of Clayton Chandler and Drew Hudson.

'So who was this guy?' Sam pointed at Clayton Chandler.

'He's the man who got the key to open the back door of the Suta Springs bank for Wolf Cotton and his gang,' Danny said. 'At a guess, I'd say Cotton was holdin' his gamblin' marker; a marker he couldn't pay, an' usin' it to blackmail Clayton into gettin' the key.'

'Clayton?' Sam said. 'Sounds like you knew him.'

'Yeah, I knew him,' Danny said, after a moment.

The two men walked back to the main street where Kate Hudson was being cradled in her aunt's arms. The girl was sobbing uncontrollably.

'She know her brother is dead?' Danny asked.

'Guess she does by now,' Sam said. 'Listen, I need to go talk to Travis Emery, he's our undertaker. He's got some — uh — clearin' up to do.'

31

Chester Darrow was roused from his usual whiskey-induced siesta by a hand shaking his shoulder.

'What'n hell — ' he began.

'Easy, Ches, it's only me,' Danny said. He was sitting on the edge of Chester's desk.

Chester wiped the sleep from his eyes with the backs of his hands. 'Danny? You back?'

'Yeah, I'm back,' Danny acknowledged.

'Things work out?' Chester's mouth seemed to be full of sand and he was having trouble getting the words out.

Danny sniffed, 'Oh, sure, they worked out.'

Chester caught his deputy's sardonic tone. 'What happened?' he asked, moving his feet from his desk and struggling to sound businesslike.

Danny carefully summarized the events that had taken place in Red Creek and in Latimer. He took his time, realizing that the befuddled sheriff was having trouble taking it in.

Chester listened with growing bewilderment. 'Clayton Chandler! Judas! It's makin' my head hurt!' He pulled open a desk drawer and extracted a half-empty bottle of red-eye. He took a quick swig and held it out to Danny, who shook his head. 'So what do I tell Boyd Chandler about his son?'

'The truth,' Danny said.

'His wife died a coupla days ago,' Chester said. 'Funeral's fixed for tomorrow.'

'Maybe it's as well,' Danny said. 'At least Ada Chandler never knew that one of her sons indirectly caused the death of her daughter-in-law.'

Chester stared at Danny. It occurred to him that his young deputy had grown up some in the past few days. Sounded years older than he had when he'd left.

'You had time to tell Ellie Hall about all this?' he asked, eyeing Danny closely. 'She'll be needin' to know about Clayton Chandler.'

Danny slid off the edge of the desk. 'Reckon I'll do that now,' he said.

'An' I reckon you'll take some pleasure in it,' Chester said, a smile twitching at the corner of his mouth.

Danny coloured. 'If she needs a shoulder to cry on, well . . . ' He moved towards the door.

'Hold on!' Chester said. 'What about the rest of the money from the bank? You ever find it?'

Danny grinned. 'Sure. What's left of it.' He walked across to a chair by the door and picked up a money belt that he had tossed there earlier. He threw it to the sheriff.

Chester caught it, then winced. 'Hell, it's full of holes an' — an' what's this? Dried *blood*!'

'The money inside is full of holes, too,' Danny told him. 'The belt was round Drew Hudson's waist when he

226

was shot in the stomach an' spilled his guts. Undertaker in Latimer found it. Gave it to Sheriff Lewis, who gave it to me to bring back. Might be a few dollars that're usable. Wouldn't count on it, though.'

Chester dropped the belt on his desk, a look of disgust on his face.

'What's wrong, Ches?' Danny said, smiling.

'There are times when I wish people would let me have my damned siesta in peace!' Chester growled.

THE END

We do hope that you have enjoyed reading this large print book.

Did you know that all of our titles are available for purchase?

We publish a wide range of high quality large print books including: **Romances, Mysteries, Classics General Fiction Non Fiction and Westerns**

Special interest titles available in large print are: **The Little Oxford Dictionary Music Book, Song Book Hymn Book, Service Book**

Also available from us courtesy of Oxford University Press: **Young Readers' Dictionary (large print edition) Young Readers' Thesaurus (large print edition)**

For further information or a free brochure, please contact us at: **Ulverscroft Large Print Books Ltd., The Green, Bradgate Road, Anstey, Leicester, LE7 7FU, England. Tel:** (00 44) **0116 236 4325 Fax:** (00 44) **0116 234 0205**

VIOLENT MEN

Corba Sunman

Hilt's fury comes from frustration. A nasty leg wound prevents him from resuming his hunt for the outlaw Buck Dunne. With his pursuit for the killer interrupted, Dunne will be long gone before Hilt can get his hands on him. But whilst Hilt believes that all the trouble in the county is over, unbeknownst to him, there are more rotten apples in the barrel with big trouble still imminent. A gun-crackling showdown with Buck Dunne is surely looming . . .

SHOWDOWN AT
DIRT CROSSING

Jack Dakota

Hal Kramer rides into Dirt Crossing to discover that things have changed drastically. Why is the saloon closed down? And what's behind the mysterious tracks in the snow? Aided by one old-timer and his wife, Kramer takes on local despot Zebulon King and his ruthless gang. But faced with overwhelming odds, can he help a group of outcasts taking refuge in the high mountains, as well as the town itself? Who will help him in the final showdown?

GHOST RIDERS AT SHOTGUN BLUFFS

Robert Anderson

Zak Carter was a boy when the Ghost Riders arrived on the bluffs, shot down his parents and hustled him out at gunpoint. Now he's returned for his inheritance. Zak starts romancing the lovely Sarah Jo, who has also caught the eye of the renegade gang's sadistic leader. When she is kidnapped, Zak promptly straps on his gun and sets out to find her. Now he must break the outlaws' grip on the town . . . or die in the attempt.

THE SECRET OF DEVIL'S CANYON

I. J. Parnham

When Mayor Maxwell and his daughter are brutally murdered, feelings in Bear Creek run high. And when the killer is caught and sentenced to life in prison, the townsfolk demand a lynching. So Sheriff Bryce calls in Nathaniel McBain to spirit the killer away through Devil's Canyon to Beaver Ridge jail. Nathaniel, just one step ahead of the pursuing mob, loses ground, then realizes that he's facing an even bigger problem: his prisoner may be innocent after all . . .

VALLEY OF THE GUNS

Rick Dalmas

Zack Clay is looking for a quiet life, but he hasn't reckoned on range-grabbers Dutch Haas and Burt Helidon bringing in sundry gunfighters to hassle him. Clay meets fists and boots with the same, gunsmoke with gunsmoke. In the end, they hang a badge on him. Then things really hot up in Benbow. But the hustlers, gunslingers, the wild trailmen and townsmen who put dollars before citizens all find that stubborn Zack Clay won't go down without a fight . . .

THE SKULL OF IRON EYES

Rory Black

In a remote valley, led by Will Hayes, six miners strike pay dirt. A fortune in golden nuggets is hidden in the dense landscape. The only obstacle to prevent their taking it back to civilization is a small, isolated tribe of natives, but Hayes has a dastardly plan . . . However, after they ruthlessly kill a child, her body is found by the infamous bounty hunter Iron Eyes. And he vows to discover who killed her — and see justice done . . .